THE HIPPOCRATIC DECEPTION

SUSAN LEE WALBERG

This book is a work of fiction. Any references to actual events, real people, or real places are used fictitiously, and any resemblance to actual events or places or persons, living or dead, is entirely coincidental.

Copyright © 2022 by Susan Lee Walberg

All rights reserved. No part of this book may be reproduced or used in any manner without written permission of the copyright owner except for the used of quotations in a book review.

First paperback edition October 2022

Book cover design by Jerry Todd

Interior book design by Kelly M. Carter

ISBN 978-0-9998605-4-0 (paperback)

ISBN 978-0-9998605-5-7 (ebook)

susanwalberg.com

1

JUSTINA

Justina woke with a start, confused for a moment about where she was. It was still dark as she peered at the glowing red numbers of her alarm clock. *Jeez, it's only five o'clock!* Rubbing her eyes, she sat up, wondering what had awoken her.

A door in the hallway clicked quietly and she heard soft steps going down the stairs. *Jose! What is he doing up!?* She started to lie back down, then thought better of it. What would that child get into with no supervision on the first morning in a new home? The trip from Mexico City had been long and difficult for her and her father, but this little boy had just spent his first night in America and a new home.

"All right, I'm coming," she mumbled to herself.

By the time she had wrapped herself in a bathrobe and made it downstairs, Jose was already scoping out the contents of the refrigerator.

"Jose!"

Jose whirled, eyes wide. "Tina … I'm thirsty," he said, shutting the door.

"It's okay, Jose," Justina said, regretting her sharp tone, which clearly startled the seven-year-old boy. "You just got up so early! Let's get you some juice." She reminded herself how much was new for Jose, and to be patient. He was such a smart child; his mastery of English already was amazing, and he seemed so able to quickly adjust to anything that happened to him. She sometimes forgot all he'd been through. She gave him some orange juice and the remainder of yesterday's animal crackers, now a wrinkled bag of large crumbs, and sent him back upstairs to try to go back to sleep.

She debated going back to bed herself, but it seemed pointless when she knew she would just lie there thinking about all the things she needed to do now that she was home. School was the first thing, and getting her head back into the law school mindset wouldn't be easy. It had been so hard saying goodbye to Daniel when he went back to school in Maryland. It left a big hole in her heart, but they had agreed it was time for them both to finish their degrees before they could move on with their lives-hopefully together. Justina sighed, thinking about what the future could hold. It would be hard to focus on school after the reunion in Mexico City with her boyfriend, and then having to say goodbye again.

And the other thing was getting a job. Everyone at school already had internships or jobs lined up, and her unplanned time in Mexico hadn't helped on that front. She wondered about the internships she had applied for and cringed as she recalled sending out her brief résumé with its sad little summary of achievements and no real work experience. But her volunteer work at the hospitals would surely count for something—or so she hoped. She knew the competition could be fierce; lots of ambitious young lawyers in New York and she certainly wasn't at the top of her class.

So much to do! She also needed to empty out her apartment in the city, now that she was moving back home to help take care of Jose. She still wasn't sure how well that would work, recalling some of the battles she had fought with her father in the past. Moving back in with him could be challenging and hadn't been part of her plan.

Sighing, she turned on the coffee machine and glanced at her laptop on the kitchen counter, where she had plugged it in to recharge the night before. "Okay, let's see what's going on," she said to herself once she had a cup of coffee in her hand.

She hadn't checked her emails in a couple of days, while they were traveling, so there was a long list to scroll through. One from yesterday, from the neighbor in the city who was watching her cat, making sure Justina was back in town. Justina answered that one right away. She had to go get that cat!

As she scrolled down, her eye was immediately drawn to an email from McIntyre, Jones, and Hancock, one of the law firms where she had applied for an internship. A jolt of adrenaline hit her veins. This was the job she wanted the most, because it was the firm with a health law position. She clicked on the email, fearing a polite rejection, and was ecstatic to see that they were inviting her for an interview with one of the partners, Peter Hancock! Excitement turned to worry when she realized the email was nearly two days old. *I hope they don't think I'm not interested!* She quickly typed an acceptance and apologized for her delay, citing travel.

She glanced through her remaining emails, but her mind was on the possible job. She had a strong, positive feeling about it. It was time to get to work and start doing something that would make a difference. This really looked like the perfect opportunity! What to wear was an issue, however, and her suits were at the apartment in the city. One more reason to go clean out that place today. And she had to let Daniel know! He was probably the only one who understood her anxiety about the job and her need to prove herself.

Her thoughts were interrupted as she heard footsteps on the stairs. "Oh no, not again," she grumbled to herself.

Her father, Victor, appeared instead of Jose, freshly showered and dressed to go to the office. Although he looked rested, his face was serious as he greeted her.

"What's up, Papa? Isn't it way too early to be going to work?" Justina asked, immediately worried. Her father was usually imperturbable and certainly didn't head into the office before the sun was up.

"I got a note from the senator, my boss who never sleeps, early this morning. Or late last night, depending on how you look at it. There's been a lot of press coverage from our trip to Mexico City, particularly related to Jose's rescue, and it's going viral. He wants me in early to figure out a strategy for handling it." He paused, pouring a cup of coffee.

Justina struggled to shift her mind back to their recent time in Mexico. "Why is that a bad thing? I would think it would be good press?"

"Yes, it is. But it's a distraction. The senator wants to announce his run for the presidency soon. So we have to deal with it right away."

"Well, what are the stories?" Her father had been in politics her whole life, but ever since her mother had died many years ago, he had stayed mostly behind the scenes in order to raise his only child. Being in the news was definitely not a typical event for him, so Justina found it intriguing.

Her father's lips formed a displeased grimace. "You can look it up. 'Local Heroes Save Orphaned Boy in Mexico Earthquake,' typical clickbait stuff." Justina couldn't understand why he was aggravated by it, but then again, she never did really understand some of the politics her father dealt with every day.

He sighed, taking a large swallow of coffee and glancing at the wall clock. "Anyhow, enough of that. You are the designated babysitter today. I have a mountain of things to do at work, especially with this latest drama. So I'm going in now and may be late getting home."

Justina felt her mood flip to irritation. "Papa, are you serious? I need to go into the city and empty my apartment, get the cat ..." She trailed off as she realized her father would have little sympathy for Hercules, the cat Justina had rescued and adopted, much to his chagrin.

She knew what was coming when she saw his mouth set in a tight line. "Justina, before I ever filed papers to be Jose's guardian you agreed totally that it would take everyone to make this work for him and for all of us. I'm his guardian, but you made a deal with me, as part of this family. I did not intend to bring him here if we were just going to leave him with a babysitter." He held his hand up as she started to object. "It's not fair to him. Take him with you to the city. He can help you with that cat." His tone indicated the subject was closed.

Justina knew she was defeated, and that her father was right about Jose, even though she would never admit it. "Okay, but Papa, I want you to know, there is an internship I applied for, and I just got an invitation for an interview. I have a very good feeling about it …" She paused, seeing the look on his face, but pushed forward. She couldn't keep letting him treat her like a child.

"Papa, I *need* to do this. I'm way behind on getting a job and I'm afraid there won't be many more good opportunities this quarter. I'm getting too old to have no experience, especially with graduation right around the corner. Please don't give me a bad time."

"Justina. We have only been home twelve hours and you already have an interview lined up? What is the rush? I thought we agreed that you would move home and help with Jose, at least while he's getting adjusted. Now you tell me you plan to go to school *and* work?" She could see his jaw clenching and knew what that meant. This was what she had feared about moving back home.

"Papa, it's the perfect job, it's a health law internship. We have Celeste, too—she's helped out around here for years, and she's like family. I fully intend to help with Jose, but I am taking this job if I get an offer!" *I can be stubborn too. He ought to know that by now,* she thought.

Her father gave her a glare. "This is a bad idea, m'ija. You just remember I said that."

2

THERESE

Reverend Mother Therese Marie Devereaux placed the phone receiver in its cradle and looked up at the clock on the wall, hoping it would give a better answer than the one on her desktop. Stifling the urge to curse (an old habit she still struggled with), she logged off her computer and started gathering up the files for the evening's class she was scheduled to teach. Not for the first time she wondered if taking on responsibility for the hospital's Pastoral Services Department all by herself had been a good decision. Between the training commitments she had made and her new executive-level responsibilities, there was no time left over. She stuffed her files into a large black canvas case, then put her fingers to her lips and transferred a kiss to a slightly yellowed photo of a small boy. *At least the work keeps me busy,* she thought as she grabbed her coat from the hook.

A knock at her open door interrupted her thoughts, and she uttered a sigh of frustration. Another delay. She injected a friendly tone into her voice. "Come in!"

Therese recognized the young woman, Angela, as the nursing director. The woman glanced at Therese's coat in hand. "I'm sorry to bother you, Mother Marie. I can see you're trying to get out of here … but I have an emergency. Can I talk to you for a minute? I need some advice, and I don't know where else to go." Her voice crackled, like she was either very nervous or trying not to cry.

Noting the anxiety in the woman's eyes, Therese set down her bag. "I have a minute. I'm already late, anyhow," she admitted, wondering why the nursing director would be coming to her, especially in such a state.

Angela looked up and down the hallway outside the office, then shut the door. "It's the clinic. There is something going on there-I think maybe drug diversion. And I suspect a lot of people may be involved. I don't see how they could get away with it otherwise." She spoke in a rush, as if she had to blurt it all out at once before she lost her courage.

Stunned by the statement, Therese dropped into her seat. "Angela, this is serious. Why are you bringing this concern to me? And why do you think this?"

"General counsel is out of the country for weeks. A lot of folks have up and vanished, if you haven't noticed. And Michelle, the compliance officer … she disappeared, too. Quit, supposedly. But what you might not have heard … Michelle was gunned down in her house the night she quit her job! The police called it a robbery, but she was shot in the back, nothing stolen!" Angela had a sheen of sweat across the dark skin of her forehead and cheeks, and her eyes had the frantic look of a cornered animal's.

Therese couldn't believe what she was hearing. "But—" she began and was quickly interrupted by the panicked woman.

"Please. I don't know what to do. The doctors down there … they aren't right. I'm sure they somehow ran Michelle out of here, and I don't know what else they might have done. Medical staff, and Dr. Al especially, were always yelling when she came to do an audit." Therese could see the other woman was on the verge of crying but blinking to hold it back.

"Angela, what proof do you have? I mean, these are very serious accusations. If you have proof you need to report this, but it's going to cause a huge uproar, you know that. The hospital president needs to know, but only if you are sure of what you are saying."

Angela nodded and took a deep breath. "Yes, I know. That's the issue. There are some very suspicious things I've seen and heard. You know the nurses all come to me. They don't even want to work for Dr. Al, and they say he is abusive. And the residents … they complained to my nurses that the doctors aren't even there to see patients in the clinic, but lots of patients come in to get pain meds and the residents are expected to take care of them, which they aren't supposed to, not like that, with no supervision whatsoever."

"But do you have proof—"

"I can't prove it by myself, but I think that's what Michelle was working on when she got, uh, removed. Someone needs to look into it." She appeared to hesitate, fiddling with her ID badge. Therese waited.

"They seem to all come in a group, too. The patients, I mean," she clarified. "They come all one after the other, all with the usual complaints. You know, headaches, back pain. They are in and out fast, with their prescriptions. I can tell the residents aren't comfortable with it, but they aren't saying anything, they just keep seeing the patients." Then she added, with a wry twist of her lips, "I guess they need their jobs, too."

Therese sat in stunned silence, not sure how to respond. "So, you think the compliance officer was already looking at this?" If that was true, surely there would be a record.

Angela shifted her weight, nodding, and leaned against the door. "Here's the thing. I don't know if Dr. Shoemaker or anyone else running St. Matthew's might be involved or even knew what Michelle was looking at. You know how those doctors can't do anything wrong, in the eyes of administration. Why is that? And I don't want to wind up gone or dead like Michelle. I'm afraid I'll be next, everyone knows all the nurses come to me and Dr. Al was extremely nasty to me earlier, when he brought a couple of residents up on the floor. More than usual. I know, I sound paranoid." She seemed to realize her words were coming out in a torrent and clamped her lips together.

Therese watched the woman shifting her weight and fidgeting with the hem of her green scrubs. She reminded herself of her executive role as the desire to dodge this pile of trouble nearly overcame her. She needed to help Angela, even though she had no idea how to do so. And although Angela's suspicion of someone from the hospital killing the compliance officer seemed far fetched, it was alarming that the woman clearly believed it. Some of the other allegations certainly seemed more credible, or at least worthy of investigation.

"Okay, Angela, how about this. I will talk to Dr. Shoemaker. That will keep you out of it. Nobody will ever need to know you're the one who reported this to me. I trust our CEO. I don't think she's involved in anything like what you're suggesting. Can you do me one favor, though? It would help me if I had a list or a summary of the specific incidents and issues that you are concerned about, since I will probably muddle it up. Okay?"

Angela nodded, and her body appeared to relax. "Thank you so much, Mother. I know it's not your problem, but … I had nowhere else to go. Everyone knows that we can trust you."

Therese felt the weight of responsibility settle on her shoulders. "Don't worry, honey. We'll figure it out," Therese said, standing to give Angela a quick hug. "You don't stress out about this. Go home and take care of your little angel, okay?"

Angela smiled. "Yes, and thank you so much. Just don't tell them it came from me, that's all I care about … I'll have you a list in the morning."

"Of course," Therese responded, and she sighed, looking

at the clock again. *Well, maybe I will make it back to class by the break. Good thing I have a trainee there to help out ...*

3

JUSTINA

Justina's life had assumed a frantic pace from the moment she got the email from the law firm confirming her interview. She'd had two days to empty her New York apartment, find a suit that looked acceptable, and prepare for the interview. And that was on top of adjusting to living in the same house with her father and a seven-year-old orphan! She mulled over all the events of the past few days as she sat in New York traffic, grateful she had allowed plenty of time to get from Long Beach into the city.

Taking Jose to New York City had been an experience for both of them, and bringing Hercules, her cat, back to the house had created a new layer of chaos above and beyond the activity of an energetic little boy in a new home.

Her father wasn't happy with her. Not at all. First the job interview, and then the cat. But she was determined about both, and her father recognized that, so they had something of a truce. Besides, her father was inundated with media and work demands, so he wasn't as focused on controlling her life. It was a blessing.

Finally arriving at the address, Justina looked up at the towering, shiny building that might house her first real job. She felt a thin layer of sweat form on her forehead as she guided her car into the underground parking garage and her nerves kicked in. She found a parking spot with surprising ease, which she interpreted as a good omen, especially since it was near the elevator bank. Taking a deep breath, she took that big step into the elevator.

When she got to her floor, Justina went immediately to the ladies' room. She picked a tiny piece of white lint off her navy skirt and smoothed her hair, which was pulled back in a square gold clip. As she looked in the mirror, she realized she was chewing on her lip and stopped, reapplying a light coat of pink lip gloss. *I'm as ready as I will ever be,* she told herself as she stepped out of the restroom and through a wall of glass into the opulent hallway of McIntyre, Jones, and Hancock. The suite of offices was too quiet, with the plush blue carpeting absorbing the sound of any movement, and no voices could be heard. The olive-skinned secretary, whose placard identified her as Sari, looked up from her keyboard as Justina approached. Her smile was warm and friendly.

"Are you Justina Gonzalez?" she asked, glancing at her computer screen as if to confirm.

"Yes, I'm here to meet with Peter Hancock," Justina said, looking at her watch for the third time in as many minutes.

"I'll let Mr. Hancock know you're here. You'll also be meeting with another associate, Carmen Oliver. Please have a seat, they should be ready shortly. Can I get you a coffee or glass of water?"

Justina thought she had probably already had too much coffee, considering the way her nerves were jangling.

"No, thank you, I'm fine."

She was only seated for a moment, distracting herself by looking out at the expansive view of downtown Manhattan, when a tall, slender Black woman in a moss-green suit appeared from down the hall.

"Justina?" she asked, and at Justina's nod, she introduced herself as Carmen. "Come this way, and we'll meet with Peter Hancock in the conference room."

Peter Hancock was a stocky blond man with bright blue eyes and a tan that suggested a love of golf or sailing. His smile was warm as he shook Justina's hand. After the perfunctory conversation about weather and traffic, he told her about the firm, and the healthcare practice specifically. Once he had asked her about her classes and grades, he asked her about her interest in healthcare.

Justina had no work experience to relate, so she focused on her volunteer experience assisting the social workers at St. John's Hospital after Hurricane Sandy and helping as an interpreter at the hospital in Mexico City during earthquake recovery. She had thought about this for the past two days and decided it a better topic to focus on rather than her mediocre grades or lack of career focus over the past three years.

At the mention of Mexico City, a glint of recognition lit up Carmen's face.

"Are you the daughter of Victor Gonzalez?" she asked. "I saw his story online this morning, and I knew you looked familiar. The *New York Times* had a lovely picture of you and your father. When you mentioned the earthquake, it came to me. Am I right?"

Justina felt caught off guard. Her father had mentioned doing an interview, but she hadn't really been paying much attention since she was so focused on this possible job and getting settled back at home. She nodded, not wanting to reveal her lack of awareness, and Peter Hancock jumped in. "Yes, I read that article as well. When I saw your name on our interviewee list, I didn't make the connection. You have had quite an adventure this past year. I imagine it has given you a unique perspective on healthcare. You're practically a celebrity." He smiled and leaned forward, looking at Justina with increased interest. She found herself getting more comfortable, and Peter Hancock, in particular, was so engaging. She felt her confidence growing, along with her desire to land this job. What a great place to work!

"Yes, I mean, not yes that I'm a celebrity, but I have come to love working in the healthcare environment, even in crisis mode. I never thought much about it until I volunteered at the hospital. But I was so impressed with how hard those people work and their importance in the community. I really loved being part of such meaningful work. That's why I applied for this job ..." She trailed off, realizing she was starting to ramble in her enthusiasm. She reminded herself she was at an interview, not a social function.

The two attorneys looked at each other and smiled, and Peter Hancock spoke, his voice warm and inviting.

"It's nice to see so much passion, Miss Gonzalez. That's what we want to see in our associates, and our healthcare clients certainly like to have dedicated representation. I think you will do quite well in this field. Carmen, do you have any additional questions?"

"No, I don't think so, at this time. It was a pleasure to meet you, Justina. We'll be making our decision very soon. We want to move this along as quickly as possible. Would you be available right away?"

"Yes, absolutely." Justina nodded vigorously. "We would just need to get Celeste lined up to take care of Jose … Sorry, I'm just thinking out loud. Thank you so much for your time. I just want you to know I would be very interested in working with you, and I hope you will consider me." She remembered her well-rehearsed closing line, just in time, as the attorneys stood to end the meeting.

Peter Hancock smiled. "Thank you for coming in today. I enjoyed talking to you. You'll be hearing from us."

Justina forced herself to walk calmly to the elevators, maintaining a composed expression. *I think I got it,* she thought, wanting to squeal in excitement. *Oh my God, how cool would that be?* Her thoughts quickly shifted. *I need some decent suits if I am going to actually be a real lawyer, working with clients!* And then, *I can't wait to tell Papa! And Daniel!* She realized she was getting ahead of herself. She had to get an actual offer before she started telling everyone she had a job. But it felt like it went so well, despite her starting to chatter a couple times. *Oh God, I hope they don't think I am an idiot, jabbering away like that ... I certainly wasn't being very lawyerly!*

By the time she got to Long Beach, she had gone back and forth three or four times, alternating between confidence and angst. She could feel where she had sweated through her blouse, and her skirt was pinching her waist. She couldn't wait to get back into a pair of leggings and a sweatshirt.

She was surprised to see her father's car in the driveway when she got home. He never left work early.

"Papa, I'm home from my interview," she called out. "Where are you?"

"I'm in the kitchen, m'ija," he answered. She entered the kitchen, where he stood in his favorite navy-blue pair of running pants, stirring a pot of frijoles.

She stopped in her tracks. He only usually cooked when he had an excess of free time, which was almost never, or when something was bothering him, and he needed to relax. Jose, as well, was being strangely quiet, sprawled out on the floor and engrossed in building something out of Legos. The whole vibe in the house felt odd.

"Papa, what are you doing home?"

He adjusted the burner and put a lid on the pot of simmering beans.

"You remember my boss had me do a media interview? Well, the article came out first thing this morning, and it created a problem for him because of some background political stuff the reporter dug up. Long story short, Samuel told me to take a leave of absence so things can calm down. Too many reporters calling, and even the president himself was irate." Her father took a big swig out of his glass of red wine. "Not a good day, m'ija."

Her father was clearly upset and anxious. She went over to him and put her arms around him, giving him a hug. "I'm sorry, Papa."

He gave her a squeeze and smoothed her hair back. "I'll be fine. It was just kind of a shock. The senator isn't blaming me. He just needs to stop the drama. Anyhow, cooking always relaxes me, so we'll have a good dinner. How was your interview?"

She was pleased to note that he didn't look irritated with her when posing the question, and she had begun telling him about it when the phone rang. She felt her heart lurch when she saw it was from the law firm. She had only left there two hours earlier!

When she answered, she was shocked to hear Peter Hancock himself on the other end of the line. He got right to the point, after greeting her. "Justina, we've talked it over here after your interview, which was our last one. We all feel that you would be a good fit for our firm, if you are still interested and available."

Stunned, she could barely respond. "Yes, of course I'm still interested!" she said, and gave her father a thumbs-up.

"That's wonderful," he said. "We're very excited for you to join our team, Justina! And, in fact, I believe we have an interesting assignment for you right out of the gate, if things go as expected. It's one reason we wanted to make our decision quickly. I'll have our HR person call you and send you over some paperwork later today."

After ending the call, Justina looked at her father, feeling a goofy grin spread across her face. "Oh my God!" she said. "I just got a job!"

4

THERESE

The email flashed on her screen just as Therese was shrugging into her blazer to go get a cup of coffee. "Confidential Emergency Board Meeting" was the header. *Ugh, now what?* She scanned the first few sentences to get past the corporate-speak and find the purpose of the meeting and the time. *Five o'clock. Tonight. To discuss retaining an attorney to investigate internal allegations of impropriety.* Of course she was expected to attend; she was the one who took the complaints to the CEO and hospital president, Dr. Barbara Shoemaker.

Therese leaned back in her chair and closed her eyes. "Lord give me strength," she murmured. Although she believed that her faith made her strong, she admitted to herself that she was afraid of a couple of the physicians. They could be so nasty mean. And she couldn't forget Angela's suspicions about the compliance officer's untimely death, although they were far fetched.

After giving herself a moment, she punched the extension to Dr. Shoemaker. Surprisingly, the woman answered immediately.

Therese got straight to the point. “Am I going to have to discuss the whole list of issues that were relayed to me? I mean, I’m concerned about certain individuals hearing of this and figuring out the source. We don’t want any retaliation going on here. How much are we sharing with the board?”

The CEO sighed heavily into the phone. “I understand your concerns, Therese. On the other hand, we can’t perpetuate a culture of hiding the truth out of fear. I’ve been thinking about this. The board needs to know we have serious allegations, and they need to approve bringing in independent counsel.”

Therese was alarmed that the hospital president wanted to hire attorneys. That seemed so serious. “Isn’t this something we can handle with our own review? Bringing in attorneys will go over like a lead balloon!” Her anxiety about the hostile doctors ratcheted up tenfold.

“I understand, but our key internal people are either out or their positions are open. I think the best approach is to frame this as an issue Michelle had been looking into before she left, with a subsequent complaint. And we are not going to raise those other suspicions about the robbery that resulted in Michelle getting shot, I want to be clear about that. That is conspiracy talk and won’t help our case. I do want you to state you’ve also heard concerns, but I don’t want to make this about you as the ‘source.’ We don’t need people spreading rumors and making assumptions about where this complaint originated."

"I've not been spreading rumors or engaging in conspiracy theories!" Therese shot back, offended at the suggestion. None of this was her doing.

"I'm not saying *you* have, but we both know it's always an issue around here. You have a great deal of influence with the board, and you have credibility, based on your role. I think we will have an easier time if you support the need for a review. We won't call it an investigation. Also, I am planning to remind them that we are currently without our attorney and compliance officer, and we don't want to delay responding to reported allegations. And this meeting will not include anyone associated with the clinic, since they are specifically mentioned in the complaint."

Therese felt a small amount of relief at that, but she knew how the doctors on the board reacted if they thought any of their colleagues were being accused of something. "I'm still not so sure this is a good idea. General counsel will return in a few weeks."

"Therese, I need you to back me up on this. You know how the doctors can be. They stick together. We shouldn't shirk our responsibilities because it's uncomfortable. I just need you to confirm you're aware of concerns and support a review." Dr. Shoemaker sounded weary, and Therese realized this wasn't easy for the other woman, either.

"Yes, okay. I can do that," Therese responded, a feeling of dread forming a heavy ball in her gut. "Let me rearrange my schedule. I was supposed to teach a class this evening."

"Thank you. And just so you know. I've already put a call in to Peter Hancock about getting an investigation going. I told him I needed board approval, but he said they can do it quickly if need be." She paused, sighing again. "I should have given you a heads-up in advance, I've just been so overwhelmed with this as well as other things going on."

"It's all right. We'll get through it," Therese said, hoping she sounded reassuring when she felt totally the opposite.

The board meeting went as she expected and as the CEO had feared. Copies of the list of issues were passed to the members with the understanding that they be returned at the end of the meeting to preserve confidentiality. The directors who were nonmedical members of the community, such as the banker and the real estate broker, immediately agreed that any serious allegations should be immediately investigated. The physicians, who were prevalent in the group, reacted defensively for the most part and suggested that the former compliance officer, Therese, and even the CEO were being alarmist and would create a hostile work environment toward the physicians if outside attorneys were brought in.

"Why don't we wait until our own attorney gets back?" one portly physician demanded. "This is just a waste of money and an insult to the professionals in the clinic. It doesn't sound to me like you even have any actual credible allegations. This feels like some sort of witch hunt to me," he huffed, crossing his arms over his chest.

Another physician member, a thin woman whose dark brown hair was skinned back tight, pursed her lips and nodded in agreement.

The chief medical officer, Dr. Pascale, watched and listened to his colleagues before nodding.

"Dr. Shoemaker, with all due respect, perhaps it would be best to wait and handle this internally."

The board chair, a very polished Asian man who owned a financial advisory firm, finally spoke up. "I don't believe that we are properly exercising our fiduciary duty if we know of such allegations and do not act promptly," he said. "We are all professionals; we all understand that serious complaints must be evaluated timely and objectively. I would ask that we use attorneys who can exercise extreme discretion and not cause undue disruption." He paused, looking at his colleagues.

"Just having them here creates a disruption," Dr. Pascale said, crossing his arms over his chest in solidarity with his colleagues. "It sends a message to the physicians that every time a disgruntled employee complains they will get investigated."

"I appreciate your concern, Dr. Pascale. But I feel strongly in this case that we cannot defend inaction." The board chair scanned around the table to evaluate reactions. Seeing a number of grudging nods, he said, "I move to approve the hiring of an attorney, to be selected by Dr. Shoemaker, to conduct this investigation. The investigation should be under attorney-client privilege, with reports back to this board. Can I get a second?"

One young doctor in scrubs raised her hand cautiously. "I

second the motion."

The meeting concluded with a majority voting to do the investigation and with only three physicians voting no. The board chair reminded them about the confidentiality of the meeting, gathered the copies of the list, and bid the group good night.

After the board members filed out of the room, Therese reached over and patted the CEO's arm.

"Well, we got through that! And you did well. They didn't take our heads off!"

Dr. Shoemaker smiled, but it was more of a grimace. "Yes, we got through it. But I think the worst is still to come. We didn't have to deal with Dr. Al and his clinic pals. Wait till they hear about an investigation at their clinic. I'm not looking forward to that one bit."

Therese walked out, checking her phone, which had chirped in her bag. It was a text from her intern, giving an update on the training class. As she started to respond, she was stopped by Dr. Pascale, who stood in her path to the back door.

"Therese, can I have a word?" he asked.

Alarm sparked through her veins at his serious tone.

"Of course, Dr. P." She forced a smile and tucked her phone back into her bag as casually as she could.

"I know you are new to this role, and I want to make sure you get off on the right foot here." He smiled.

Uh oh. "Certainly ..."

"You need to understand how important it is for this hospital that we don't alienate our physician partners," he said. "The doctors are the ones who bring in our patients. If they quit practicing here, well, we won't have patients in our beds. Do you follow me?"

"Well, yes, of course."

"I just want you to make sure you don't get a reputation for causing trouble. I'm sure you know that the nursing staff here can be very militant, and they are not above spreading rumors and conspiracy theories. As a leader at this hospital, you will need to keep a distance from such behaviors if you want to be successful. Do you understand?"

She could feel her anxiety giving way to anger. Swallowing back her instinctive response, she nodded. "I certainly don't intend to get involved in any troublemaking or conspiracy theories. However, it is also important for me to be a trusted resource for all staff, including physicians and nurses, and to do the right thing, regardless of who may not like it. In this instance, I became aware of serious allegations. I had a duty to report that. Surely you are not suggesting that I cover up this type of report, *Doctor*?"

She regretted her sarcastic tone as she saw Dr. Pascale's face begin to flush.

"Well, *Reverend Mother*, what I would suggest is that you tend to your flock and leave the medical staff to me if you want to be successful here. That's all I wanted to say, just a well-intentioned word of advice." With that he turned and walked away, leaving Therese feeling both angry and alarmed.

5

JUSTINA

Justina arrived early for her first day at her new job, eager to get involved in what would hopefully be an important case. She had heard from other classmates about the grind of intern work, lots of boring research and drafting meaningless documents. She felt so fortunate to maybe get started right away on a real case.

Sari led her to a small windowless office and explained the company's email system and various shared drives and that they were still waiting for her to get set up with the IT department. She was given a folder of company policies, a confidentiality agreement, and a code of conduct to review. It was quiet, and nobody had come by to greet her. She felt invisible. She flipped through the documents, her thoughts wandering.

Life at home was crazy hectic these days, and it had been difficult to study, even though her father was home more now. In theory that meant she wouldn't be watching Jose as much, freeing up her time, but in reality, it had been the opposite. Her father's recent publicity had led to a call for him to run for a congressional seat, surprising them both. Justina knew her mother had often encouraged him to run, but after she was killed, many years ago, he had lost the heart for it. Suddenly his behind-the-scenes advisory role was in the forefront, and people looking for a fresh face were pushing him to run. She was so proud of him and thrilled at seeing him so excited about something again, but she was also anxious about what this would mean at home. She needed to excel at this job, and keep up at school, plus take care of Jose, and be supportive of her father. It just seemed like a lot … She reminded herself of Daniel, and their plans, and the burden seemed much more worthwhile.

Her thoughts were interrupted when Carmen appeared at her doorway, a thin manila file folder in hand.

"Welcome to your new home!" Carmen said with a friendly smile. "I guess you heard you may be working on a new case right away?"

"Yes, when Peter Hancock called me, that's what he said."

Carmen nodded. "Yes, the client has confirmed they want to move forward. We're going to be looking into some complaints of possible drug diversion at St. Matthew's Hospital. They're a good client of ours, and they want us to do an attorney-client privileged investigation, which one of our senior attorneys, Frank Osbourne, will be leading. But we want you to go along and help with the interview and notes. You'll be going over there with Frank to meet with the hospital president and a couple of other executives to get the process started. It will be a good learning opportunity for you. Okay?"

Justina was impressed. It sounded like a very important case. "Of course! Just tell me when and where, and I'll be there!"

Carmen smiled and handed her the folder. "We don't have much information yet, but here's what we have, so you can get oriented to the case. We have some other materials on the hospital, as well, in our shared drive, if you have access already, for additional background. This is probably not a big deal; these sorts of concerns are often false alarms. But the hospital has had some trouble before, so they are very cautious. And it's politically sensitive, in terms of the physicians involved, just so you know. Their in-house attorney is out of town, which is why they called us. Frank will come find you when he finishes his current meeting."

Justina was perusing the folder before Carmen had even turned to leave, eager to start on her first real case.

Impatient to get started, she devoured the file from St. Matthew's, although, as Carmen had stated, there wasn't much. There were the notes taken by an attorney at the firm during the call from the hospital, with a brief outline of the concerns as well as a printed list of issues. Justina looked it over but couldn't tell who had written the list; probably someone at the hospital. The notes showed the hospital president was the one who made the call to McIntyre, Jones, and Hancock.

According to the file, one of the nurses had gone to the

vice president of Pastoral Services, a woman named Therese Devereaux, reporting a concern that some of the physicians were involved with a drug diversion scheme. The nurse had gone to the chaplain because she was afraid to go to anyone else, for fear that it would be traced back to her. The nurse reported that the compliance officer had left suddenly, and the nurses were afraid to go up against the physicians. The head of Pastoral Services had asked the nurse to document her concerns. *Oh, so that's where the list came from.* According to the attorney's notes, the comment was made by the nurse that the physicians "owned" the hospital and were doing whatever they wanted. *Wow, this sounds serious,* Justina thought. She couldn't imagine how to begin to tackle such a case and was eager to get started.

Frank Osbourne arrived at her office within the hour. Frank, according to Carmen, was experienced with cases like this as a former government prosecutor and investigator. She was immediately intimidated by him; he was tall, with broad shoulders and long legs, and his dark hair was graying at the temples. *He looks like a fed,* Justina thought upon meeting him.

Frank didn't waste much time on pleasantries as they gathered their laptops and headed for St. Matthew's, although he was friendly enough. They rode together to the hospital, with Frank giving Justina some background on the hospital and some information on common drug diversion issues that can come up in a hospital. Justina followed along in fascination, not wanting to miss a word. This was the kind of stuff you read about. She kept quiet, listening. She was determined to make a good impression and not show her inexperience. This was her first case; it was critical that the firm see she was an asset so they would offer her a real job when she finished school and passed the bar exam.

Frank explained what he needed from her: she was to take notes of all the interviews and help with document organization and review. He went over the rules of attorney-client privilege with her and explained the process of the investigation. By the time they arrived, she felt confident that she could hold up her end, although she felt a twinge of anxiety when they were shown to their assigned conference room. Suddenly it became very real.

Their first meeting was scheduled with Dr. Barbara Shoemaker, the hospital president who had called and engaged the law firm. Justina wasn't sure what she was expecting, but the woman running the hospital was not what she would have imagined: tall, slender, with her light brown hair cut in a practical bob, with no attempt to cover the traces of gray. Although she was wearing a conservative gray suit and practical low-heeled black pumps, Justina was surprised at how attractive and gracious she was. The woman greeted them warmly and expressed appreciation for their quick response.

"Peter Hancock and I go way back," she explained to Justina with a smile. "I know I can always count on him to take care of us in a crunch."

Frank, not surprisingly, got down to business quickly, and Justina took detailed notes, mostly on Dr. Shoemaker's reiteration of the facts in the file and Frank's guidance about the process. As Frank got into more details with Dr. Shoemaker about the specific interviews and documents that he wanted, she began to feel a bit overwhelmed.

Apparently, the CEO felt the same way. As Frank went down the list, Barbara rubbed her temples, as if fighting the onset of a terrible headache.

"This stuff always happens at the worst time," she said. "For the first time in years, Greg takes an extended vacation out of the country. Now I have this!" She gestured to the list of allegations on the table in front of Frank.

"Yes, I understand," Frank said calmly. "But you want to have a thorough review in order to put this to rest. You don't want to create a whistleblower situation where a staff member goes outside the hospital to report wrongdoing."

Barbara grimaced. "Where is my general counsel when I need him? He would normally be handling this," she explained as she glanced at her phone. "Anyhow, I will have my assistant, Mina, help you set up whatever meetings you need, and if you give me the list, I will let them know what is going on. And thanks for coming on such short notice. This is all we need right now." She paused. "Oh, and this must be as low key as possible. The physicians on the board were not supportive and we need to try to not rock the boat any more than necessary."

"Of course, that's usually how it works," Frank told her. "Can you see if Ms. Devereaux is available now while we're here? It would help to hear from her first about how this all came about before we really dig into additional interviews."

"Certainly. I'll have Mina track her down. She'll help you set up the other meetings, as well. Feel free to go to her with anything you need. I need to go now. I have another meeting, but Mina can help you. Give Peter my regards, okay? Tell him we need to get together again soon." She looked at her phone and wasted no time leaving the conference room.

Mina, a smooth-skinned young Filipina, immediately appeared with a notepad in hand.

"Barbara said I should help you set up some meetings?" she asked.

Frank gave her detailed instructions and asked her to call Therese Devereaux to see if she could meet them while they were on-site.

"You mean Mother Marie," she corrected. "I'll locate her for you."

"Okay, thanks," Frank said, and looked at Justina with a shrug, as if to say, *I don't know, either ... we'll find out.*

After Mina left, Frank stretched, yawning. "I'm going to track down a cup of coffee while we wait. Can I get you anything?"

"Some water would be nice," Justina said, flipping through pages in her laptop and filling in details she hadn't captured. After he left, she marveled at the fact that she was sitting alongside a former government prosecutor, investigating a possible drug crime. This was the sort of issue you read about in the news. She was mulling over her good fortune to be involved in something so important when there was a light tap on the open door.

"Can I help you?" Justina asked, not sure how to respond to the woman at the door and wondering if perhaps someone else was scheduled to use the conference room.

"I don't know. I was called down to meet with some attorneys? My name is Therese Devereaux."

Justina stood, smiling. "Yes, come in. I'm Justina. My colleague Frank will be right back. We're the ones you are supposed to meet with. Thanks for coming so quickly." She managed to hide her surprise at the appearance of the reverend mother, who was an exotic beauty in a boxy brown pantsuit that did nothing to detract from her very feminine figure. And then there was the question of this woman's name. That was certainly something she could straighten out while they waited for Frank. After offering the other woman a seat at the conference table, Justina said, "I'm sorry. We have some confusion about your name." She looked at her notes. "Is your name Therese, or Marie?"

"Well, it is both. My proper name is Therese Marie, but I can't very well be called 'Mother Therese,' right? That would be unseemly! So staff here know me by my middle name," she said, a melodious lilt in her voice as she explained. Her large almond eyes sparkled with humor, and Justina immediately liked her.

"I see." This woman sure didn't fit any stereotypes of a reverend mother that Justina might have had in mind, and she couldn't help but smile at Therese Devereaux's explanation. "We'll get started in a minute. Frank should be right back. I'm an intern, so we'll need to wait for him."

Therese leaned back, crossing her legs. "I thought you looked very young to be an attorney. But then, I am getting old. Everyone looks young to me these days!" she said with a laugh, as though perhaps the statement was true, but wasn't bothering her in the slightest.

"No, I don't think so, you don't look old in any way ..." Justina began, as Frank entered the room, and Therese stood to greet him.

Justina made the introduction, and Frank handed each of them a bottle of water. He took a long sip of his coffee and began giving his disclaimer about their roles as legal counsel and explaining confidentiality. Once the preliminaries were completed, he began the interview, first asking the reverend mother how she had come to hear the complaints.

"It was very odd, actually." Therese frowned. "The director of nursing, Angela Jackson, came to me just as I was getting ready to leave one night. I remember it clearly, because I was supposed to be teaching a class and was running late. I'm afraid I was a bit distracted at first, trying to get her to come back the next day, but she insisted. She told me that we have a compliance problem at the clinic, maybe drug diversion, and that some of our physicians are involved."

"Did she say which physicians?" Justina asked, when Therese paused. Frank shot her a look that she couldn't decipher. Had she overstepped? It seemed a logical question.

"Well, the two physicians down there are Dr. Al-Basri and Dr. Powers, they run the clinic. We've had other complaints about Al-Basri, but mostly just personality issues. Anyhow, she said she thought there might be some drug diversion going on with some of the patients that were coming in, and some problems with 'fraud.' I will admit, I wasn't at all sure that she was bringing me a legitimate concern. I mean, the nursing staff get into disputes with the physicians all the time, and Angie can be very vocal in defending her nurses. So I was kind of, like, really? Why are you bringing this to me? It just seemed very unusual. I'm not the person who should get those kinds of complaints."

Frank nodded, considering. "And who, in your opinion, should be getting those concerns?"

"Well, I guess the attorney. Or the compliance officer. Certainly not the head of Pastoral Services. I couldn't figure that one out." Therese shrugged, and Justina noted she was fidgeting with the badge hanging around her neck, the only sign of nervousness.

"Did you ask her?" Justina piped up, forgetting again that she was supposed to just be taking notes. It seemed the obvious question, and Frank gave her another look, but then nodded to their interviewee to continue. Justina reminded herself of her role and hoped she wasn't going to be reprimanded. It was hard to be quiet when she felt herself getting wrapped up in the case already.

"Oh yes, you can bet I did. I wanted to get out of there. I was late," Therese said emphatically. "But she said, 'The lawyer is out, and the compliance officer is gone.' She told me it had already gone on too long, and she was afraid people would get hurt."

Justina stopped typing, looking at Frank for his reaction, suddenly feeling very out of her depth and not even tempted to jump in on this one.

Frank was silent for a moment and took a sip of coffee. Finally, he said, "Do you know why she thought people would get hurt? And what happened to the compliance officer? I know the attorney is on vacation, but we haven't heard the story on the compliance officer."

Therese sighed, looked at Frank, at Justina, and then down at the table, considering. Finally, she said, "Angela said she thinks that there are more people involved than we might expect, and that they are very powerful. She talked about the clinic but didn't name names. And then the thing with Michelle, the compliance officer, is, she was fearless, and the doctors got upset with her all the time."

Justina looked at Frank, who seemed to be waiting for the reverend mother to continue. Since he wasn't asking, she did. "Why were they upset with her?"

Therese frowned. "Whenever she did an audit or came to tell them about a policy they didn't like, they would complain that she was making their work harder. But it didn't stop her. She wasn't a whiner or someone who was easily intimidated. Recently she was looking into some issue at the clinic and then she suddenly gave her notice. That night, she was killed at her home in a robbery. Everyone on the leadership team here, and the police, are saying it was just a robbery; nobody wants to admit that it was very unusual. Although the staff have a different opinion. No other robberies in her neighborhood, which is typically a very safe one, and nothing stolen. The whole thing smells bad. Dr. Shoemaker won't even talk about it, calls it a conspiracy theory."

"So, she quit her job, then was killed?" Frank frowned.

"I don't know exactly what happened," Therese said, her expression troubled. "But I can tell you this much. She wasn't planning on leaving her job. It was very sudden. She just went in to HR and gave them her notice and some story about a personal problem. Then that very night someone broke into her house and shot her in the back."

Justina froze in her typing. Suddenly this case was about more than fraud or drug diversion. Someone had already died! It had never occurred to her that she could be getting involved with dangerous people where lives might be at risk. She recalled her father's initial warning and wondered if he had been right.

6

JUSTINA

Justina mulled over the case all evening but didn't mention anything to her father. She knew what his reaction would be, and she feared he might be right. He would never want her safety at risk by dealing with dangerous people. On the other hand, although she felt apprehensive, it was that much more important to help figure out what was going on so it could be stopped. And really, the compliance officer's death could have been totally unrelated. But it didn't feel that way.

Justina arrived at the hospital the next day earlier than she had expected. Traffic between the law school and the hospital was lighter than normal.

Since she was early, she stopped and got her visitor's badge from the security desk and then went looking for the clinic. She knew it was attached to the hospital, on the main floor, so she went exploring. It seemed important to see the actual place they were investigating. She found it without difficulty and wandered in.

The waiting room was full, with a vast assortment of patients. There were a couple of harried-looking mothers with crying children, an elderly Black man in stained khakis with his arm in a sling, a couple of young Latino men with no identifiable problems, and a poorly dressed bleached-blond woman who was nervously jiggling her leg and chewing on her fingernails. There was a heavyset, dark-skinned woman in pale blue scrubs working at the desk, focused on a computer screen.

As Justina was checking out the clinic, a white-coated man with olive skin came out from the back and complained loudly to the woman at the desk about how she had scheduled patients. He had a heavy accent, but his reprimand was very clear to Justina and all the patients in the waiting room. When he finished with the cowering woman at the desk, he looked up and made eye contact with Justina. In that split second, she realized that she stood out from the patient population based on her black suit and laptop bag.

"Can I help you?" he asked her, in a less-than-friendly voice.

"No, I'm sorry. I just made a wrong turn," she said, moving to leave the way she had come. *That's all I need, to get one of the doctors complaining about me,* she thought. Even though she hadn't done anything wrong, she could see his displeasure, as if she was invading his territory without permission. She wondered if he was one of the doctors running the clinic and felt a ball of anxiety in her stomach, warning her that he probably was one of the physicians in question.

She made her way back across the expansive lobby, crowded with scrub-clad men and women as well as clumps of patients and families looking at directional signs or hurrying to their appointments. She thought of the dead compliance officer. How many of these people would be comfortable coming here if they knew? No wonder the CEO and others wanted to ignore the killing and let it go as a robbery. She rode up in a crowded elevator, sharing her space with a large group of young people in green scrubs who appeared to be residents, based on their badges. They paid little attention to Justina as they openly discussed a case they had just worked on. Justina thought about the privacy laws she had recently spent hours reading but didn't feel she could say anything. Stay in your lane, she reminded herself.

When she arrived at their assigned conference room, Frank was already set up, laptop open, and reviewing the day's schedule with Mina. The plan was to interview the nurse who had originally reported concerns, Angela Jackson, and meet with the two physicians who had primary responsibility for the clinic. Once they had the initial conversations, they would determine which additional interviews would be needed. Justina also still had to go through the files from the compliance officer to see if there was anything of interest.

Angela Jackson arrived on time and had either run up the stairs or was having an anxiety attack, judging by the gloss of sweat shining on her dark skin. She stood inside the door for a moment, eyes darting like she might decide to run away.

"Please, come in and have a seat," Frank told her with a smile. "We won't keep you very long."

The nurse glanced at the window that provided a view of the busy hallway outside.

"Can we shut those blinds?" she asked, motioning to the window. "I don't want anyone seeing me in here with you all. No offense," she added, with the barest twitch of a smile.

At Frank's nod, Justina jumped up and pulled down the blinds, blocking the view. Angela finally sat in the chair nearest the door, pocketing her phone and picking up a stray pen that was lying on the table. After giving her the standard opening instructions about confidentiality, Frank got right into it, asking her to provide them with the details of her concerns.

The nurse took a deep breath and looked down at her hand clenching the pen before responding. "We have two physicians down there," she began. "There is Dr. Powers and Dr. Al-Basri. We also have residents working in the clinic, and a physician assistant. I don't know what is going on exactly, but we have a lot of patients come in who don't seem to have real medical issues."

When Angela paused, Justina looked at Frank to see if he was going to ask the obvious question, which he did. "If they don't have medical issues, why are they there? Have you reviewed the records?"

Angela nodded. "Yes. They always have a complaint. But most real patients that come in, you can tell if they have a problem. Their body language, how they communicate. A lot of times you can just look at them and know why they are there. I've been a nurse a long time. And another thing, there's a guy who brings patients there, I've seen him outside with different groups of people. Those patients rarely see one of the doctors; it's usually one of the residents. So it looks like a batch of patients get dropped off, and they have very short visits. A lot of times we only see them once, which is also odd. They always get a prescription for Schedule II pain drugs. Almost always. So I looked up a few of those charts, because something seemed odd. The charts I saw all said headaches or backaches. You know, those things that the frequent flyers always say."

Frank nodded, and Justina tried to capture everything. She felt stupid but had to ask, "What do you mean, frequent flyer?"

Angela looked her over and gave a short laugh, the first time she had managed a real smile since coming in the door. "I can see you are very new to this," she observed. "A frequent flyer is a patient who comes in, often to the emergency room or clinic, with some pain issue, like headache, that can't be disproved. They are looking for drugs. After a bit we know them all. But they move along when they get cut off."

"So how many patient records did you review?" Frank asked. "How many are we talking about here? I mean, you always have some level of drug seeking to manage. What makes this seem different to you?"

Angela sighed. "Dr. Al-Basri caught me looking at the

files, and he was very upset, told me I wasn't qualified to practice medicine and had no business in his records. That's one thing. I mean, it's normal for me to check over the charts. It is not inappropriate. I am very picky about our documentation, especially with residents here. They are still learning and need to be supervised. Or at least they are supposed to be."

Frank nodded. "Right. I would think that's your job, checking that."

Angela nodded. "Exactly. And then, another issue: these patients are being brought here, by the same person, which is something I have never seen in all my years, plus, like I said, they usually just come in once. Most frequent flyers come until we cut them off. Also, I know that the compliance officer came down one day and started looking in our system. I don't know why. But Dr. Al made a scene in front of the patients. Michelle stood up to him, but he threatened to talk to Dr. Shoemaker about her interference with medical practice. And now she is gone—the compliance officer, I mean. Totally gone. As in murdered." She paused, taking a deep breath, hesitating.

"Go on," Frank encouraged.

"I know he has some very powerful friends, and he brings in a lot of business to the hospital … I think there is something very wrong here. It might not sound like much proof, but I feel it, you know? It's not right." She looked at her hands again, rolling the pen back and forth between her fingers.

Justina typed as fast as she could, trying to focus on the

task at hand rather than allowing herself to think too much about what the woman was saying. Wanting to be sure, she asked, "He who? Who are you referring to just now? Dr. Al-Basri?"

Angela nodded, looking back and forth at Justina and Frank, as if uncertain she had said too much. Frank nodded encouragement. "Go on," he said, and Justina realized his strategy was to say as little as possible to keep people talking.

"Well, another thing," Angela continued, after thinking about it. "Those residents. They are not allowed under the rules to just see patients and write prescriptions for narcotics with no supervision. I can't say for sure, because they all work some crazy hours. But looks to me like those doctors aren't checking the charts or seeing any of these patients the residents are handling. But none of us can say anything. I'd be out a job. Or worse."

Justina thought back to the man she had seen in the clinic that morning. If that was Dr. Al-Basri, she could imagine how ugly he would be to someone questioning his records.

"Do you think someone here was involved with what happened to the compliance officer?" Frank asked, and Justina was grateful for the direct question, but feared the response.

Angela's eye's widened, and a look of alarm crossed her face. Her next words came out in a rush. "Look, I wish they hadn't called you all. I mean, I don't really know that anything is wrong, it was just a feeling, mostly. I shouldn't have made that list. And I need my job. I don't want any trouble. I'm not accusing anyone of anything!"

Justina started to ask, but Frank got there first with the obvious question. "Why do you think your job would be in jeopardy?"

Angela shook her head. "People sometimes disappear around here. I don't mean, like, they are found dead in a river somewhere, well, except for Michelle, but they just suddenly aren't here anymore, and there is no warning, no goodbye party, no announcements. So we just keep quiet and do our jobs."

"But you did speak up, so you must have felt like it was important," Frank observed.

Angela again had a cornered look on her face. "I only went to Mother Marie because I got freaked out about Michelle. One day she was in the clinic, getting yelled at, and then she had suddenly quit and was killed in a mysterious 'robbery.' I never meant to start this whole thing. I didn't know who to talk to; I don't trust HR and the chief medical officer always defends the doctors … So I went to Mother Marie."

"That's totally understandable," Frank said calmly. "You say that people disappear. Do you have any opinion as to how or why that happens? Other than Michelle, I mean. Or who might be involved?" When Angela started shaking her head no, he clarified, "I am just asking for your opinion. It is totally confidential. It just gives us an idea of what has been going on here. If there is something wrong, we need to fix it, right?"

"I really don't know, okay? I just hear things, rumors. And I notice things, like I said. But I can't say more than that, I just don't know." She pulled her phone out of her pocket and sat up straighter in her chair, as if preparing to bolt.

They couldn't get Angela to say any more, and she seemed as though she regretted what she had told them, as she looked back and forth between her phone and the pen she was twisting through her fingers. After Angela left, Mina poked her head in to see how they were doing and to let them know about their next meeting. "Dr. Powers can meet you now, if you're ready," she offered. Justina wondered how this doctor would compare to the other physician, who she was already starting to fear.

Dr. Powers entered the conference room shortly, bringing an entirely different type of energy with him. He was stocky and deeply tanned, his close-cropped light brown hair fashionably spiky. Justina figured him to be in his early forties, although the energy in his blue eyes and sparkling smile make him seem ageless. He appeared so open and friendly, especially compared to what she had seen and heard about the other physician, Dr. Al-Basri, that Justina was caught off guard. He smiled engagingly at them both as he entered the room, and Justina immediately felt more relaxed, pushing the fears from the last interview to the back of her mind. If she needed a doctor, she would not hesitate to go to him.

The physician relaxed into his chair, sitting back and crossing his ankle over his knee, adjusting the crease in his beige trousers as Frank went through his spiel about why they were there, confidentiality, and thanking him for his time. Justina admired the physician's expensive Italian leather shoes … they looked like some her father had admired when they were shopping in the city but said were too expensive. Clearly the clinic was paying well.

"Hey, it's fine. If there is anything going wrong, I want to help. Please. Feel free to ask me whatever you need to. I have been around here a long while, and I am more than happy to share with you what I know about the clinic, the hospital, and all the problems here." He smiled and glanced down at his vibrating phone, moving quickly to switch it off.

At Frank's urging, Dr. Powers walked them through the organization of the clinic and hospital, which didn't really add much. As they got past the general preliminaries, however, Frank asked him about anything he might have noticed in the clinic that was out of the ordinary or inappropriate.

As he considered the question, Dr. Powers frowned and looked at Justina and then Frank. "You know, I can't say that there is anything actually wrong," he began. "But I don't like how Al treats the staff. And I know that patients have noticed it. It's not an issue for the lawyers, though. It's just not how I think things should be run."

"Al?" Justina asked, just to be sure who he was referencing.

"Sorry. Dr. Al-Basri. Lots of us call him Al. Anyhow, he rips up the staff in front of patients. He's a good doctor, but his behavior sometimes … it's just not what I like to see in our clinic. But I don't think there is anything inappropriate going on. No, not like what you might be looking for."

Frank thought for a moment. "What sorts of things does

Dr. Al-Basri get upset about?"

"Oh, you know, just scheduling problems, too many patients scheduled at the same time. Or someone second-guessing his records."

"Were you at the clinic when he had a dispute with the compliance officer about his records?" Frank asked.

Dr. Powers shook his head. "No. I heard about it in the physician's lounge, though. Michelle was just doing her job. That's the kind of stuff I'm talking about. I don't think he meant to cause a problem, but he did. You know, with staff. They don't like to work with him."

"What specifically did you hear about that incident?" Frank asked. "I understand this is just secondhand, but it might be helpful to understand what was going on at the time."

Justina couldn't wait to hear the response. After what Angela had said, what would the physician have to say? She bit her lip to stay silent.

"Nothing much. I heard someone went and complained to Mother Marie. Al was actually grumbling about that the other day. I'm not sure if it's true or how he heard it."

"And what happened after that?" Frank asked.

Dr. Powers shrugged. "I don't think anything happened. I haven't seen Michelle back in the clinic, that's for sure."

"Do you know why the compliance officer was going through his records? Did she say there was a problem, to your knowledge?" Justina had to ask. She couldn't believe that this physician was that uninformed.

Dr. Powers shifted in his seat and glanced at his silenced

phone. "I don't really like to say this," he began. "But I do think it had to do with him supervising the residents. You know, I'm really not comfortable talking about this, I don't want to bad-mouth a colleague, a good physician, on nothing but rumors. I think you were brought in here for no reason. I don't have any personal knowledge of Al doing anything wrong. It was probably a routine review, you know. Supervision of residents is always an issue that the compliance people monitor. You should be talking to him, you know."

Justina nodded, typing up the question and response. She had so many questions but knew she shouldn't interject again, so she waited for Frank's follow-up question.

"Fair enough," Frank said. "And I understand this is all just hearsay, and it's confidential. We're just trying to clear though a little smoke to see if there's any fire under there. We will be talking to Dr. Al-Basri, and he will get his chance to tell us what happened, don't worry."

"Well, if that's all for now?" Dr. Powers asked, his hand on his phone and feet pulled under his chair, ready to stand.

Frank held out his card. "Yes, thank you for your time, Doctor. Feel free to give me a call if anything comes up that you think we should know about. Hopefully, we will be finished up here very soon."

"No problem, happy to help. We all want the hospital to do well and be run right. Let me know if I can do anything further."

With that, Dr. Powers slipped out of the conference room.

Justina looked at Frank. "Well? What do you think?"

Frank pursed his lips, pondering. "We have Al-Basri next. It will be interesting to see what he has to say. Dr. Powers seemed pretty straight-up, so I think we have some management issues there, but maybe not anything that we need to worry about. Some physicians can be temperamental, but it doesn't mean they are doing anything wrong."

"But what about that whole thing with the compliance officer? And those drug patients?" Justina couldn't get the idea of the compliance officer getting shot out of her head, not to mention batches of patients getting pain medications in such an unusual way. But she was still learning, she reminded herself.

"Yes, we definitely need an answer on that one. We need to see what Human Resources says, and what the hospital president has for an explanation. If it doesn't add up, we will need to do more digging. You don't want a compliance officer being thrown out when there are allegations floating around. That's a major red flag. Regardless of any theories about the robbery, the fact that she gave her notice and immediately left with no warning … I hope all of this has a rational explanation. We haven't really heard anything concrete yet, just speculation. We'll know more once we go through those files."

Justina nodded, inwardly cringing. She wasn't sure what she was even looking for.

As if reading her mind, Frank said, "I want you to check for anything that appears to be an audit or investigation file, any notes on issues in the clinic or that came in as a complaint. I'm not expecting you to decipher chart notes, okay? Just go over anything related to the clinic, in particular."

"Okay," Justina agreed. "I can do that."

The meeting with Dr. Al-Basri was very brief and less than friendly. The physician was in a rush and made it clear that his time was too valuable to spend discussing complaining staff and "uppity" nurses. Justina was relieved he wasn't being as unpleasant as she had witnessed him being downstairs in the clinic, but it was clear he was trying to hold his aggravation in check.

Dr. Al-Basri gave short responses to every question and wasn't willing to offer any actual information. After about ten minutes, he said, "I'm not sure this is the best use of my time. Is there anything else specific I can answer? We have some very lazy nurses and staff, and they are always complaining. My job is to take care of patients. I don't need Administration and Nursing nosing around in my records, wasting my time. We have a room full of patients right now, so if we're done here?"

"Of course, Doctor." Frank appeared unperturbed, even though he had been asking questions and getting nowhere. "I know you're busy. We will follow up with you if we need to. Thank you for your time."

Dr. Al-Basri nodded curtly and left the room. No sooner had he exited than Dr. Shoemaker poked her head in.

"How did it go with Dr. Al?" she asked.

Frank chuckled. "Well, I can't say he was interested in actively helping us."

The hospital president shook her head. "Yes, I figured as much. He's a good doctor but very challenging to deal with at times. I just wanted to tell you that we have lost another one. Angela just turned in her notice; she said she had a family emergency out of state and wouldn't be coming back in the near future. Seems like a lot of people are having those sorts of troubles these days." She frowned. "I don't like what's going on here, but I can't pin it down. Hopefully you can figure it out quickly."

"Speaking of that," Frank began. "Can you tell us what happened to Michelle, your compliance officer?"

Dr. Shoemaker sighed. "She resigned with no notice as well. Said she had some personal health issues, needed to take some time off, indefinitely." She shook her head in disapproval. "It was very unlike her. The woman never missed a day of work and always planned any vacation time months in advance. So unfortunate what happened to her afterward, too."

"Did she give you any idea of the problem?" Justina asked. She couldn't get past what had happened to the compliance officer. She kept hoping to learn something that would make more sense than what she had heard so far. Frank gave her a sideways look, but didn't appear bothered.

"No. Nothing. But she sure created difficulties for me. I had to try and explain to the board, of course, and I had no answers. She seemed upset, wanted to go right away. It's a free country, I couldn't stop her. She knew that by giving no notice she was sacrificing her outstanding vacation pay balance, under her employment contract, but she didn't care. She just wanted out of here. Very odd."

Her sadness seemed genuine, Justina thought, but she also didn't see any sign that the CEO suspected foul play. Pushing her luck, Justina said, "It sounds like some of the staff found the robbery and shooting suspicious?" She wasn't sure she should go there, but sometimes Frank seemed too cautious. She wanted to hear what this woman thought.

Barbara frowned. "Yes, I've heard that, and I'm sorry they've been spreading those rumors to you. There is no evidence, that I'm aware of, that it was anything other than a random robbery." Justina got the feeling she had maybe pushed too hard; the CEO didn't look pleased. She looked to Frank, deciding it was time for her to get back in her lane.

Frank nodded. "Well, if you do hear anything else about that, please let us know. For now, we'll keep you posted as we move forward."

After the hospital president left, Frank and Justina exchanged looks.

"Well, that can't be a good thing," Justina said. "About the compliance officer, I mean."

"No, it's certainly not," Frank agreed. "Seems like she was scared, and it didn't sound like she was one who scared easily. If so, she was in the wrong job. But it's definitely a concern. And the nursing director, now, too." Frank shook his head. "Something is definitely not right here."

"I hope it wasn't out of bounds for me to ask her about the robbery. I just can't get that out of my head. I'm not a big believer in coincidence," Justina said, wanting to test her boundaries with Frank before she got herself in trouble.

"You surprised me," Frank said. "Most new attorneys aren't comfortable doing that. I'm fine with it, so long as we stay on topic."

Justina smiled and considered that a green light to be more than a scribe. That was a good thing, because she was having a hard time keeping quiet.

7

JUSTINA

Justina decided to take the boxes of files home to work through, after checking with Frank. She felt guilty about Jose, never having enough time for him, but she wanted to add value to the investigation and show Frank she was an asset. She really didn't know what she was looking for, but at least she could be at home while she worked on it. She felt a sense of urgency to uncover the truth.

The first box was full of mundane business documents, policies and work plans, corporate documents, and organization charts. She pushed it aside. *This isn't going to be too hard, if that's all it is,* she thought, disappointed. The next box yielded a folder documenting hotline calls. Apparently, the hospital had an anonymous hotline where employees could call if they wanted to report a concern. Many of the calls were about scheduling complaints and other typical human resources types of things. Then came one that had been called in anonymously. The allegation was that patients' privacy in the clinic was being violated because employees with no business in the charts were caught reviewing patient records. The complaint didn't name names but did refer to administration. In addition, the caller stated that people should be worrying about their own jobs instead of interfering with the practice of medicine, which they were not qualified to do. Justina read over it several times. Dr. Al, maybe? It sure sounded a lot like him. Was he sending a not-too-subtle message to the compliance officer to stay away?

A note was scribbled in the margin. "Talk to Barbara." There was nothing else attached to the complaint, and Justina noted it was dated just a few days before Michelle had left. Justina tagged it with a bright pink sticky note so she could find it easily later.

The last printout in the folder was another anonymous complaint about the clinic, and this one named Dr. Al-Basri specifically.

"Dr. Al-Basri is scheduling too many patients, and he doesn't see them. He isn't in the clinic when he is supposed to be and has residents seeing the patients. He isn't supervising the residents, but he's billing for those patients."

The note in the margin, dated a month earlier, was "Pull sample—Dr. Al. Call Jen for audit." Justina didn't see anything else relating to that complaint, and all that was left in the folder was a spreadsheet report of the hotline calls, dated merely a week earlier. Justina scanned the report, locating the entry about Dr. Al. The status documented that the complaint was still open. Justina pulled another pink sticky note loose and stuck it to the report.

On a mission now, she dug through the other files in the box, looking for anything relating to the clinic or Dr. Al. Nothing. Privacy audits, a couple of payment error reviews, and some routine reports to the board. *What happened to those audit files?* Maybe the CEO had them. But nobody mentioned that during the initial meeting. Concerned, she texted Frank. “Found hotline complaint—Dr. Al. Looks like audit was to be done but no file. Thoughts?”

Franks response was immediate. “Need to talk to Barbara and admins. Make sure no access to that office before we got there.”

Knowing that she would have to wait until the next day to talk to hospital staff, Justina started putting together a timeline to organize the order of events.

1. Hotline call
2. Michelle goes to clinic to review records. Dr. Al sends her away.
3. Michelle resigns. Murdered at home.
4. Angela goes to Mother Marie
5. Hospital calls the firm
6. Mother Marie meets with us
7. Angela meets with us
8. Angela resigns and leaves
9. Audit file can’t be located

What next? There wasn’t much else to do from home, but

it was eating at her. She couldn't just put it away. So many unanswered questions. She made another note: "Next Steps."

1. Talk to Dr. Shoemaker and admin staff about audit report and compliance officer's office—who had access?
2. Check with Mother Marie and HR—any more info about Angela leaving?
3. Find out about other staff who would know what's going on in the clinic
4. Who is Jen? Might have audit.
5. Research rules about residents

Just as she was starting to look up some rules, Jose came bombing in the door with Celeste on his heels.

"Tina, I am home!" he yelled, as if she didn't know. "We had ice cream!"

"Yes, I guess you did." She smiled at the evidence smeared all over his face and dribbled down his bright green T-shirt.

He dumped his SpongeBob backpack onto the floor, rifling through it.

"I made art," he announced, producing a wrinkled drawing that appeared to be a family of stick figures and some creature that could have been a large cat or dog, or maybe a small dinosaur.

"That's great, Jose," she told him. "Why don't you put it on the fridge, so Papa can see when he gets home."

"Okay," he said, before calling, "Kitty, kitty, come here! I made a picture of you."

Well, I guess that answers that question, Justina thought, exchanging smiles with Celeste as the other woman put on her coat to leave. Celeste had changed so little since she had been Justina's baby-sitter years before. There was a bit more gray in her short black hair, and her plump lap was a little plumper, but she was still the same sweet woman who had held Justina in her lap after her mother had died and her father was at work all the time. Justina reflected that she and her father would never have made it through those bad times without this calm and reliable family friend. And now she was keeping things running by helping to manage Jose, which clearly wasn't the easiest job!

It wasn't long after Celeste left before Hercules scampered into the dining room, looking for a safe space under Justina's chair. *Looks like I'm done working for the day,* she thought, as Jose crawled under the table.

Justina turned some music on and took out some steaks to defrost. *Haven't seen Papa much in a while,* she thought. As if on cue, the front door slammed and he appeared, looking a bit more tired than usual but in good spirits.

"You read my mind, m'ija," he said, eyeing the steaks. "I haven't eaten since a stale doughnut this morning in the car."

"Coming right up," she said, dropping a large scrape of butter into a pan with some rice. "How are things going? It's been forever!"

Her father dropped his suit jacket over the back of the chair, peeled off his tie, and unbuttoned his collar. "Ahhh," he sighed with satisfaction. "That's better. I tell you what.

That firm you are working for is wonderful, to me at least. They are practically funding this campaign. You better keep making them happy!"

"Oh great, no pressure there." She joked, but was proud of the fact that her law firm had decided to contribute to her father's campaign. One more sign that she was clearly working for the right people. And, bonus, her father wouldn't be complaining about her job anymore! "I don't think they have any problem with me, but I know a doctor or two who might want me to take a permanent vacation!"

She was starting to tell her father about her day when his phone chirped. He looked up from the device with a puzzled expression.

"Better hold on to the dinner for a minute," he said. "Marci is stopping by. She didn't say why."

"Well, that's odd," Justina said, wondering why the senator's public relations person and her father's colleague would be visiting them and adjusting the burner under the rice.

Marci arrived like the whirlwind she always was, her loud red sports car serving to announce her presence. Justina had always been fascinated by Marci, who was a brash New York girl-from-Queens who had grown up street smart, but who now was widely respected in the political world for her ability to not only strategize, but to get pretty much anyone to do her bidding. Her network and access to information was as legendary as her brightly colored signature stilettos. Justina had seen the woman work a room, one minute being a charming flirt to get a hardened editor to put her guy's story above the fold, the next minute doing hard negotiating with a reluctant corporate donor and walking away with a big commitment. She was known to be a chameleon, seeming to sense how to approach pretty much any situation and establish a rapport with her target.

Justina sighed. Marci's energy seemed like too much today, and she was still preoccupied with all the questions about the investigation swirling in her head. She wasn't in the mood for politics, but when she opened the door and saw Marci in a baggy T-shirt, leggings, and flat canvas sneakers she immediately knew something was off. And she realized, with a shock, that Marci was also clearly pregnant. How had her father never mentioned that?

"Hey, Justina," Marci said, her smile as perky as ever as she gave Justina a hug. "Is your handsome papa anywhere around?"

Justina heard her father coming up behind her, laughing. "Well, Marci, look at you. I leave the office, and this is what happens? They confiscated your shoes?" He chuckled, and Justina was happy to note how relaxed he appeared but also a bit surprised he didn't have more to say. "Care for a glass of wine?" was all that her father asked Marci.

Justina couldn't believe her father was so oblivious. He was usually the first one to notice anyone's appearance, especially a woman's. Better just to wait this one out and see what she says, Justina thought.

Marci shook her head, the first time she had ever turned down wine that Justina could recall. But of course, it made perfect sense, considering! "Not today. I'm just here for a few minutes. Can we sit down and talk?"

"Of course. What's going on?" Victor asked, motioning to the couch.

"Well, you know Samuel is running for president now, and his campaign is high octane," Marci began, and they both nodded as she continued. "Things are going great, but I have some exciting news." She smiled, her face lighting up. "After years of trying and pretty much giving up, Jon and I are going to have a baby!" She gestured to her little baby bump, and Justina saw her father finally realize.

"That's wonderful!" Victor exclaimed. "I know you have wanted that for years!" He looked her over. "How did I not see that?"

"Well, I didn't want to talk about it while it was early, so I adapted my work wardrobe a bit to cover it up. I have had a miscarriage before and I'm superstitious. But my news is not all good, at least for my career.," Marci said. "I'm a high-risk pregnancy according to my doctor. My blood pressure is high, and I have preeclampsia. Which means that, even though I have a pretty mild case so far, I'm not able to run a presidential campaign. I am supposed to stay away from stress."

"What are you saying, Marci? You're off work?" Justina asked, disbelief in her voice. Marci was a political animal; she couldn't imagine the woman sitting home knitting booties. This bit of news certainly was interesting! Although she didn't see why it warranted a personal visit.

"Yes. Apparently I am a 'geriatric' mother, so with the high blood pressure I am supposed to take it easy. I'm only about 6 months along, so it's critical to try and get this baby to term, or at least as close as possible. I can't lose this baby, so I have to just deal with it." Her face was serious as she went on. "The senator has someone good to replace me, but it still sucks. In fact, that part of it sucks even more. He might find my replacement easier to deal with than me … and this campaign was the opportunity of a lifetime."

Justina could imagine how frustrating that would be, now that she was getting so entrenched in her own work. And she was just getting started. Marci had been working toward this for years. Her father shook his head. "No, nobody could replace you, Marci. You are a force of nature. But even more important, how do you feel? Are you doing all right?"

"I am. That's the hard part. I have too much energy to just sit around. But that's why I'm here. I'm hoping you can help me out."

"Of course! What can I do?"

"It's more of what I can do. I want to help you run your campaign, Victor. No charge. I'm going crazy already, and I've been following your progress, of course! Samuel has, too, and he has no problem with me helping you while I'm off of his campaign. It's legal, and I don't need the money: I'm on leave, I have benefits. So, I am all yours if you will have me."

Justina couldn't believe the brash and confident Marci was looking needy, and her father appeared equally shocked. "Marci, anyone in New York would beg to have you, at any price. I would be a fool to not want your help. But I don't want you to put your health or your baby in jeopardy. I couldn't bear it if I was responsible for anything happening to you."

"I know, and I am not promising to do anything full time. And if I start having problems, I will have to go to bed rest. The doctor already told me I can do something part time, nonstressful." She smirked. "The doctor doesn't understand that stress is like vitamins or oxygen for me. It's more stressful for me to not be actively doing something."

Justina and her father both laughed at that comment. "Well, I would love to have your help, Marci," her father said. "It sounds like you've already thought through any possible problems. I admit, although I've run plenty of campaigns, it isn't the same when you're the candidate and trying to do it all yourself. It's a bit overwhelming."

Marci nodded. "Exactly. You will have a hard time being successful without help." She shifted in her chair and reached into her bag, pulling out a small notepad. "Now. How are you set for donors?"

Seeing that her father was now occupied, Justina returned to the kitchen to finish dinner. She was glad to see her father getting support, especially from Marci. She couldn't help wondering, though, how all this would play out here at home. She was already feeling overloaded. She sighed, turning the burner back on. It would work out.

8

THERESE

Therese stuck the last piece of a stale bagel from breakfast in her mouth, wishing for more hours in the day. Her corner of the floor was quiet and dimly lit, since most of the administrative staff had gone home to their families hours ago. Stomach growling, she tried to recall if there was any food at home that would be quick to fix. She couldn't recall the last time she had been to the store. *Life is sure different living alone*. She looked at the picture of her boy, Mateo. *I'm sorry, baby. I would rather be with you ...*

Her thoughts were interrupted by brisk footsteps coming toward her office. *Now what? Every time I want to get out of here!*

Dr. Al-Basri wasted no time with a courtesy door knock.

"Reverend Mother," he began, his tone somehow making the title an insult. "What can you tell me about this?" He waved a piece of paper under her face, and she could tell it was the now infamous list of clinic allegations.

Therese felt a swift surge of panic rise up in her stomach.

"What do you mean? And how did you get that?" she asked, hoping to stall for a minute while she figured out how to respond. All the copies of that list had been collected at the board meeting. Or so she had thought.

"Do you think I don't know what's going on around here? I want to know where this garbage came from and why you took it to Barbara." He folded the paper lengthwise and tucked it inside the pocket of his white lab coat. He stared at her, unblinking, waiting for an answer.

Calm down, she told herself. To the physician, she said, "They are anonymous concerns. It is not my job to evaluate them, which is why I gave them to Dr. Shoemaker. She thought they should be reviewed sooner rather than later, just as a precaution."

"You are creating a very unacceptable situation, *Mother.* I understand that now we have attorneys nosing around in the clinic, trying to find something wrong. I already saw one of them down there the other day. I have told administration repeatedly that we are already understaffed and barely able to take care of the patients. Who, I might add, have nowhere else to go for care. So if we can't help them because we are answering ridiculous questions from know-nothing attorneys, you are responsible. How does that fit with your *mission*?"

"Dr. Al, I'm sorry, but we have to investigate any legitimate complaint—"

"It's NOT legitimate!" he roared, drops of spittle shooting out along with his angry words. "You have no idea what you are doing. You should go back to your monastery or wherever they found you and quit interfering in the practice of medicine. I am tired of explaining this to idiots like yourself. You will call a halt to this, tell the lawyers it was a joke, I don't care. I am sick to death of this harassment. You make it stop or I will."

Before Therese could respond he turned and stomped out, slamming her door as he left.

Therese could feel the heat in her face, and her hands were shaking. *What in the world have I gotten involved in?* She leaned back, closing her eyes to say a quick prayer for strength.

9

JUSTINA

Justina's phone pinged as she was clearing dishes off the dinner table. It was Frank. "Sorry to bother you at home, Justina. We had a development, and I wanted to let you know, so we can be prepared tomorrow."

"Sure, no problem. What happened?"

"Mother Marie, Therese Devereaux, had a surprise visit from Dr. Al. He had a copy of the list and was furious. He was very threatening to her, told her to make the investigation go away. She's pretty upset, as you might imagine."

Justina gasped. "Oh my God! How terrible! So where is she now? What do we do?" She couldn't believe someone threatening the beautiful reverend mother, of all people.

"She is all right for now. I told her to go home but to be vigilant, lock the doors, that sort of thing. I don't know what's going on here. It may be just smoke, but it looks like we may have stumbled onto something that could be pretty high stakes for someone. Or it could be just this doctor's usual way. Anyhow, just be aware. For now, is there anything helpful in the files?"

Justina told him what she had found in the compliance officer's box so far, and then updated him on her list of to do's. "We need to find a person named Jen," she said. "It looks like she was involved in the audit somehow. Maybe she has the files or other information?"

"Okay," Frank told her. "Bring that hotline information with you tomorrow. We'll also circle back with Therese. I want to hear what was said, word for word, once she's calmed down."

"Yeah, sure, okay," Justina answered, trying to focus on the tasks at hand. "Frank, what do you think is going on here? This is really creepy!"

"If I had to guess, there's some sort of fraud scheme going on in the clinic. Maybe there was something to that drug diversion allegation. We just don't have enough information yet, mostly a string of odd events and vague suspicions. We need to track down any audit reports, too, asap. But we don't start making assumptions about what or who at this point, right?"

"Right, of course. See you tomorrow."

After a restless night and a light morning class load, Justina arrived at the hospital ahead of schedule, with a heavy feeling of dread and anxiety in her stomach. *And I thought this was going to be a cool and interesting job,* she thought. She decided to stop and check on Mother Marie/Therese first. She couldn't imagine how she would feel if she had been threatened like that. So scary! It just added to her concerns about the compliance officer's death not being a random crime.

After getting directions from the security desk, Justina found the Pastoral Services Department and the reverend mother's office. Therese looked no better rested than Justina felt and was nursing an extra-large white paper cup of coffee, about half-full. Justina asked her to join them in the conference room to go over the details of the confrontation with Dr. Al.

"Sure. I honestly wish I was never dragged into this, but sometimes staff prefer to come here rather than their boss or HR, you know? It's a safe place, and they feel comfortable that I won't go telling anyone what they have said." She paused. "Except that I did, didn't I? I guess this is my penance." She grimaced and took a swig of coffee. "Now Angela is gone, and the good doctors are after me."

Justina was at a loss for how to respond. She thought back to her files from the day before. "Therese, who is Jen? Someone who would have something to do with an audit."

"We have a few Jens that I know of, probably more. One in pharmacy, one in nursing … oh, and yes, one in medical records. That's probably the one. You want me to walk you down there?"

Justina looked at the clock. "No, not yet. Let's go touch base with Frank. He should be here by now. Can you come with me? I know he wants to talk to you right away."

Therese agreed. As they rounded the corner toward administration, they saw Barbara Shoemaker standing with her back against the wall in an intense conversation with Dr. Al. He saw them right away and frowned. After saying something else to Dr. Shoemaker, he turned and left, striding off in the other direction.

Justina looked to the hospital president, expecting a greeting or comment, but the woman instead looked down at her phone, which was buzzing, and disappeared into her office without acknowledging them.

"Nice," Therese said. "Looks like we're popular around here." She sounded flippant, but Justina could hear concern in her voice and was surprised by the noticeably different attitude emanating from Dr. Shoemaker.

"Let's see what Frank has to say," she suggested. She was hoping he had some great guidance or insights, because she was feeling way over her head, involved in something she didn't understand and that was starting to unnerve her.

Frank seemed calm, as always, and looked like he had not missed any sleep. "Sorry for what's happened to you, Therese. Justina, can you get the door?"

Frank walked the reverend mother through the events of the night before, Justina taking note of each word.

"So did anyone else know of this meeting with …" Frank looked at his notes. "Angela?"

"Well, Dr. Powers knew something, somehow, because he came and asked me if there were any concerns he should know about. I thought that was very weird. Like, why would he come to me, unless he knew something?"

"Did he explain?" Justina probed.

"Kind of. He said he had heard some rumors, and Dr. Al had been having a fit about all the scrutiny and wasted time. It seemed like Dr. Powers just wanted to make sure nothing was wrong, and to maybe look out for the reputation of the clinic. Everybody knows folks come to me," she added.

"Did he seem angry?" Justina couldn't picture the warm and friendly doctor she had met being temperamental.

"No, not at all. Dr. Powers never loses his cool. He was almost too pleasant. He seemed more concerned that something might be wrong, like he wanted to fix any problems. I didn't tell him much, because of confidentiality. I just told him that there were some rumors about possible overprescribing, but that I didn't know anything about it. Quite frankly, I really didn't want Dr. Al back down here yelling at me, or at the nurses, so I tried to play it down. I'm sorry. I shouldn't have said anything. He caught me totally unaware."

"Of course, you did the best you could in that situation. And you didn't tell him it was Angela?" Frank asked.

Therese shook her head.

Frank pondered for a moment. "It seems to me that anyone could have known that someone came to you if the docs were talking about it. Who else might have seen Angela with you?"

Therese considered the question. "Well, there are residents in and out at all hours. Sometimes administrative support staff. Barbara works crazy hours, but her office isn't that close by. And, of course, various physicians and nurses. It's a hospital. We have folks here all the time. My department isn't right in the middle of patient care areas, of course, but the residency program is operated just down the hall; the chiefs, the coordinators, and the residents are around pretty much day and night."

"Okay, so we can't really eliminate anyone at this point. Let us know if you remember anything else that might help. Now, we need to figure out what happened with that hotline audit."

"Therese says that Jen is in medical records. She can walk us down there," Justina said to Frank.

"No, I don't think we want to be seen doing that at this point," he said. "I don't want to get anyone else on the radar for helping in this investigation. I think right now we need to keep it as low key as possible." Looking at Therese, he asked, "Could you go find her and send her up? Or we can get Mina to help."

"Sure, of course," Therese answered, and stood. "Tell me, do you really think I'm in danger? Or that anyone is? I'm really starting to wonder who I can trust. It's a horrible feeling when you find out your coworkers might actually do you harm. And in a hospital, of all places. Whatever happened to the Hippocratic oath that the doctors take? That whole 'do no harm' thing?" She tried to laugh, but it fell flat as her eyes sought out Frank's for reassurance. She smoothed back her hair in a nervous gesture and seemed reluctant to leave the safety of the conference room.

"I can totally understand your fears," Frank said. "I did tell Security, so it's not a bad idea to have someone walk you out to your car at night. And if you are really nervous … Do you live alone? Do you have someone to stay with you or somewhere you can go for a few days? I don't want to overreact, but we also want you to feel and be as safe as possible."

"I will be fine. I'll just have Security walk me out. And I will keep my doors locked. I could stay with my sister, but she's too far away, and I really don't want to bother her. She's a single mom with two little ones. I'll be fine," she said, and Justina wondered who she was trying to convince. *I wouldn't want to go home alone if someone was threatening me,* she thought. Especially after what happened to the compliance officer!

After they interviewed Jen in Medical Records, who hadn't heard about any audit, they wrapped up for the day, early because Frank had another case he was called to help with. Justina had plenty to do for school, which was being sadly neglected, so a short day worked out for her. She was also hungry, really hungry, so she headed down to the cafeteria, figuring it would be quicker than stopping somewhere.

She had barely sat down with her oversized salad bar lunch when a voice over her shoulder asked, "How can such a lovely young lawyer be left to eat alone?"

She turned her head, surprised to see Dr. Powers standing there with his own lunch tray. "Can I join you?" he asked, smiling engagingly.

Who could resist him? I bet nobody ever does! Out loud she said, "Of course, that would be great." But she wondered why he would want to sit with her rather than the other doctors and residents, or in the privacy of the physician's lounge.

Dr. Powers seemed very at ease, taking his time eating his soup and sandwich, and asking her about herself, how she ended up in law school, all the usual chitchat. She told him about her experience with Hurricane Sandy and volunteering at St. John's Hospital, the recent trip to Mexico City, and then ended up telling him about her dad's campaign and Jose. It was so nice to have someone to just talk to. She felt like she hadn't had a social conversation in years and found herself forgetting that he was actually a potential target of their investigation and, of course, the client.

"Oh, yes, Victor Gonzalez! He's your father? How exciting. Yes, I've seen a couple stories online about him. It looks like he's off to a great start. You must be proud of him … and he of you, of course, having such a smart and gorgeous daughter!"

Justina felt herself blushing, flattered that this very attractive doctor was flirting with her. She decided to ignore the compliments, mostly because she felt way out of her league with him, so she stuck with talking about her father.

"Yes, I'm proud of him. He really wants to make a difference, not like a lot of politicians. He's especially interested in working on drug trafficking and drug addiction issues. He's been very lucky to get lots of donations, so many people believe in him—" She stopped, embarrassed. "Sorry, I'm jabbering." She looked down and began attacking her salad with unwarranted interest.

Dr. Powers reached over and patted her arm. “It’s wonderful for him to have such great support. I don’t blame you for being excited.” He was smiling at her, warm and welcoming, and she felt herself melting just a bit.

He finished the last bite of sandwich, scooping up the last drops of soup with the crust. “Well, I should get back to the clinic. Don’t want to get in trouble with Dr. Al.” He laughed.

Justina smiled. “Well, I don’t blame you for that! He seems pretty, umm, formidable,” she observed, not wanting to say anything too negative about his colleague.

As he arranged his dishes and trash on the tray, he asked, “By the way, how is your project here going? Is everybody being cooperative? Any problems I should be working on? How long will we have the pleasure of your presence?”

“I’m not sure how long it will take, I’m new to this. Most everyone has been helpful …” She thought of Dr. Al but didn’t want to bring that up. “You know, some key people aren’t here, which makes it more difficult to find out what happened with hotline calls, issues like that. But Therese has been helpful, even though she’s getting nervous.”

Dr. Powers stopped in the middle of picking up his tray, frowning. “Why would she be nervous?”

Justina realized too late that she probably shouldn’t have mentioned it. “Oh, it’s nothing, you know, just that people get anxious when there are investigations, and the lawyers are involved.” She tried to make light of it and recover from her blunder.

He smiled again, that stunning white smile that was

matched by his sparkling blue eyes. "Of course, I'm sure it's very upsetting. But please, if something comes up and you need help or find anything wrong that I should be fixing, please give me a call." He reached into the deep pocket of his white coat. "Here's my card with my cell number. Don't hesitate to call me. I'm very protective about that clinic and want to know what's going on. Okay?"

Justina nodded. "Yes, sure, I can do that."

A phone chirped from one of his pockets. "Oops, looks like I'm being summoned. It was lovely to share lunch with you, Justina." He patted her shoulder and headed to the cafeteria conveyor belt to drop off his tray.

Justina watched him go, struggling with mixed feelings. *What was I doing talking about the case to him? I am* so *not supposed to do that!* She felt anxiety rising in her chest and tried to talk herself down. *I didn't really tell him anything, and he is a good guy—no harm.* Once she had the stress reaction tamped down, she thought about the lunch. *Why in the world would he want to sit down with me? He could almost be my father's age!* But he sure didn't behave like her father, and her reaction to him was not daughterly, either. *And he's probably married! He didn't mean anything by flirting. He probably does that with everyone, gets whatever he wants with charm.*

As she thought about that, she stopped short, remembering another situation where she had been tricked by a charmer. *I've done this before,* she thought, recalling an attractive smooth talker who had tried to use her to get a job with her father. *I need to not be so naïve! But what could he possibly want with me anyhow? It's probably just his way.*

She shook her head to clear the thoughts and made a mental note to call Daniel. She had other things to do, things more important than obsessing over this meaningless encounter.

10

JUSTINA

Frank and Justina attacked the list of action items early the next morning, enlisting Mina's help to identify employees and residents at the clinic. Despite Frank's reassuring demeanor when interviewing the potential witnesses, none of them offered any new information. It seemed to Justina that they all were worried about keeping their positions, based on several comments made about the employees who were no longer there and the fear of retaliation.

"Is it unusual for employees to be so afraid to talk?" she asked Frank. "I mean, it's confidential, and they are protected, right? But if people around here tend to disappear, then maybe it's understandable …" She trailed off, as Frank nodded.

"Yes," he agreed. "People are always worried about retaliation, but usually once you explain the confidentiality rules, they start to relax. This is a very nervous group. Of course, Angela just departed with no warning, so it's very fresh. And residents, of course, worry about their careers." He started flipping through his notes, with a slight frown on his face.

"We're not getting any closer with these interviews," he said. "We need to bring in some auditors to look at those clinic charts. Particularly since we can't locate any audits here that the compliance department requested. It's a very big open question. We can't really do much more or solve this until it's been reviewed by outside auditors, and we get their opinion."

"So what will we be auditing?" she asked, her inexperience troubling her again.

"First, we get some reports that show what the doctors billed for, what services, what diagnosis, that sort of basic information. The auditors can tell by looking if it appears typical or if there are any obvious anomalies. Then, based on their initial review, they can pull a small sample to look at the chart notes as compared to the bills, or a larger sample. We want to look at billing issues, supervision by the physicians over the residents, and, of course, excessive prescribing of regulated pain medication without appropriate documentation." She nodded, grateful that Frank didn't seem to mind teaching her the basics.

"That won't be a popular decision." Justina's mind flashed to Dr. Al. She wouldn't want to be the one to tell him.

"Mm-hmm," Frank agreed, distractedly, already scrolling through the contacts on his phone. "Can you get Mina to have Dr. Shoemaker come in when she has a minute? We need to keep her informed. I'll get the auditors lined up."

Frank managed to get some consultants scheduled to do

an audit before the CEO stopped in. Justina was not surprised when Dr. Shoemaker expressed concern about the audit or, more specifically, Dr. Al's response.

"He's already complained about his staff gossiping because you are here," she said. "Even Dr. Powers seemed less helpful than usual. This will be bad for the hospital if those two decide they aren't happy practicing here. Not to mention if they poison other physicians as well."

Justina listened in surprise. Dr. Powers had seemed very helpful, and Dr. Shoemaker was the one who called them to come in the first place. But she was starting to understand that there were a lot of political and financial ramifications. More than she had ever imagined possible.

"We will make every effort to not be disruptive," Frank assured her. "But we'll need one administrative person from the clinic, or maybe from Medical Records, to help coordinate. Also, we need some reports pulled so we can see a summary of the patients and claims. The auditors will then select the records to audit. But in the meantime, we do need some help pulling those reports."

The CEO threw up her hands. "I'm already short on staff. This is going to put a strain on our records department." She paused, looking at Frank., "I know, I know. It's what needs to be done. Anything else?"

"Just that we will conduct this audit under attorney-client privilege, so it will all go through me, and will be highly confidential. You've had one allegation reported to Therese, there was a hotline complaint, a potential audit we can't find, plus the sudden resignations that could be related. This is not something we can ignore. A good audit will show if there are any concerning patterns related to claims or billing that indicate a potential problem. That's for your protection, okay?"

Barbara Shoemaker looked a bit overwhelmed but nodded. "I'll get you the people you need to pull some reports." She left the room with a sigh, her shoulders seeming to droop more than they had been just a few minutes earlier.

"When will the auditors get here?" Justina asked, realizing that this detail hadn't actually been mentioned or even asked about.

"First thing Monday," Frank said. "We want the claims summary report as soon as possible. Then the records will be pulled, with no advance notice to the clinic. We can't allow any opportunities for creative editing."

Justina nodded. "What else can I be working on?" She was eager to be doing something. This process seemed too slow, with so much at risk.

He glanced up at the wall clock. "We need to find out some more about the prescription issue. What pharmacy the clinic patients use, and if there's a way to cross-check the prescriptions against clinic and prescriber records." He paused. "I kind of want to keep this low key, at least until we have to pull any additional records or reports. The auditors will flag anything that needs extra scrutiny on that front, but we need to better understand the process, if anything unusual is being done."

"Maybe Therese can help us. She seems to know a lot

about what's going on in the hospital," Justina suggested. "I can stop at her office on the way out and ask her. That way she won't be seen down here again, if that's causing a problem for her."

"Good idea," Frank agreed. "But let's both go. I need to hear it from her myself, and I want to see how she's holding up."

The reverend mother was putting her coat on when they arrived at her office, with a security guard waiting outside to escort her. The lines around her eyes and mouth appeared more pronounced than Justina had noticed before, and even her skin tone seemed less healthy. She did attempt to smile in greeting, although it didn't reach her eyes.

"Hey, Matt, you don't need to hang around," she told the burly redheaded guard, who looked like he had maybe been recently in the military, judging by his very high and tight haircut. "Do you guys need much time, or can we just walk out?" she asked, looking at Frank.

"No, we'll walk you to your car. That will be fine," Frank said, acknowledging the security guard with a nod.

As they walked down the deserted hallways, Frank asked her about the clinic and pharmacy. "Do the clinic patients fill their prescriptions here at the hospital usually, do you know? I'm not sure of the best way to research the prescription issue without raising red flags until we have to. Just wondering if you have any thoughts."

They walked down a hall and around a corner before Therese responded. "You know, that's a good question. I never thought about it, but it seems that a lot of the clinic patients use the pharmacy across the street. I'm honestly not sure if the owner has some deal with one of the doctors or offers better pricing. But now that you mention it, I have heard some rumbling from the pharmacy director that we have a retail pharmacy, and the clinic steers patients across the street." She stopped walking. "What does that mean?"

Frank tucked his hand under her elbow and nudged her to keep moving. "That's what we will find out. That's very helpful." He stopped speaking and smiled at a gaggle of women in pale blue scrubs passing by with sandwiches and paper soup cartons from the cafeteria.

As they exited the back door of the hospital, Justina was startled as a breeze threatened to rip the door out of Frank's grip.

"Wow, looks like we're getting a little storm! I didn't hear about that," Justina exclaimed, as her hair blew across her face.

"Yes, looks like," Frank concurred. When they got Therese to her little black car, Frank again touched her arm. "Hey, we'll get this sorted out. I want to do a little digging about that pharmacy. Just get home safely and try to relax, okay?" Justina noted with surprise the serious expression on his face. *Wow, he's actually worried!* she thought. She felt a jab of anxiety as she realized that Frank was concerned. Although everything happening had been alarming, the fact that Frank took it in stride made it somehow seem less frightening. Now, though … Justina pushed the thought back as she pulled her jacket tighter against the cold breeze.

Therese smiled, a tight and unconvincing gesture. "Thanks, yes, I know. It's just been a long day. A long week, actually, and it's not over yet. But I'm glad you're both here, please know that. Whatever is going on needs to be uncovered and fixed." She glanced nervously at the string of cars streaming into the employee parking lot. "I think I should get going," she said, clicking her key fob to unlock the car door. Once her car door was open, Frank bid them a good night and turned back toward the other end of the parking lot. Justina lingered, still worrying about the reverend mother. Digging into her laptop case, she pulled out one of Frank's business cards and a pen. She scribbled her own contact information on it.

"Here's my cell number and address," she told Therese. "Feel free to call me if you need anything or just want to talk. I know how it feels to be alone in an empty house. Especially on a stormy night." She didn't know what else she could do, but she was worried about the other woman's safety.

Therese took the card. "I'm sure it's all fine," she said, "but thank you. That's very kind."

As Justina drove home, she tried unsuccessfully to massage her knotty neck muscles at red lights. *This is sure not what I ever imagined,* she thought. *I never thought my friendly neighborhood doctor could be a crook! Or even a killer! And poor Therese!* She fretted, imagining the woman going home to a dark, empty house, knowing that someone potentially dangerous was very mad at her.

Her thoughts were quickly dispelled, however, when she arrived at her own brightly lit and noisy home. Jose had a new favorite thing, a cartoon with dinosaurs and robots in outer space, and he really thought she would enjoy it as much as he did. She was finally able to disengage his grip as he tugged her toward the television by asking if he knew what was for dinner and if, by chance, there might be ice cream.

Fortunately, her father wanted to order Chinese food, which was a good option in Justina's mind, as she couldn't quit thinking about Therese and the threats at the hospital. She barely tasted her dinner as she watched the sky getting darker and heard branches scratching the windows as they were blown about by the gusty wind. Even the weather reflected her sense of foreboding, and she couldn't help but wonder what would come next.

11

THERESE

The windshield wipers could barely keep up with the sudden torrent of pelting rain that bombarded her car as Therese made the slow drive home. She kept going over the events of the past weeks, trying to think of any bits of information that might help the lawyers. This drama needed to stop. It was keeping her awake at night and distracting her attention from her work.

The young lawyer, Justina, was such a lovely girl, Therese thought as she sat at yet another red light. The parade of brake lights ahead seemed endless, blurred through the streaky windshield and driving rain. As the wipers thumped and the green lights changed to red yet again she thought of Justina giving her that business card with her information. Therese couldn't suppress a smile, imagining that sweet little thing protecting her from the angry doctors. It was a thoughtful gesture, though, and one that she appreciated.

After finally arriving at home, Therese hung her dripping coat in the foyer and stepped out of her pumps, noticing that she had somehow managed to get mud on them. She dropped her bag on the couch and flipped on the television, more to dispel the quiet in the house than to watch any particular program. The local news was talking about the storm, with the newscaster being filmed live at the beach with violent surf in the background. The reporter struggled to keep the hood of her rain jacket on, with the wind whipping it relentlessly. "Yeah, we're having a storm," Therese mumbled to the television. "Tell me something I don't know!"

As she realized she was reprimanding the reporter for reporting the news, Therese scolded herself. "Sister, you need an attitude adjustment! And maybe a glass of vino!" She took off her blazer, draping it over a kitchen chair, and went in search of a bottle of wine.

Once she had her wine and was changed into a pair of soft velour lounge pants and T-shirt, she realized she was well beyond hungry. The refrigerator was a sad reflection of her hectic schedule, with an unopened bag of browning salad mix, condiments, and a carton of orange juice three weeks past it's best-by date. "Good grief," she muttered to herself. The freezer was a bit better, a few steaks only mildly freezer burned, bags of vegetables, and a stack of frozen dinners. The steak would be way too much work, so a frozen dinner it would be. None of the options sounded good, but she pulled out a lasagna with meat sauce that she knew was unlikely to resemble anything even close to the picture on the box. She decided it would keep her alive another day. Maybe. She scraped off the chunks of ice crystals, wondering how long it had been in the freezer, and stuck it in the microwave.

Once it was heated, she put the sad little dinner on a plate and took it to the living room. As she settled on the couch with her phone handy and her glass of wine in hand, she started flipping channels to see if there were any good old movies on that might be more cheerful than news. Settling for something on the Hallmark Channel, she took a swig of wine and was just starting to eat when a loud crash erupted around her, shards of glass flying everywhere.

Therese jumped up, panic flooding her entire body. Her living room picture window was shattered, and a large rock rolled across the floor. Not seeing anyone directly outside, Therese grabbed her phone, heart pounding, and ran to the back of the house, locking herself in the bathroom. With trembling hands, she dialed 911 and told them what had happened while trying to control her unsteady voice. After their assurance that the police would be there shortly, she hung up the phone and slid to the floor, leaning against the bathroom door. Shaking and trying not to cry, she listened to hear if anyone was coming into her home through the broken window. She couldn't hear anything. *What do I do if someone comes in? Please, God, let the police come quickly,* she prayed.

It felt like an hour, sitting on the floor listening for any sound of an invader coming into her home that was now open to the world. She focused on her breathing and her prayers, trying to keep herself together. Finally, she heard a car door slam and the police, knocking and calling out. *Thank you, Lord!*

When she opened the front door, she saw two police cars and three officers on her doorstep. "Please, come in," she said, trying not to cry in relief.

Now that the police were there, she could survey the damage. The rock had come right through the center of the glass, destroying not only her window but also her table of framed pictures near the couch. As she recited the events of the evening for the police, she started shaking again, seeing how close the rock came to where she had been sitting. One of the officers, a blond female, had her sit down.

"It's a shock," she said, "But you're okay. Just sit down, and we will take a look around."

Therese nodded and sat down, noticing her dinner and wine, undisturbed on the table, which seemed surreal given the glass all over the floor and rain coming in through the open window. She gulped down the wine. "I'm sorry," she told the officer, who had seated herself in an adjacent chair. "I just … I've never been so terrified. So helpless …" The tears refused to be held back anymore, and Therese felt herself breaking down, unable to stop it. "Not during Katrina, not even when I lost my son …" Her thoughts felt jumbled and random as she buried her face in her hands, and the officer patted her on the shoulder, talking in a soothing voice.

Wiping her eyes, Therese looked at her broken photos. Her favorite picture of Mateo, her son, was smashed, along with two other family photos taken long ago, before Katrina had turned their lives upside down. She reached for the picture of her son and started picking the pieces of glass out of it, trying to preserve the photo itself which fortunately hadn't been torn or scratched. "This is my son," she told the officer, then corrected herself. "Was my son. He died years ago," she said, and then set the photo aside, willing herself not to let it trigger another round of crying.

"Therese, can you think of anyone who would want to hurt you?" the officer asked. "Do you have any enemies?"

Therese visualized Dr. Al, yelling at her in her office, then the indirect threats from Dr. Pascale. She imagined the police going to the hospital and questioning them.

"No, I don't know of anyone who wants to hurt me," she said, cringing inwardly.

They were interrupted by a knock at the door. It was Skip, the neighbor from across the street. "Holy crap, Therese!" he said, eyeing the damage. "I saw the police, wanted to make sure everything was okay …" He surveyed her broken window and the rain that was gusting in. "We gotta get this thing covered," he said. "I can fix that for now, okay?" Therese barely had a chance to reply before Skip was out the door, on his way back home to get whatever materials could cover the window.

"Looks like you have a good neighbor," the officer commented. "Very lucky!"

Therese felt a wave of relief for the second time that night. "Yes, Skip can fix anything, and he's always watching out for me. I am lucky."

She could tell the officer was looking at her closely, trying to see if she was going to have another meltdown. Finally, the woman asked, "Do you have somewhere to go tonight? A safe place? You might want to stay somewhere else until this window gets fixed. Any family nearby?"

"Well, my sister, but I'm not sure …" She thought of the long drive to her sister's home, and the house full of kids. She couldn't face that. Then she thought of Justina's offer. Just for one night, until she could figure out her plan. "Yes. I have a safe place to go."

It was nearly an hour later, after Skip, along with his wife and teenage son, got the window covered and the glass swept up. Therese tried to clean up the water that had blown in and salvaged her photos. The police had not found any evidence to help identify the rock thrower, but they wrote their report, took the rock, and told her they would be in touch. Therese knew they were unlikely to ever find the perpetrator, especially since she was pretty certain what it was related to and the police had no idea to look in that direction.

She grabbed her phone to call Justina, but her battery was dead. She remembered that she had forgotten her charger at home that morning. It was lucky she had been able to call 911! Jeez, what next? Maybe a hotel? She felt tears pushing the back of her eyeballs, trying to burst out again. "Stop it!" she said out loud to herself. "It's done, I'm fine."

Trudging up the stairs, she resolved to pack an overnight bag and find a hotel. Once in her bedroom, she could see the tree branches waving wildly in the moonlight, and she could feel a slight breeze where her window had been left open, blowing her sheer curtain. "Oh great," she muttered, seeing where water had leaked all over the windowsill and was dripping onto her carpet. She tugged on the sash, but the frame seemed stuck, the wood swollen from the moisture. Maybe she should have upgraded to new windows with aluminum frames, like that salesman had recommended, she thought randomly. As she leaned in, putting her palms under each side to wrench it loose, something crashed against the glass, right in her face.

Therese jumped back, staring at the window, which now had a long crack from the top corner to halfway down. She could feel her heart pounding and couldn't move, glued to the spot in the middle of her room. *Breathe. Think,* she told herself. After several deep breaths, she still couldn't quell the panic. *I've got to get out of here!*

Running downstairs, she grabbed her purse, phone, and keys and headed toward Long Beach.

12

JUSTINA

With bellies full of Chinese takeout, Justina and her father traded stories of their day, and Justina noted an edge of concern in her father's voice and face as he reviewed the issues around donors, campaign finance, and his opponent, D. J. Jefferson. She tried to focus on his concerns, feeling as though she had let down both her father and Jose lately. She didn't tell him about the threats at the hospital. There was no point in getting him worried about her on top of everything else.

"I'm just looking ahead," her father was saying. "Jefferson has enormous support and resources. I have a lot of little donors, but the big bucks are just a few key donors, mainly your law firm. I need to get more of the big dogs on my side to fight back against Jefferson's smear machine. It's just beginning, but I think he's trying to plant seeds against me. Thank God for Marci. If anyone can get this train on the track, it's that woman—"

"What's seeds, Papa?" Jose asked while marching his toy

dinosaur across the dining room table.

With a tired smile, her father said, "Seeds are what you put in the ground. To grow a plant. Like flowers, or fruit." However, the child was clearly more interested in his toy, introducing it to the delights of General Tso's chicken.

"Anyhow, Marci warned me that Jefferson's gearing up to get ugly. He hasn't really had a serious challenger, and he's determined not to have one now. Marci said we absolutely can't trust him. So"—he took a sip of wine—"it may be a rough campaign. And it won't last long if we can't get a solid base of donors."

Justina could see he was worried, but she knew her father. "Papa, what can he do to you? You have led such a clean life! There is nothing he can say about you. I have no doubt you will beat him!"

"I hope you're right, m'ija. You know that truth isn't always the problem. It's the lies from 'anonymous sources' that we need to be aware of. And we can fight back, but that requires money. It always comes back to money. Thank God for Marci. I have total faith in her ability to work some magic."

Justina laughed. "Yes, if anyone can make it happen, it's Marci. She's a force to be reckoned with. I almost pity Jefferson if he tries anything!" Her father smiled at that, and she could see he was relaxing.

After Justina cleaned up the remains of their dinner they moved to the family room, where Jose alternated between his cartoon channel and chasing the cat with his dinosaur. While her father had his laptop open, going over potential big organizations that were inclined to donate to political campaigns, Justina was on her own laptop, researching regulations for medical residents, trying to figure out how residents could be involved in whatever was going on at the clinic. There were so many angles to explore, and she had so much to learn. It was frustrating to be so focused and so worried but not really knowing which direction to look first. Her inexperience was a handicap, one that she intended to correct as fast as possible. Not only was she worried about the threats, but she was determined to help solve this case and to prove her worth to the firm. And to herself. Plus the threats to Therese. She just couldn't get that out of her head.

The wind was picking up again, and rain had started stinging against the windows. A large branch slapped the pane right behind Justina, giving her a start. Now fully distracted, she went upstairs to get a sweater and made Jose put on some slippers.

"It's getting chilly, Papa. Do you want me to light a log?" They had a supply of pressed logs that they could put in the woodstove for a bit of heat. Justina liked the little stove and had fond memories of huddling around it with Daniel during Hurricane Sandy, even heating up food on top of it when the power was out. Now it was less of a necessity, but the house felt drafty, and the stinging rain seemed to put a chill in the air.

Her father peered at her over the top of his glasses. "What? Oh, whatever you want, m'ija," he said and went back to his laptop.

Justina started getting a simple fire going in the woodstove. Jose and Hercules came to observe, the cat winding around her ankles as the log flared up. Jose crouched next to her, chattering and warming his toy dinosaurs. She was about to return to her laptop when the shrill screech of the doorbell made her jump and sent the cat flying out of the room.

Justina looked at her father, who frowned, then went to the door, opening it cautiously with the chain on.

Therese, with stringy, wet hair and widc, frightened eyes, stood on the porch. "I'm so sorry to come here," she began. "I'm in trouble." And tears started to flow down her cheeks, mixing with the raindrops.

"Oh my God! What happened to you?" Justina shrieked. "Get in here! Oh my God!" She tugged on Therese's arm, pulling her in while holding onto the door so the wind wouldn't blow it wide open.

Jose ran up beside her, stopping short and dropping his dinosaurs at the sight of the bedraggled woman dripping in the foyer. Her father's glasses and laptop were completely set aside as he stood, looking to Justina for an explanation.

Justina was focused on Therese, however. "What happened to you? Here, take off that wet coat!" she fussed, helping with the soggy jacket.

"Justina, I am so sorry to come here. But the police asked me if I had a place to go, and I just said yes so I could get out of there. I was going to go to a hotel, my phone was dead," she rambled, then she took a deep breath, and Justina jumped in.

"The police? What happened?" Justina asked, stunned and alarmed.

"The police came to my house because someone threw a rock through my front window. I know it was deliberate, no way was it an accident. Then something smashed into my bedroom window … You had said to let you know if I ever needed help." She laughed, shakily, surveying the family. "I'm not sure it's even appropriate. I probably shouldn't be here. I just panicked, I didn't want to have to explain this whole thing to anyone else, and frankly, I was scared to be alone," she said, taking a deep breath. "I can go," she stated, looking from Justina to Victor.

Justina reached past Therese and double-locked the door. "No, you're not going anywhere. It's fine, you need to be safe. Nobody would look for you here. Papa, this is Therese, Mother Marie, from the hospital where I'm working on that case. Therese, this is my father, Victor, and Jose, my … brother?" Justina paused as she stumbled over the introduction but was more focused on Therese.

Her father stepped forward and held out his hand to welcome the reverend mother, concern all over his face. Justina hoped he wouldn't say much. She knew she had told him more than she probably should have about the hospital case, although not much about Therese's role in the drama. It was probably just as well she had told him something about it, though, so she wouldn't have to start from scratch explaining. At this point it was more important to help Therese.

In his usual fashion, her father immediately offered

something to eat or a drink. Before long they were seated back at the dining room table, after Justina insisted on food and wine for their guest. Jose, of course, was excited to have company and was hopeful that he would have a viewing companion for his cartoons. Justina took him upstairs, instead, and he was mollified with a bubble bath so the adults could talk without interruption.

"I can't prove it, of course," Therese stated, once she had calmed down and had some takeout and a glass of wine. "And of course we don't know who is behind this. But I think that someone was trying to give me a stronger warning. What else could it be? My neighborhood is so quiet, and my house is way off the street, nowhere near a main road."

Justina couldn't believe how things were unfolding, but before she could comment her father spoke up, frowning. "Why would they be going after you? I don't understand."

Therese explained how she had been brought into the situation, with Justina adding in details from her perspective. "And you did call the police, you said?" Victor asked.

"Oh, yes. Absolutely I did! But they wanted to know who might have done this, and I couldn't tell them because I don't know. I couldn't tell them that we have a possible fraud, or drug diversion, or whatever, at the hospital. Right? I mean, what do I say? If I say something like that, then we have police come to the hospital and start questioning the doctors and administration. I couldn't do that. It's such a mess."

Justina nodded in agreement. "I would think that would only make things worse," she said, picturing how angry Dr.

Al would be if police showed up to question him.

Therese raked her hair back, still damp from the rain, and leaned into her glass of wine. "I am so grateful to be here. I can't tell you. You can't imagine how I felt, like I couldn't tell the police anything, and couldn't involve anyone else. I mean, what could I say? And I was all alone in that house, with no protection …" Her beautiful almond eyes started filling with tears, and she visibly blinked them back. "This is not right; I know I shouldn't be here. I'm creating a problem for all of you now, too."

Justina shook her head no, and her father replied, "Nonsense. You stay here as long as you need. Nobody will look for you here, and this house is secure. Someone is always home, you will be safe."

That was all the persuasion the exhausted woman needed. It wasn't long before Therese nearly fell asleep on the couch while they were talking. Justina could see her eyes getting heavy so she gave her a T-shirt and pajama pants to sleep in, showed her to the spare bedroom, and they called it a day.

13

THERESE

Therese awoke with a start at the sound of a garbage truck outside and could tell by the bright sunlight that she had slept much later than usual. It took her a minute to remember where she was and all the events of the night before. She fought back a wave of mortification. *I can't believe I showed up on a stranger's doorstep in the middle of the night! They must think I'm a lunatic!* At least the house was quiet; maybe everyone was gone, so she wouldn't have to face them just yet. Especially in the skimpy white T-shirt and pajama bottoms Justina had lent to her. Not her best look.

Creeping down the stairs, she was dismayed to find Justina's father in the kitchen, making coffee. She wished she had put on her clothes from the night before, although after the trip through the rainstorm they were wrinkled and smelled musty. *It's not bad enough I showed up here like a drowned cat, now I'm half-naked in front of a stranger!* The coffee smelled wonderful, though, and it was too late to hide.

Victor appeared freshly showered and shaved, making Therese feel all the more disheveled. "Ah, good morning," he said easily, as if it was a normal day. "Coffee?"

She found herself smiling at this good-looking man offering her coffee. "I would love some," she admitted, planting herself on a kitchen stool to try to conceal the skimpiness of her sleepwear.

Placing a large red mug of steaming coffee in front of her, he asked, "Did you sleep well? We were worried about you last night." She could see the concern in his eyes and felt like she was blushing under his scrutiny.

"I think I slept too well, thanks. I am usually up before the sun." Pausing, she added, "It's so quiet here. Is Justina already gone?"

"Yes, she took Jose to drop him off early. She has morning classes, but I have a hard time keeping track of her these days." Victor poured sugar into his own black coffee and asked, "Have you thought what you will do about the house? How long do you think it will take to get fixed?" Then he quickly clarified, "Not that I am hurrying you out of here, not at all. I'm just wondering what will happen." He stirred his coffee, looking a little perturbed with himself at the unartful question.

Groaning, she said, "I need to call one of those glass places. They always advertise fast service. But it's a very large picture window and probably will have to be ordered. I don't know if insurance covers it. Plus, the window upstairs was cracked. I still don't know how that happened."

She stirred her coffee and took a large swallow. "Ahhh, that's what I needed!"

Victor set his coffee down and looked at her intently. "It would be much better if the police knew the whole story, don't you think?" She could see he was worried for her, and it warmed her heart. Nobody had shown much interest in her well-being in a very long time.

"I appreciate your concern, Victor. I really do. But there's no way I could suggest to the police that this was related to the situation at the hospital. I have no proof of that, and sending the police there to ask around would probably be the end of my career, at least as far as St. Matthew's is concerned."

"I understand that. But still, I don't like the idea of thugs going around terrorizing people with no consequences. Maybe the police will find something, anyhow. We can hope."

Therese shrugged. "Maybe. But they didn't really have anything to go on. They were going to talk to a couple of neighbors, but my house is kind of isolated, with the trees and shrubs, set back from the street. Someone could easily do it without being seen."

Frowning, Victor said, "You won't feel safe there until it's resolved, and I don't think you should go back there until they know who did it." He took a sip of coffee, then continued, "You should stay here as long as this is going on. Nobody would connect you to us, and certainly wouldn't expect you to be staying here."

"I'm hoping the hospital investigation will go quickly and put this whole thing to bed, one way or the other. And I appreciate the offer, but I don't want to put your family at risk, if someone is following me. I can go to a hotel, or my sister's." She smiled. "You already did enough, letting me crash here with no notice. Justina is so sweet, you know. She knew I was scared the other day and said to let her know if I needed any help. She's such a sweetheart!"

Victor chuckled. "Yes, she is. She is all heart, always ready to help anyone. She's just like her mother, that way." He smiled, appearing lost in thought for a moment, then added, "You will talk to the attorney doing the investigation at the hospital, right? See what he thinks?"

"Yes, of course. In fact, I should get moving. I need to go by the house and put some clean clothes on. Last night I wasn't thinking clearly, I just wanted to get out of that house. But I need to see it in the daylight and figure out what I'm doing."

"I mean it about you staying here, Therese. Please don't argue it. I can handle anyone who comes around here. It's no problem. In fact it's nice to have some company over coffee!" He smiled. "Okay? You agree?"

"Sounds like I don't have a choice." Therese laughed, partly out of relief and partly at Victor's insistence. She could tell he was used to getting his way. "I do appreciate it. And I will earn my keep. I am very talented in the kitchen, you will see!" She drained the rest of her coffee. "Now, I need to get going, lots to do today! And thank you, I do feel safer here. Being all alone last night, when that happened … I never knew that kind of fear before."

Victor nodded, his face serious at her last comment. “There is no reason for you to go through anything like that alone again,” he said. “I mean it when I say I am glad you’re here.”

14

JUSTINA

Justina yawned and wiped her watery eyes. A quick peek in the rearview mirror confirmed that she looked tired. Even her hair looked dull. She had very nearly fallen asleep in her class that morning, which was evidenced by the way her notes were full of incomplete sentences and unrecognizable abbreviations. *Not sure how long I can do this,* she grumbled to herself as she grabbed her laptop case and prepared to face another day of the investigation.

Her sleep the night before had been restless, with odd, threatening dreams, and she woke up feeling sweaty. She hadn't had nightmares in a long time and had hoped she was past it, but the whole thing with Therese had been downright scary. *I'm not sure this is what I had in mind with this job,* she thought. *I was thinking about helping people, not facing down bad guys.* And she knew she was out of her depth, on top of it all.

When she arrived at their assigned conference room, Frank was there with a tall, skinny young man that Justina hadn't seen before. "Hey, glad you're here," Frank said when he saw her in the doorway. "Justina, this is Scott. He's been running some reports for us. We're looking at the claims, which providers are billing the most visits, and for what conditions. We're looking for any odd patterns, issues like that. He was just explaining the report to me. Mostly, however, we'll let the auditors analyze it and use it to select the charts to audit."

"Okay," Justina said, slowly, not sure what that meant for her, and briefly shaking Scott's outstretched hand.

Frank continued, "Scott was just explaining the medical records at the clinic, how they are switching from paper to an electronic system in a couple of months. Some pieces are electronic, though, like the labs. Anyhow, that doesn't matter for today; we just need the schedules. We want to see if the days our doctors were on the schedules match the days that they billed, as well as any trends that jump out at us. The auditors will go over that, but I wanted to get a look for myself first."

"There are a lot of claims billed under Dr. Al, more than I would expect to see in a day, even with residents seeing patients. So that's one thing to check." Scott gestured to a spreadsheet in front of them.

"Dr. Al?" Justina asked. "But he's not in the clinic as much as Dr. Powers, right? I thought we were told that Dr. Powers is on-site more? Or is he? So what does that mean? He is billing for patients he doesn't see?" This was so confusing, and she struggled to remember what they had learned about the doctor's schedules during the various interviews; the report was very detailed, with a tiny font size, and her bleary eyes were not helping. She blinked hard, twice, to help focus.

"That's what we want to figure out," Frank confirmed. "Let's get the schedule for a couple of these specific heavy days, both for the physicians and residents, but also a list of patients seen." Turning to Scott, he said, "Do they have a signature log, so we can compare signatures?"

Scott nodded. "Yes, I can get that." Turning to Justina, Frank explained. "When you have a lot of people seeing patients, the hospital usually keeps a log of each one's signature, since sometimes it's hard to read them." Scott snorted a laugh at this, but Frank continued. "It also helps the auditors to confirm a signature is legitimate. Not a fake. Understand?"

Justina nodded. Frank was so patient with her lack of experience.

Frank's phone pinged and he glanced up at the clock, sighing heavily. "I am supposed to be on a conference call for another case. Justina, can you and Scott get those schedules and signature logs? Pick a couple of dates, maybe the ones I marked up, and get the staffing and patient schedules for those dates. Okay?"

Without waiting for her response, Frank picked up his phone and began dialing. "Oh, and try to keep this low key, if you can. I know it might not be possible. Work with the person who does scheduling, or some other backroom office person. No need to bother the doctors with this, unless it can't be avoided. Just because of the drama. We have every right to pull those records. Got it?" Justina nodded, glancing over to Scott to see if he looked comfortable with their task.

"Yes, sir," Scott affirmed, and Justina was relieved to see that he looked confident. As they walked down the hall, Scott asked her, "So, what is going on here? Frank didn't tell me anything, just that it's a review the CEO requested, and that it's confidential." His green eyes were inquisitive, and he glanced down at the paper in his hand as if the answers might be there.

"Umm, well, I can't really get into it much, just that some concerns were raised, and Dr. Shoemaker wanted to make sure there weren't any problems. And since the attorney and compliance officer aren't here, well, she decided to call us." Justina was pleased with her nonanswer, although Scott seemed earnest and honest. *Keep your mouth zipped,* she reminded herself.

"Oh, I see. Well, it might not matter, but the compliance officer was asking me for some similar reports before she left. She was also looking at the pharmacy, but I don't know what issues she was investigating."

Justina's ears perked up. *And now the compliance officer is mysteriously gone!* "What did she find, do you know?"

"No." Scott shook his head. "I never actually talked to her after that. I left the reports in her office. She wasn't there when I dropped them off, and so I didn't hear what she thought. I mean, she probably wouldn't have told me anything anyhow; it's not my business. I just pulled the data off the system. It was like right after that I heard she left. She might not have even ever had a chance to review them, I don't know." He shrugged.

Justina thought about the boxes from the compliance officer's office. *Those reports were not in those boxes!* she thought. *Somebody else got them.* And *knows what we are looking at!*

"Scott, do you have the specifics of what she requested? Like, was there an email request, something like that? It would really help if we could compare it to the issues we're reviewing. And maybe it would also show us some additional matters we should be looking into." Justina felt some adrenaline starting to pump, her lethargy totally gone. They were definitely on the right track!

"Yes, staff have to fill out a request form for any ad hoc reports. I'll find it for you today."

We're getting somewhere now! she thought. Her enthusiasm turned to anxiety, though, as they entered the clinic and saw Dr. Al at the front desk, with his back to them. Justina grabbed Scott's arm and pulled him back around the corner. "Is there a back door into the office area? Any way to be less obvious and talk to that scheduling person? Can someone in the back room get us that info? I'd really like to avoid Dr. Al if we can. Plus we don't want to make a scene here in front of patients."

Scott gave her a wide grin, nodding. "Yeah, he scares me too! And I know we were told to keep it 'on the down low.' Suits me just fine! Come on, this way."

They found their way to the clinic's back office, and Justina didn't see either of the physicians she was hoping to avoid. Scott introduced her to Tina, a tiny Filipina with black-rimmed glasses almost too big for her face, and explained their request. "Sure, I can do that, easy," she said, and logged in, referencing the spreadsheets to pull up dates. "I got it right here, for this date … let me print, and we'll do the other one … Okay, there's your staff schedules, now patient logs."

Justina watched the girl's fingers fly across the keyboard and pull up long lists of clinic visits on the dates in question. Justina looked at the info on the screen. "This is great; we have all the specific times. That's what we need!"

Nodding, Tina hit the 'print' button, then retrieved a think blue folder labelled 'signature log' from a shelf over her desk and handed it to Justina. "Do you want the sign-in sheets, too? We scan and save those, if that would help."

Justina nodded, feeling like they were hitting the lottery. This girl seemed unusually eager to help. "Awesome. Yes, thanks. I appreciate it!"

The humming printer was starting to wind down when a loud voice broke up the calm in the room. "What is going on in here?" Dr. Al stood in the doorway, with Dr. Powers right behind him.

15

JUSTINA

Justina felt a jolt of guilt and panic when Dr. Al-Basri barked his question at them. She looked over at Scott, not sure who should answer, but he and Tina were looking over at her expectantly. She realized with a sudden flash that it was her job to step up and respond with some degree of authority. She was no longer *The Student*, now she was *The Lawyer*, at least in the eyes of these two employees. *Yikes.*

She swallowed her anxiety and smiled, trying to project confidence. "We are pulling patient lists and schedules to help the auditors pick the records to review," she said, modifying the truth a little just to make it sound less serious. "The auditors will want to get samples from different days and different patients," she added, hoping that sounded convincing.

Dr. Powers spoke up. "What specifically is this audit for, exactly? We want to help, of course, but we have concerns if you take charts out of here; we need them for patient care. You never mentioned doing an audit." His tone was still civil, but it was clear he wanted a real answer and wasn't happy.

"I'm sorry we didn't mention it." Justina felt her cheeks getting hot and her adrenaline starting to push upward. "It just came up. There were some open issues in the compliance officer's files. We are just making sure we wrap up any open matters, since she isn't here. It's just to cover everyone, so any questions can be put to rest." Pulse racing, Justina congratulated herself for what she hoped was a convincing and somewhat innocuous explanation.

Dr. Al frowned. "What 'open matters'? Are you saying we are under an actual investigation by the hospital? What are we being accused of? We are seeing so many patients here, and training residents, and you want to get in the way of our work, to question our honesty?"

Justina wished she could run away. She was not prepared for this. "No. I'm sorry. You know I am working for Frank, the attorney Dr. Shoemaker hired. I'm not comfortable getting into details. I'm new to this, okay? I'm not trying to play a game with you, I just don't think I can give you more information." She knew she was rambling, but then remembered what Frank had said. "This is a confidential review, it is privileged. So you should talk to Frank or Dr. Shoemaker. I'm not able to discuss it, I'm sorry."

Dr. Powers smiled, clearly trying to smooth it over. "We don't mean to put you in a compromising position, of course. You understand we just were not expecting this, and wanted to know what was going on," he said reassuringly.

Dr. Al wasn't buying it, though. "Yes, I will be talking to

Barbara. I'm feeling harassed lately. I don't know why I am being targeted; there are plenty of others around here you should be looking at, not me!"

Dr. Powers shot a sharp glance over at him. "Al, I think we have created enough drama. No need to shoot the messenger. We'll talk to the CEO," he said, the last part directed at Justina and the others. "Thank you, Justina. We know you are just doing your job," he gave Dr. Al a warning look and a nudge to leave.

As soon as the doctors were out of sight, Justina let out a deep breath. "Whew. Sorry about that. They sure aren't happy."

Tina laughed nervously, and Justina noticed the girl looked terrified. "It's okay. But you should take those reports and the signature log and go, before they think of something else," she said, watching the door where the two physicians had just loomed.

"Yes, absolutely. We caused enough trouble for one day!" Trying to make light of it, Scott pulled the documents off the printer, flipping through to make sure there was nothing in the pile that they shouldn't have. "Okay, let's go," he said, the relief in his voice evident.

When they got back to the conference room, Frank didn't seem surprised to hear how the doctors had reacted. "Now we wait for the CEO to hear about it, and see where that takes us," he stated.

"No need to wait, I've already heard from our doctors down in the clinic about the disruptions your staff have caused." Dr. Shoemaker stood in the doorway, her skin looking flushed and eyes unnaturally bright and glassy.

16

JUSTINA

Justina wearily hefted her laptop bag out of the passenger seat and trudged up the steps, pushing the front door open. It was such a relief to be home. *Oh my God, what a day!* she thought, feeling desperately grateful to be off work for three days, until Monday. After the not-so-thinly-veiled reprimand from the CEO, she had left the hospital exhausted and worried.

As she dropped her bags in the foyer she was greeted by a welcome assault on her senses: a delicious scent saturated the air, wafting from the kitchen, and Jose was singing some little song in Spanish and squealing, apparently also in the kitchen. Stomach rumbling, Justina ventured toward the source of all the activity, feeling simultaneously too tired to deal with anyone but also hungry and remorseful that she'd been neglecting Jose. And wine was in the kitchen. If there was ever a day for wine, this was it.

Jose was sprawled on the kitchen floor with some handheld game entertaining him, while Therese was surrounded by fresh vegetables, a baguette in a white paper wrapper, and a couple of pots on the stovetop, steaming and bubbling. Clad in a pair of formfitting black sweatpants and a baggy red T-shirt, hair up in a scrunchy, she looked right at home presiding over the kitchen activities.

"Wow," Justina said, surprised to find Therese there, preparing a home-cooked meal. Both she and her father had a limited repertoire in the kitchen, so a change-up after a long day was welcome. "What is all this? You totally did not need to be the house chef! Not that I'm complaining," she added, sniffing the air in an exaggerated fashion. She was determined to not dwell on the hospital drama, at least for a little while.

"Don't be silly. I love to cook and it's therapy for me. It takes my mind off less pleasant things. Plus I can't justify cooking just for me, anyhow, and I miss fixing real dinners for a family." A sad look flitted across her face but was gone before Justina could even be sure it was there. "Shrimp Creole. A N'Orleans favorite," she said with an exaggerated drawl and a smile. "One of my favorites from my hometown."

"Well, it smells fantastic!" Justina said. "You're spoiling us!"

Despite her determination to push the stress of the day into the background, Justina wanted to talk to Therese about the day's events. It was hard to think about anything else, even with Jose showing her his high score on his game every five minutes and Therese avoiding anything upsetting. When her father got home, she knew she had lost her window of opportunity to talk with Therese; he had his own drama going on, and Jose was looking to take center stage, bouncing from one of them to the other every time he got a new high score.

It wasn't until after dinner, once Jose was occupied upstairs with a bath and Justina was cleaning up the kitchen, that she informed them that the hospital administration, by way of the two doctors, was frustrated with the work they were doing there. The interaction had actually been almost hostile, but Justina didn't want to tell either of them that. No need to create unnecessary drama.

Her father frowned, taking a seat on one of the kitchen barstools. "I don't trust these people," he said flatly. "And both of you could be a target. One already is, and they have shown that they are willing to make threats. Who knows what else they might do? One thing I will do: I am going to call the chief of police here in Long Beach and tell him we had a threat."

"I don't know if that's a good idea," Therese began, but he quickly cut her off.

"No, I won't tell him anything about you, Therese. The fewer people who know about you being here, the better. I can tell him it is related to my campaign. But at least then they will keep an eye out. I will stay out of it, for now. But only with that condition. And you both make sure nobody follows you when you leave the hospital. Okay? Those are reasonable steps. I'm serious."

Justina knew her father and gave Therese a look that clearly told her there was no option. "Okay," she agreed, and Therese nodded.

"It's not bad to have the police watching out for us," she conceded. "But I'm sorry to bring this to your doorstep."

Justina was about to argue that point when her father's phone buzzed. "Looks like Marci is hard at work," he commented as he read the screen, his mind clearly already elsewhere. "She has started doing some opposition research and wants to share. If you ladies will excuse me?"

"Of course," Therese said, with Justina nodding. Her father was already on his feet and absorbed in his phone.

"Looks like we're on our own," Therese commented.

"Yup. Let's go relax a bit before Hurricane Jose blows back downstairs," Justina said, welcoming the chance to have Therese alone.

They took their bottle of wine and settled onto the couch in the living room. "Much better," Therese commented. "I feel like I haven't taken a moment to breathe in weeks. My life is usually so much more predictable."

Justina realized how little she knew about this woman who was now sharing her house.

"So, Therese, what is your story? I can't say I've ever sat down and drank too much wine with a reverend mother before!"

"Well, we're pretty much all alike," Therese joked.

Justina laughed. "Somehow, I doubt that; you don't look like any priest I've ever run across. But seriously, I'm curious about you. How did you end up leaving New Orleans, and coming to New York? And becoming the Reverend Mother at a big hospital? It can't be easy."

Therese took a long, slow sip of wine, and Justina was starting to wonder if she was going to answer. Finally she did.

"Well, I'm not originally from New Orleans, first of all. I was born in Miami, but we moved to New Orleans when I was ten or eleven. So that's where I spent most of my life. I came to New York after Hurricane Katrina. That's really when my life changed ..." Her face clouded and she took another sip of wine, her dark almond eyes focused on some distant memory.

Justina reached over and put her hand on Therese's knee. "How horrible, I know that was so much worse than Sandy ... What happened to you?" She wasn't sure if she should even ask, but Therese looked like she was far away, already reliving the past.

"I had a good job at a hospital in New Orleans. I hadn't been there for too long, maybe three years, and was going to school at night. I thought I had everything in life all figured out ... my career, a great group of friends I worked with, even my own little house. Something I never had growing up."

She paused, taking a sip of wine, and Justina reached over to refill her glass. "Go on," she encouraged.

"Anyhow, that's how I met Philippe, my future husband. He was a driver for one of the medical transport companies that worked with the hospital. He was there a lot with a couple of our dialysis patients who couldn't drive to their appointments. He was a beautiful man, with this amazing accent … he came from Haiti, so he spoke French. I could listen to him talk all day; I think I fell in love with that first." She smiled, remembering. "Philippe was very gentle with those patients; I remember one older lady in particular. She always joked that he was her 'date' when he came to get her. He would kiss her hand and act very gallant with her. She loved it …"

She paused and took a drink of wine, reflecting.

"We didn't date very long before he proposed. I was head over heels in love. My mama told me it was too fast, but I didn't care. He was the love of my life."

Justina watched the range of emotions flow across Therese's face: happy memories, sadness, loss. Her eyes still had a faraway look as she sipped her wine, so Justina did the same and just listened to this lovely woman's story.

"I got my degree in social work, and my promotion, almost at the same time I had a positive pregnancy test. I had such mixed feelings; I always wanted to be a mama, but it was much sooner than I intended. Anyhow, Mateo, a gift from God; that was my baby. And he truly was—as soon as he was born, I was in love with him. I had no more doubt about how important this baby was to me."

"That's the picture in your office?" Justina asked, recalling the framed photo.

Therese nodded, smiling with memories. "The trouble began when I had to go back to work. I didn't want to. Philippe did not make very good money, and he didn't want me to stay home. I knew I had my job waiting, and I loved the work, but still …We fought about it, but I couldn't go against my husband. Now I think differently."

Justina scrunched up her mouth, thinking of her father's domineering ways. "I can imagine," she murmured, not wanted to stop the flow of this story.

"Anyhow, I am telling you so much more than you want to hear, I'm sure. I'm sorry. I don't let myself dwell on these things very often, and after a few glasses of wine, well …"

"No, please, I want to hear your story. You continued working, as a social worker there, at the hospital?"

"Yes, I stayed there, but it was hard. I couldn't always leave on time, and it wore me out, emotionally. Philippe was always angry with me. He wanted me to work and bring home money but also thought I should be a better mother. I couldn't do anything right. But Mateo was a very healthy and happy baby, he seemed to thrive, even with our schedules and fighting …"

She paused and looked at Justina, sadness filling her eyes and tugging her full lips downward.

"When Katrina came, I was at the hospital. I had to be. Which, of course, was just one more instance of my poor mothering, according to my husband. Anyhow, Philippe and Mateo were at home when the levees broke, trying to ride it out in the upstairs. Nobody really understood, at least we didn't, that there really could be fifteen or twenty feet of water, flushing people out of their homes, or trapping them inside." Tears filled her eyes. And she looked down, taking a sip of wine to compose herself. Justina listened, horrified as she imagined the scene.

Therese's voice crackled with emotion. "Philippe lost Mateo in the water. He was holding on to a tree branch with one arm, and our baby with the other … a powerful wave washed over them and pulled Mateo away." Now she was openly crying. "I'm sorry, some things you never get over. I still have nightmares."

Justina leaned over and took her hand, stroking it, at a loss for words. "Oh, Therese … I am so sorry. I can't begin to imagine how awful …" She wished she hadn't asked Therese about her past. It was obviously still with her every day.

Therese sniffled, trying to finish her recounting without a total meltdown. "I know, it's hard to even fathom. I was, of course, at the hospital so I had no idea. It's not like we were able to pick up the phone and call. Philippe eventually came to the hospital to find me, I don't even know how long it was, that whole time was like one long nightmare. Our hospital was trying to get patients out. They were bringing boats and helicopters, up on the roof. But there was nowhere to take those people. We had disabled people, people on ventilators, dialysis, oxygen … people who had just had surgery and shouldn't be moved. Brand new babies and mothers, fragile old people."

Justina nodded, thinking of the tragedies she had seen after Hurricane Sandy. But she hadn't lost anyone.

As if reading her mind, Therese continued, "You know how hard it is when there is no power, no elevators, nowhere for people to go and no way to get them to safety. So I was in the middle of trying to figure out who we could evacuate, with communication virtually impossible and everyone underwater. And then, of course, even getting these people up to the roof for a helicopter was a nightmare. So Philippe somehow showed up, in the middle of all that, to tell me our son had been … washed away … and of course it was my fault."

She buried her face in her hands, openly sobbing. "I'm sorry, too much wine I think. It's making me emotional," she said between sobs, her voice breaking and mascara drawing black rivers down her cheeks as she looked at Justina with red eyes swimming in tears, trying to smile.

"Please, don't. I'm sorry I asked. I can't imagine what you went through." Justina couldn't find the right words, so she just stroked Therese's hand.

"I think I need a glass of water," Therese sniffled, trying to regain some composure. "I'll be right back," she said, and headed to the kitchen.

Justina wiped her own eyes and fished around in her sweatshirt pocket for a crumpled tissue to blow her nose.

Therese reappeared with two glasses of water. "In case you want one, too," she said, offering a glass to Justina. Justina noticed Therese's hand was shaking, causing the water to slop a little. Therese didn't seem to notice.

"Anyhow, not much else to tell. Ultimately, I went to Houston, survived the famous Astrodome disaster. Philippe stayed in New Orleans to search for Mateo. There were so many places that our baby could have ended up, and with so many agencies trying to help, there was no single way to verify anything. So we figured I would go to Houston and see if Mateo had ended up there somehow. Thousands of people were taken there. We figured if someone found him, he would be taken out of New Orleans if they couldn't find the parents. And of course, he was very young, he couldn't explain who his parents were or where to look for them. Philippe stayed to continue searching. And I think Philippe didn't want to even look at me. I know he blamed me for being at the hospital instead of taking care of our son, even though he didn't come out and say that."

She paused, looking down and struggling not to fall apart. "Philippe found our baby, he had to identify him at the morgue," she said, then a loud sob ripped out of her. Justina moved over to sit closer to Therese, wrapping her arms around her while she let loose crying.

Between sobs, she lamented, "I couldn't even go back and see my baby. There was no way to get back. Philippe told me not to come. He said it would just make it worse for me. He said"—she gulped hard—"he said I wouldn't want to remember our baby like that." Justina held her as she cried, tears of her own streaming down her face. She tried to soothe Therese, smoothing her hair and letting her cry.

Justina got a couple of Tylenol and a damp washcloth for Therese after the storm of crying subsided, leaving her with a headache and a blotchy face.

Therese took the washcloth, obediently laying it across

her eyes and resting her head against the back of the couch. "I'll be fine. I don't let myself think about those times very often, although Mateo is always there, a part of me."

"I'm sure he is," Justina responded, trying to imagine how a mother could survive such a loss and go on. "So is that when you came to New York?"

"While I was still in Houston, Philippe told me he couldn't face going back to our old life, and he wanted a divorce. We already had problems but losing our home and our baby was just too much for him, he just wanted out. I think he just wanted to escape everything and start over. Once we lost all we shared, it seemed pointless to stay together. It's not that simple, of course, but I wasn't surprised. And I had nothing to go back to, really. Some of my best friends at the hospital were scattered and gone, and the thought of seeing Philippe all the time, well, it just seemed like it would be harder to heal. So I took a job in New York. I didn't even go back to New Orleans, the city was so devastated, and our home was destroyed." She sighed and turned the washcloth over to find a fresh, cool patch of material.

"Anyhow, to make a long story short … too late, I know," she said, finally smiling, "I was so destroyed when I came to New York, I found the local church and started going regularly. I found a lot of solace in the congregation there. I was not only grieving for my baby, but for my whole life. I felt like a failure at marriage and, really, as a mother as well. Through the support, and all the help I got, well, they really saved my life. I realized that the church was my calling. The church was very supportive of my goals, helping me get back to school and go through the process … so here I am."

"Well, I'm so glad you are here," Justina said, overwhelmed by the story she had just heard and knowing that anything she could say would be inadequate. Therese was a truly amazing woman who had been through so much.

"I feel the same way," Therese said. "And to think that it's all because of some bad people that we've gotten to know each other. Every cloud truly does have a silver lining."

Justina nodded in agreement. "Let's just make sure they don't find out *how* well we've gotten to know each other. I could imagine Dr. Al would be none too pleased to know we're having girls' time and sleepovers!"

"Well, let's just make sure he doesn't find out."

17

JUSTINA

Monday morning found Justina back at the hospital with Frank, getting the auditors set up in the clinic. Neither of the two physicians came into the back office, much to Justina's relief. Frank had managed to placate the irritated CEO with a promise to minimize any disruption to operations and to keep her informed. The auditors went over the lists and reports, picked the files to review, then printed copies of it all to take to review outside of the clinic. That was the agreement, in order to keep the audit off the employees' radar as much as possible and, Frank speculated to Justina, to prevent the employees from talking to the auditors. The auditors were tasked with not only reviewing the chartnotes and signatures against the claims billed, but also to flag cases with pain complaints and prescriptions.

When she arrived at the conference room, a very thin Black woman in light blue scrubs approached her just outside the open door.

"Excuse me," the woman said. "Are you one of the lawyers here investigating the clinic?"

"Yes," Justina said, glancing at Frank inside the conference room to make sure he was listening.

Frank nodded. "Yes, we are doing a review at the request of Dr. Shoemaker. How can we help you?" He beckoned them to come in.

Justina and the woman entered, and Justina shut the door. She noticed the woman glancing at the window to make sure the blinds were closed. This wasn't the first person to do that, she noted to herself. Once seated, the woman hesitated to speak, scratching her short, tight braids and then glancing at her phone. Finally, she began.

"Okay, so I heard you guys are investigating stuff at the clinic. I don't know anything that's going on there, not really, just heard staff in the lunchroom talking about the audit you all are doing. I work in the lab mostly, but I seen some funny stuff and I thought I maybe should tell you."

Justina opened her laptop, looking at Frank, who nodded. "Of course. Can we get your name?"

The woman bit her lip and scratched her head again. "Do I have to? I don't know what's going on, but I don't want to be on anybody's list, you know?" She slouched down in her chair, and Justina wondered if she would change her mind about talking to them.

"Well, you don't have to, but we won't be able to follow up with you if we have more questions," Frank said. "It's confidential," he added and explained about attorney-client privilege.

"How 'bout I tell you what I know and then we'll see if you still think you need my name. I really want to stay out of it, and this may not be anything."

"Fair enough," Frank said.

She nodded. "Okay, so I work Monday through Friday, and I go outside to smoke on my breaks. We're not s'posed to smoke on the hospital campus, and they are real strict about that. So I found I could go across the street from the clinic and sit in that bus stop. You know, right in front of the pharmacy and med supply store? It's dry, you know, when it rains, and I can sit down and have my smoke."

"Um hmmm," Frank murmured, encouraging her to keep going.

"Well, so, I seen this white van coming into the clinic parking lot, and the driver brings a bunch of people to the front of the clinic. Happens all the time. I thought at first he was a medical transport guy or something, but he doesn't wear no uniform and those folks he's driving don't look like they from a nursing home or anything. They look like homeless, you know? Kinda dirty looking. Probably smell, too," she said, wrinkling her nose.

"Okay, so this guy drops off people and then leaves?" Frank prompted.

"No, he walks them to the door, then he parks the van and waits. Those folks come out, one by one, you know, and most goes over to the pharmacy, that one across the street by my bus stop. Then they get back in the van, and once they all come back he leaves with them." She paused, took a deep breath. "So it just looks weird to me. I never heard of groups of people like that coming together to a clinic, not like families or anything, just individuals, look like. And then, why do they go across the street to that pharmacy, you know? We got a pharmacy inside. It's right by the lab where I work. But I never seen one of those scruffy people down there. Oh, and those people, none of them look like they need a clinic. You go in there, see who's at the clinic, they usually is folks with injuries, pregnant, or a sick kid, and you can kinda see why most of them are there."

"Hmm, yes," Frank said. "Tell me about the van, is there a logo or anything?"

She shook her head vigorously. "No, sir. They got that stuff on the windows where you can't see in. It's just a plain white van. I can't say he comes every day; my break isn't always the same, either, but it does seem like he's there a lot on Fridays. I seen 'em twice on a couple of Fridays, when I had an afternoon break out there, too."

"So, what do you think is going on," Frank asked. "Have you heard anyone talk about it?"

"I don't know. I mentioned it once to my friend who does blood draws over there at the clinic. She didn't know, either, just said she thought the guy was helping out the doctors, getting patients in." She shrugged.

"What time does this usually happen?" Justina asked.

"Well, let's see … I go to lunch at 12:30 … so probably about one, I have my smoke after I eat," she explained.

"Okay, thanks," Frank said. "Is there anything else you

can think of?"

She shook her head. "No, I don't think so." As she stood to leave, Frank asked again for her name.

"You can find me in the lab. Just ask for Marietta. But I don't want nobody in the clinic or any of those doctors knowing I came up here, okay? I really need my job."

Frank nodded. "I won't share who we talked to, unless we end up having to talk to law enforcement." At her alarmed look, he added, "That's not likely to happen, and if it does, I will track you down and let you know first, okay? And believe me, if it comes to that there will be bigger problems for them than trying to harass you. Right? And we will protect you, they can't retaliate against you. We will be watching."

She still looked worried, a frown creasing her forehead. "Yeah, okay. I mean, if they're doing something illegal, they need to get caught. I just really want to be kept out of it."

Frank nodded, and Justina spoke up, "Thanks for coming to us, Marietta. And if you think of anything else, let us know." She took the liberty of handing the woman Frank's business card from the small stack he had on the conference table.

"Yeah, sure, thanks," she said and quickly scooted out of the office, closing the door behind her.

Justina looked over at Frank. "So, what do you think? Is this the 'pill mill' thing we heard about? Drug diversion?" She felt a small flush of adrenaline and anxiety, all at once. "This could be something pretty big, couldn't it? It would explain why they don't want anyone looking at their records!" It would also explain why they were desperate to keep people from looking at the clinic and why Therese was now living at her house.

"There's definitely something here that is not right," Frank said, in an obvious understatement. "We need to see who owns that pharmacy." He was already tapping away on his laptop, eyes scanning through the list of pharmacies to find the one across the street. "Here it is. Kal's Pharmacy and Medical Supply. Now let's see who owns it," he said as he continued typing and scanning.

Justina peered over his shoulder to watch him search the Secretary of State's site for business information.

"Whoa, here we go," Frank exclaimed. "This explains a lot."

Justina leaned in to see what he was looking at. "Wow," she said, staring at the screen.

18

JUSTINA

"Justina, did you find any documents about conflicts of interest in those boxes you took home?" Frank asked as they pondered the implications of what they had discovered.

"Ummm, no, not yet," she said, frowning as she thought back to her review of the boxes from the compliance officer's office. "But I didn't get through everything. You know we found that stuff about the hotline call and audit, and then everything went crazy." She felt a wave of anxiety, realizing she hadn't finished her task.

"Okay, well, I need you to see if there is anything in there. I want to be sure about that before we talk to Dr. Shoemaker," Frank said. "You know this makes the situation even more damaging for them. We can't have physicians writing bogus scrips and sending patients to their own pharmacy."

"Of course," Justina said. "I'll go through the rest of the boxes right away. Is there anything else I should be working on?"

"Not right now. I want to review some of our previous

drug diversion cases for this district. I'll let you know if I need you to help with additional research," Frank stated, frowning a little bit as he looked at his laptop screen. "You have those boxes at home? Why don't you go home and work on them? I don't want to create any additional drama here until I have a few more answers. I'm also going to drop by the HR department and have a casual conversation about the nurse, Angela, leaving, as well as the compliance officer. Should have already done that, but as you say, things have started moving quickly."

"Okay, I'll keep you posted on what I find. Shouldn't take long; there isn't much left, as I recall," Justina said, noting Frank's focus on his computer. *I should have finished going through those boxes,* she chastised herself. *Now it looks like I was totally forgetful about what I was supposed to be doing, or careless.*

Listening to her rumbling stomach, Justina decided to stop at the cafeteria on her way out, to grab a sandwich and bag of chips for lunch so she could eat and get home quickly. *I need to get back into that box ASAP!* she thought as she maneuvered through the early lunch line at the hospital's cafeteria deli.

"Hey, stranger," a voice said behind her, and Justina turned with a smile to greet Therese.

"Hi, yourself," Justina responded. "How's your day going?"

"I'm okay. I'm speaking with some students this afternoon, have a couple of meetings. The usual, which is fine.

No news is good news!" Therese said, patting Justina on the arm. "Are you here for all day?"

"No, Frank sent me home to … do some homework," she said, trying to stay vague in the lunchroom.

"Okay. Well, that's good. I'm sure Jose will be happy to have you home. I can pick up something for dinner, if you want. I probably won't get back to the house until around six, if that's okay."

"No worries, I'll fix dinner," Justina said. "I think my homework will be done within an hour or so. And it's my turn to cook!" This new roommate situation was really working out well. She liked having another woman in the house.

"All right. I will see you later, then." Therese moved away to pay for her cardboard cup of soup and small green salad.

Justina returned her attention to the deli counter, deciding what to get. When she glanced up, she saw Dr. Al, in line next to her at the hot food bar. He was looking right at her, frowning, and she realized he had probably heard the whole exchange. His eyes met hers directly, then he looked away without any acknowledgment. *Oh, crap,* she thought. *This is not good!*

She stepped out of the deli line, opting instead for a prepackaged egg salad sandwich, and darted to the cashier's line to pay and get out of there.

As soon as she got to her car, she sent Therese a text. "FYI. Dr. Al heard us in the cafeteria. Watch your back." Leaning her head against the headrest, Justina took a deep breath. *I hope I didn't put her at more risk. Or all of us. Now he knows she's staying with us,* she thought, as the magnitude of the lapse sunk in.

19

JUSTINA

Justina mentally prepared herself to dig into the remaining box from the compliance officer's files as soon as she got home. She felt like her heart was beating too fast as she imagined various horrible scenarios where Dr. Al came after them. She told herself she was being ridiculous, but it didn't help calm her nerves at all. That look on his face …

Once she had entered the house, she sent Celeste home and locked the door, telling Jose to stay inside and not to open the door for anyone except the people he knew. Although he had heard these sorts of instructions before, he apparently could tell Justina was upset because he frowned at her, confusion all over his face. She reassured him that everything was fine and sent him to go watch cartoons for a little while so she could dig into her belated "homework."

The box yielded exactly what they were looking for: conflict of interest disclosures. Frank had told her that all the physicians and managers were supposed to fill them out to tell if they had any financial or business interest that could conflict with their duties to the hospital. Justina found the files were set up by department, so she set aside Emergency, ICU, Lab, and Radiology before she found what she was looking for.

"Ah, here we go," she murmured to herself as she found the clinic folder. "Let's see what you bad boys admitted to!"

She found Dr. Al's form easily and scanned the pages. *"Oh, there you are,"* she said out loud; Dr. Al had listed nearly a dozen investment interests. Kal's Pharmacy and Medical Supply was placed innocuously toward the bottom of the list. *Hmmm, well, at least he admitted it.* She set the form aside and went back to the file. *Dr. Powers, where are you?*

She set the folder down and leaned back, stretching her neck and shoulders, which were getting stiff from sitting in an awkward position on the floor. Puzzled, she went back to the box. *Maybe you got in the wrong folder,* she speculated, flipping through the files. No sign of a form for Dr. Powers. As she got to the bottom of the box, she pulled out the last folder, titled "COI Reports."

A lengthy spreadsheet revealed that several individuals had not yet completed their forms, including Dr. Powers. The footer on the document was dated one month prior. Another spreadsheet, thirty days earlier than the first, was also in the file, with a copy of a memo attached. Justina scanned it quickly, noting that the compliance officer had sent a copy of the older spreadsheet to Dr. Shoemaker with the update on which management and physicians had not yet cooperated with the disclosures and a request for Dr. Shoemaker to send a reminder. There was nothing else in the folder.

Sighing, she sent a text to Frank. “Went through the COIs. Dr. A listed many investments, including the pharmacy. No form for Dr. P. Report shows it was not completed.”

Frank’s response was immediate: “Ok, we can talk tomorrow. Also got copy of emails and request sent from compliance officer to Scott requesting records. Thx.”

Putting the files back in the box, Justina stretched again, cracking her neck to relieve the tension. She nudged the box out of the way with her foot and stood up, feeling at a loss but not sure why. *This house is way too quiet,* she realized. *Why don’t I hear Jose?*

20

THERESE

Therese hefted her oversized leather bag onto her shoulder and said a last round of goodbyes to the students she had just met with at the conference center in Garden City. Although teaching and mentoring the students was the best part of her job, she was having trouble focusing.

She wondered if everything at her house was still intact. Although she knew the broken window was covered over with heavy plastic, she felt like her house was now wide open and no longer a safe place. Even though she didn't want to, she decided to stop there and pick up some more clothes and check things over. She looked at her watch—it was still early. The window repair company had ordered her glass, but it was going to take a couple more days.

Traffic seemed heavier than usual, and her jangled nerves only made it seem worse. Every block had a red traffic light. *This is ridiculous,* she fretted, pulling out her phone. *I'll let Justina know I may be late, not to wait on me for dinner.* She was halfway through her text when a loud honking behind her made her jump and drop the phone. Glancing in her mirror, she saw a white van behind her, clearly the source of the honking. The light had just changed.

She stomped on the gas, jerking forward too quickly, then chastised herself. *Settle down already! People honk in New York, get a grip on yourself.* She realized how rattled she was if a honking car startled her. *Deep breaths,* she told herself.

At the next light she fished her phone out from under the seat and finished her note to Justina, keeping a close eye on the traffic light, especially aware of the van with the impatient driver still in her rearview mirror.

She noted with irritation that the vehicle remained behind her, making her hypervigilant about the traffic lights. "Go around me already," she grumbled as the driver seemed intent on staying right on her back bumper. The late afternoon sun reflected off the glass of the other vehicle, making it impossible to see the driver in the mirror. When she finally turned onto the side street toward her house, the van turned as well, and she suddenly wondered if it was following her. As she pulled into her driveway, however, the van kept going. "What is wrong with me?"

Her anxiety stayed with her as she let herself into the house. Nothing appeared to have been moved since she had stopped by the last time, but it just didn't feel like home anymore. She felt vulnerable and exposed, even though the door was locked behind her and nothing had been disturbed. *Nothing except me,* she thought, still trying to focus on her breathing.

She realized she might not be ready to stay in that house for a long time, even after the window was fixed. Not if she felt this unsafe and nervous. She decided it was probably a good idea to take more clothes than she had originally intended, given her unease. She knew she would be back when the window was getting repaired, but other than that … maybe not until this issue at the hospital and clinic was resolved. It was just too unsettling being in the house alone.

Therese pulled a suitcase out of the closet in the spare bedroom and went through her dresser and closet, trying to plan a week's worth of work clothes. She threw in her pajamas, almost as an afterthought, as she recalled Victor watching her in Justina's flimsy T-shirt. She smiled to herself as she thought of it, recalling how uncomfortable he had been. It had been a while since she noticed a man looking her over!

That memory, and packing, helped calm her nerves, and she decided to look in the kitchen to see if there was anything that should be thrown out or taken with her. Just the ancient bag of salad and probably rancid orange juice, so she threw those out and tucked an unopened bottle of wine in her work bag. *That should do it*, she decided, taking one last look around. She glanced up at the kitchen clock, noting it was later than she thought. She hadn't meant to take so much time at the house. She checked her phone but saw nothing from Justina.

She lugged the suitcase down the front steps and hoisted it into the back seat. She realized how relieved she felt that she wouldn't be coming back to stay for a while. Although she hated disrupting Justina's and Victor's lives, they didn't seem to mind, and she felt much safer there with them. *And it's nice to feel like part of a family again,* a little voice in her head nagged, but she shook the thoughts away.

Before leaving, she decided to walk around the house, hoping to see what had crashed into her upstairs window. It was impossible to see if anyone had been walking around, since the side yard was all grassy, but there was a large branch on the ground. Looking up, Therese thought she could see where it had broken off and felt a small amount better than if she had found another large rock that didn't belong there.

She pulled out of her driveway, eager to be back to the Gonzalez house. When she got up to the main road, however, she realized her brakes felt a bit soft and her sense of panic immediately returned full force. Were they already like this? Maybe. That van had been distracting her earlier. She made a deal with herself and God: Let me get home and I'll have them taken care of tomorrow…

Traffic had gotten even heavier than before, with rush hour at its peak. Please, hang on! There was no question now that the brakes were going, as she pushed the pedal all the way to the floorboard in order to stop. Okay, I'll have to deal with this tonight. No getting around it. She tried to focus her thoughts on where there might be an auto shop along this route…she couldn't remember. "Come on, baby, just hang on…"

At the next red light, the pedal went completely slack beneath her foot. Her car didn't slow down at all as she put both her feet on the pedal, pushing into the floorboard without results. Seeing the sleek black Mercedes ahead of her, she had an instant vision of crunching metal and an angry driver jumping out, red-faced, and screaming at her, or, even worse, a small, injured child in the car crying after getting thrown from its seat on impact. And then the police would come, grilling her about why she continued driving with bad brakes, endangering other drivers. No, that can't happen! She cranked the steering wheel all the way to the right, into a bank parking lot. Come on, baby, slow down! Her car lurched up onto the parking lot curb and sidewalk, but didn't stop, and Therese cringed, bracing herself as she plowed into the brick wall of the building.

21

JUSTINA

"Jose," Justina called upstairs. She couldn't hear the television or the typical perpetual ruckus that accompanied Jose wherever he went.

Maybe he's taking a nap, she thought as she mounted the stairs. "Jose!" She looked in his room, which was empty except for Hercules, lying in the middle of the bed, flicking his tail, and looking annoyed at being awoken.

Going from room to room, Justina called out for the boy, even going up into the attic space which could be attractive to a child. Nothing but silence. Getting truly alarmed, Justina ran back downstairs, through the family room to the kitchen and pantry, even checking the wine cellar. No sign of Jose or even his usual trail of toys and unwanted shoes, socks, and other clothing—anything that could be discarded on the way to the activity of the moment.

In the kitchen Justina realized the back door was open a crack. *I know I told him to keep the doors locked! Did I lock the back door?* She couldn't remember, but certainly it hadn't been left open by any of the adults in the house. *Or was it?* She struggled to remember. *I was so focused on that box I had to go through ... What did I do?* Peering out the window, there was no sign of Jose playing outside.

Oh my God, where is he? Justina bolted out the back door and down the steps. *The shed! He's been wanting to make a camp in the shed!* Racing to the shed, she called out, again. "Jose! Where are you? Not funny, come out! We're not playing, Jose!" The shed door was swollen from the recent rainstorms, and the hinges were stiff as she tugged the heavy wooden door open. Nothing but a stack of mossy white plastic lawn chairs, a few rusty tools, and—ugh—thick spider webs that proved nobody had been in the building recently.

Justina walked the perimeter of the yard, peering in all directions to try to spot Jose playing in a neighbor's yard or the alley. It seemed unusually quiet, no movement, almost like one of those sci-fi movies where everyone is gone or dead except the hero. She pulled her phone out, in case there was a message, somehow, that would provide the answer. Nothing but a note from Therese saying she was running late. *Maybe Papa came and got him*? She quickly dialed her father, who answered on the first ring.

"M'ija, what's going on? I'm on my way home." Her father sounded tired. "I've been in meetings all day, trying to raise money ..."

"Papa, is Jose with you?" Justina interrupted. "He isn't here. I can't find him, and the back door was open." She couldn't keep the pure panic out of her voice.

"What? No, he isn't with me. I've been in the city all day. How long has he been gone?" Victor's voice was sharp, immediately focused. "What happened?"

"I don't know." Justina's voice shook as she struggled to stay focused. "He was here with Celeste when I got home. I told him to stay inside and go watch television while I did some work." She took a deep breath, trying not to cry. "Papa, he's not here. I was working, not even for an hour probably. In the living room. And when I finished, I couldn't hear him, the television was off. I don't know how he got out of the house. How could I not hear him go somewhere?" The enormity of a missing child flooded over her, and she choked back a sob. "Papa, I'm so sorry, what did I do?"

"Justina, I will be there in less than twenty minutes. Call the police. He probably wandered off, chasing a squirrel or something, you know how he is. The police will find him. Do it now and I will be right there. Okay?"

"Okay, yes," she said, gulping a breath. "But Papa … there is something you should know," she began.

"What?" Her father's tone was sharp. "What is it? We are wasting time here!"

"The doctor, the one we are investigating, who is so nasty to Therese and everyone about this investigation … He knows she is staying here. You don't think … ?" She couldn't finish her thought.

Victor was silent for a moment. "Justina, just call the police. Get them started looking. We will talk about all this later. Right now, we need to find Jose." His voice was firm, but Justina could tell he was shaken, too.

"Yes, Papa, I will call right now. You're right, I'm just so scared."

"I know. I'm sure it will be fine. I'll see you in a few minutes," he said, and he hung up.

Shaking, Justina called to report the missing child. She couldn't even remember what he was wearing nor could she stop crying as she tried to provide the police with basic information about what happened. After the call, her nerves jangled as she waited for them to arrive, pacing the house and rechecking every corner, under the beds, calling for him. She walked, again, all around the house, looking for any clue to Jose's whereabouts.

When the police arrived, she reiterated the description of what happened, although she didn't mention anything about the incidents at the hospital. She felt paralyzed with worry, with no idea what to do. The police left and she sent Frank a text, not knowing who else to ask, but he didn't answer. She found herself hyperventilating, trying not to cry and reliving the afternoon over and over, hoping to find some forgotten detail that would miraculously provide a solution.

When her father got home, Justina flew at him, throwing her arms around him and sobbing into the shoulder of his charcoal suit jacket. He held her for a moment, then pulled her back, looking at her. "Have the police been here yet, m'ija? What did they say?" Justina looked at his face and saw weariness, more than just the current crisis could have created. He didn't look good, and she hadn't noticed lately, barely spending time with him. But there was no time for that, not now.

"They took the report, they are looking for him," Justina said, trying to calm herself. Just having her father there made her feel much safer. He always knew what to do, and she felt so helpless. "Papa, it's my fault. If I had been paying attention … I don't know how he could get out of the house without me hearing him. I was right here." She gestured to the living room. "I don't know how this happened; how could I be so stupid?" she sobbed.

"Shhh, Justina, this isn't helping. He was being very quiet if you didn't hear him. He probably was being sneaky. He's a child, and we don't know what little plan he might have had. The police will find him, or he will turn up. Did you call Celeste? He might have tried to go to her house. It's not that far. Don't assume the worst," her father said, pulling out his phone. "I'll call Celeste. She might have some ideas, too."

"See? I'm an idiot. I never thought of calling Celeste," Justina sniffled as her father waited for the call to go through and then explained to the housekeeper what happened. She couldn't tell from his side of the conversation if there was any new or useful information.

"She's very upset, too," her father stated as he tucked the phone back into his jacket pocket. "She hasn't seen him, but she's going to go out walking around. He has been to her house, of course, but probably would never know how to get there. She did say he was talking about his friend Toby, and some ideas about camping out. Do we know anything about

Toby? His family, or where he lives?"

Justina shook her head. "No, I only heard about Toby the other day. They met at school, but I don't know if he lives nearby." She sighed and wiped her eyes. "With so much going on lately, I haven't been paying enough attention. I should have known who his friends are …" Her eyes started filling up with fresh tears. "I haven't been doing my job here. I don't know what he's doing, how you are doing … I'm just work and school. Now look what happened. It's not right, it's my fault."

Her father pulled her into his shoulder, stroking her hair. "We need to have faith. He's a little boy, he is out having an adventure. The police will find him, or Celeste will find him wandering her neighborhood, he will turn up. And about that hospital business … I think you are being paranoid. Internal reviews happen everywhere. People don't go kidnapping kids because they are irritated about an audit. And if someone came to the door you would have heard it. Okay?" Justina nuzzled into her father's shoulder, nodding and trying not to cry.

There was a sharp knock at the door, startling them both. "They found him," Justina exclaimed as her father jumped to the front door.

A very tall, broad-shouldered Black police officer stood on the step, and Justina knew he wasn't one of the officers she spoke with earlier. Her father, of course, didn't know that.

"Have you found Jose?" he asked immediately upon opening the door.

Justina watched the confusion cross the officer's face. "Sir, I am not here about a Jose. I am here about Therese Devereaux."

Justina ran to the door. "What? What happened? Is she okay?" Before the officer could answer, however, Therese mounted the front steps with another officer, who was carrying a large red suitcase.

"She's fine, miss," the officer responded, then stepped aside to make way for Therese. "She had a little accident, and her car had to be towed. So, we brought her here." He smiled. "Nothing to worry about! I wish all our accidents had such a good outcome." The officer's trim blond partner leaned in to deposit the suitcase in the foyer, smiled at them, and wished Therese a good day before heading back down to the cruiser parked in front of the house.

The policeman handed Therese a card. "Call us if you need anything else, ma'am," he said, then nodded to the group. "Have a good day, folks."

Shutting the door, Justina asked what had happened, while Therese frowned, seeing the effects of a hard cry on Justina's face. "What's going on here? Did I hear you say something to the officer about Jose? What happened?"

"We can't find Jose," Victor stated flatly, putting his hand on Therese's shoulder, steering her toward the kitchen. "I suspect he went off on an adventure; there is no reason to assume anything else. We have the police looking for him," he added when Therese opened her mouth to protest.

"Celeste is looking, too. Right now, I think we need to

take a few minutes and calm down. The police said the best thing is to stay here and wait for him because he will most likely show up on his own." Her father's reassuring voice belied the strain visible on his face, and Justina knew him well enough to know he was trying to keep them from falling apart. He got a bottle of water out of the refrigerator and handed it to Therese.

"What happened?" Therese demanded. "Was Celeste here with him? How did he go missing?" She settled onto a kitchen barstool, opening the bottle of water distractedly, looking from Justina to her father for an answer.

"It was me," Justina said, trying to stop her voice from cracking. "I was doing some work, here, and told him to go watch television so I could get something finished. Something I should have already done if I was doing my job properly." She could feel her eyes filling up again. "When I went to look for him, he was gone. The back door was unlocked and not closed all the way. Probably because somebody didn't want me to hear the door latch!" Guilt and fear threatened to consume her whole body as she relived the events. "It's my fault," she said, the tears breaking free again.

Therese leaned over and put her arm around Justina's shoulders. "Honey, it's not your fault. You can't have eyes on that child every minute, it's not possible! And I bet your dad is right, he snuck out on some grand adventure. If you two want to go out looking, I will stay here in case he comes back."

Justina nodded emphatically. "Yes, I need to go look for

him; I don't agree with the police. It is awful to just sit here!"

"Well, I would drive you around, but I'm a bit short on a car right now," Therese said, trying to lighten the mood. "You two go on, you'll feel better."

Victor smiled, patting Therese on the shoulder. "A very good idea, and you are exactly right. Sitting here is making it much worse. Thank you. I couldn't leave my daughter here alone to go look but sitting here is making me crazy. Justina, go put your shoes on, let's go. Let's go toward the school. He knows that route, maybe he went that way for some reason." He paused, then added, "I still want to know the whole story of what happened to you today, too. Not a good day all the way around. When we come back, and Jose is home, we will have a glass of wine and hear about your day."

Justina nodded, smiling through her teary eyes and blotchy face and jumping up to get her shoes that she had kicked off at the back door. She could hear her father and Therese talking.

"Victor, I don't know what to say, so much going on and now Jose! Did she tell you about the drama at the hospital? I'm sure it's nothing to do with this, but my mind just keeps going there," Therese said, and Justina knew then that Therese had the same worry she did. She felt both better and worse knowing that: worse, because it made her fear seem more rational and therefore likely to be justified, but better because she wasn't the only one feeling that way about the situation at St. Mathews, so she knew she wasn't imaging things.

"Well, yes, she told me a little, but we never really got the chance to—" Victor stopped midsentence as a loud knock interrupted him. "That's probably the police. Hopefully they found Jose!" He jumped up and ran to the door, almost colliding with Justina when she came running with one shoe on and the other in her hand.

Justina and her father were both surprised to see a very short, heavyset woman with auburn hair and bright green eyes standing on the steps. "Victor Gonzalez?" she asked and, at his nod, gestured to two boys cowering at the bottom of the stairs. "Does one of these little monsters belong to you?"

22

THERESE

Therese slowly relaxed as the mood around the dinner table was merry and light-hearted, except for Jose who was in the doghouse for his decision to try to find his friend Toby's house to go "camping." Jose pouted, pushing his food around, having lost his games and outdoor playtime for a week.

"I still can't believe you thought you could go to Toby's house by yourself!" Justina exclaimed, unable to let it go. "Why didn't you come ask me? Or have his mom call? What were you thinking?" Therese exchanged glances with Victor, who appeared to be suppressing a smile at his daughter's tirade.

"You were busy," Jose mumbled. "Can I be excused? I'm not hungry," he said, directing the question to Victor and avoiding Justina's eyes.

"Okay, Jose, but no games. Why don't you go up and take a bath? I'll check on you in a little bit." Seeing Jose's pout, he said firmly, "I mean it. Go now, put your plate away first."

Jose slunk off to the kitchen, and Therese could hear him

complaining loudly to the cat about the unfairness of his life. *He's has certainly become an American very fast,* she thought. Aloud, she said, "Well, he's adjusted to being here, I would say!"

Victor and Justina both smiled, and Victor topped off their glasses of red wine. "So, finally … Therese, tell us about your accident!"

Therese relayed the events of the afternoon, trying to make light of the whole thing. She did, however, share her fears that she had been followed. *What if she put this family in danger?*

"I'm sure it's my paranoia, you know, after that whole incident at the hospital with Dr. Al hearing us talk. And the rock at my house. But it did seem odd that the brakes suddenly didn't work. I'll be glad when this investigation at the hospital is over." She tried to keep her tone casual rather than let them see how afraid she was.

"Did the garage think that someone had sabotaged your car?" Victor asked, frowning. "Do they have an explanation?"

Therese shrugged; her mouth twisted into a wry smile. "They said it could possibly have been deliberate, but they couldn't say with certainty. The brake line was punctured, and the fluid drained out each time I hit the brakes until they failed. Brake lines can get leaks or punctures without it being deliberate. At least that's what the mechanic said." She didn't add that the mechanic had also said he suspected someone had tampered with it but hadn't wanted to state that as a fact.

"Should you report it to the police?" Justina asked, looking back and forth between Therese and her father. "I mean, just in case? It's not the first thing that's happened." Therese could see her own fears reflected in Justina's tone and face, her eyes wide and her voice seeking reassurance.

"I don't think so," Therese answered. "We don't know that anyone tampered with it. I don't like calling police for any possible problem when there is no proof. The issue at my house was deliberate, but this, well, we don't know." *And the police will never be able to find who did it, anyhow ...*

Victor frowned. "I don't agree. This looks like a pattern to me. Whoever did this might back off if they know the police are watching for any mischief."

Therese shook her head. The idea of sending police to talk to the people at the hospital scared her more than the failed brakes. "I think the best thing is to push Frank to get the hospital investigation done. If it is a plot against me, that's the only reason I can think of."

"I can send Frank a note to let him know what happened," Justina said. "We have been getting a lot of information, and an audit is underway." She paused. "It is scary, though. The way Dr. Al looked at me today, and then when Jose disappeared … I have to admit, that was the first thing I thought of. But I'm sure that's ridiculous, I'm just getting carried away." *No, you're not,* Therese thought. *I would have thought the same thing.*

Therese reached over and patted Justina's hand. "I suspect we both are. There is no proof that anything at the hospital was related. And we know Jose is fine, that that was just a false alarm, thank God."

"Well, it's not my decision," Victor said, his tone and expression showing that he knew it would be better if it was. "But you both be very careful. Therese, I can take you to the hospital in the morning, since Justina has classes." He held up his hand as Therese opened her mouth to argue. "I will feel much better this way. And I have meetings in the city. You can ride home with Justina." Justina and Therese looked at each other and smiled. The subject was clearly closed.

"Yes, Papa," Justina said in an overly obedient, slightly mocking tone. "You're the boss."

"That's right," Victor affirmed, smiling and draining his wineglass.

Justina had stood up to start clearing away the dishes when her phone chirped with a text message. "It's from Frank," she shared as she opened it.

Therese knew something was wrong as Justina's eyes grew large. "He said the auditors have found a number of 'very concerning issues,' at least in their very early review of the data and charts." She looked at Therese. "This isn't going to be pretty. Nobody is going to be happy!"

23

JUSTINA

When Justina arrived at the hospital the next day, Frank had already met with the auditors and was poring over some spreadsheets and other documents in their usual conference room.

"Hey," Justina called, announcing herself. "What did the auditors find?"

Frank sighed. "Well, they've only looked at a few cases so far, but we have a couple of issues here. First of all, the physicians aren't seeing the patients or supervising the care like they are supposed to, and they are billing for it. So that's an issue, although by itself not terribly uncommon. It's still a problem, though. Also, the auditors said there is an unusually large percentage of diagnoses for headaches and back pain." He frowned, flipping through the spreadsheets. "Especially those billed under Dr. Al."

"Why are those an issue?" Justina asked. Why would the diagnosis matter?

"A lot of drug seekers come to clinics and hospitals complaining of those conditions because it's harder to disprove. They know that managing the pain is usually the immediate clinical solution, and, of course, they decline any other type of treatment. Sooner or later, they get cut off and then just go elsewhere."

"Oh, that's right, the 'frequent fliers.' And it's Dr. Al seeing those patients?" Justina asked.

"Well, it's billed under Dr. Al. But we look at the records, the signature logs, the schedules ... the residents pretty much see all his patients and he's not even here most of the time, according to the schedules. He is supposed to be involved in the care and supervising the residents, even if he's not in the same room all the time; he isn't supposed to just let the residents see patients without any oversight whatsoever. And then prescribing Schedule II drugs-we definitely have a problem here."

Justina recalled the myriad of complex rules she had tried to digest around medical residents and what they could do. It was very confusing, but she could easily understand why the attending physician needed to keep an eye on doctors in training.

"What about Dr. Powers?" she asked. "He was also acting odd; they were both unhappy about the audit."

"Well, Dr. Powers has some issues, too. All his cases, if you look at his *bills*, are very complex and require a significant amount of time and decision-making. But you look at the diagnoses, and the documentation—it doesn't hold up. It doesn't take complex decision-making usually for a cold or an ear infection, for instance. He has a lot of residents, too, taking care of the patients. So, we need to dig deeper into the doctors' schedules and contracts to verify what they are committed to in the clinic as well as in other contracts and their own practices. Plus the whole pharmacy connection. But first we will need to nail down these claims and any overpayments. The clinic and the doctors can't keep money they didn't earn. The government kind of frowns on that," he said sarcastically. Justina laughed at Frank's small attempt at humor, but he clearly wasn't laughing.

"So what now?" Justina asked. "Are you going to talk to them? What happens next?" She paused, thinking. "Dr. Shoemaker won't be happy, either."

"No, she won't. This was just a probe sample. We need to do a deeper analysis and audit, determine how far back this problem goes and make a plan to pay back any money, especially to government programs like Medicaid and Medicare. But they need to stop doing business this way right now. So yes, Dr. Shoemaker is the next one we talk to. Especially given the various financial arrangements and the conflicts of interest, fraud and abuse issues, possible drug diversion …" He grimaced. "Although we need to put a stop on any further inappropriate claims, that is really not the biggest potential problem here. We may have to start a conversation with my contacts at the Department of Justice or the Office of Inspector General. Dr. Shoemaker is really not going to like *that*!"

Justina nodded in agreement. "What about the pharmacy issue? And the patients getting dropped off? And the residents' training and supervision? How does all that fit together?"

"Well, we need to talk to more of the residents, to see what they can tell us, because we're clearly not going to get anywhere with the interviews so far. But my guess is that there is some sort of drug diversion scheme on top of the other problems. There have been a variety of prosecutions where 'fake' patients are brought into a clinic by 'runners' and get prescriptions for drugs that they can then take themselves or sell on the street. Sometimes they have stolen Medicare numbers. That is where we call in the government, though. It's not our job to do a stakeout at the clinic or create risk for anyone here by raising alarms."

Justina nodded, relieved. "I'm glad to hear that," she said in a joking tone, but not really joking at all. "So, what are our next steps?"

"We'll just work through the audits, for now. They already know we are doing that, and I will talk to my contacts at the DOJ about the other issues. This type of scheme can be worth millions to the ones involved; it's a big business. If they think we are just looking at overbilling or supervision, they won't like it, but they won't get as alarmed." He paused. "Also, I got a copy of the report requests from Scott, —the ones from the compliance officer requesting pharmacy data?"

"Yes!" She'd been waiting to hear about that but had nearly forgotten. "What was she looking for?"

"Well, apparently she was interested in the same issue.

She wanted the records of patients from the clinic who had been prescribed OxyContin and other opioids and who had them filled at the pharmacy here. He said the report didn't show much commonality, so the clinic patients weren't getting their scrips filled here at the hospital. Scott said he could rerun the report if we didn't have it. That wasn't in the boxes, was it?"

"No, it never turned up," Justina replied. "I've been through everything now. Somebody must have gotten it before we got here. Scott did say he had left it on Michelle's desk, shortly before she resigned."

Frank nodded. "Yes. Someone who knew about it and didn't want it being reviewed. I'll have him rerun it." He frowned. "Plenty of things going on around here that nobody can explain."

"And, speaking of that," Justina began, and she recapped all the events involving Therese. "It's probably just coincidence but I thought I would tell you. The rock was obviously not an accident, but the car problem may be nothing."

Frank shook his head. "I don't like it, especially after Al heard she is staying with you, and she felt she was being followed right after that. I don't want to raise any unnecessary alerts until we have more information, but we also don't want to be foolish. I have a contact with the local police; I will just give them a heads-up that she's been threatened and have them keep an eye on your house. Also make sure you both have Security with you if you go out alone here at the hospital. Okay?"

"Yes, all right. You're making my dad happy, anyhow. He's been fussing. And I think has already called his friend at the local police department."

"It's just a precaution. Hopefully we wrap this up quickly, at least our part of it. Now, what I want you to do is go grab the auditors and get access to the full patient records. This report"—he gestured to the spreadsheet—"doesn't have all the details of whether there was a specific prescription or test ordered. They've given me their initial impressions, but at this point we need an audit report with details that we can rely on. Work with the auditors and your medical records person. See what you can pull out, but don't tell them details about our concerns, just that we need to see all the orders, prescriptions, and tests related to these visits. We'll start with this to confirm what I think we are going to see." He handed Justina the report. "Focus on those highlighted cases, okay? And if anyone does ask, tell them it's just to make sure we have the complete record, like it's no big deal. Got it?"

Justina nodded. "I hope I don't run into Dr. Al," she said, then added, "Or even Dr. Powers, for that matter. They make me nervous, especially now." She took a deep breath. "Okay, I'll be back."

"You'll be fine. Just let them think you don't know anything; you are just the messenger. That's the best way to keep you off their radar. And don't forget, all we really know is that we have some billing concerns. The rest of this is just supposition. Innocent until proven guilty, remember?" He smiled. "I'll talk to the CEO while you do that.

She might be more comfortable with a one-on-one discussion this time, less likely to feel threatened."

Justina chewed on her lip as she waited for the elevator. *I should check on Therese,* she thought. *Let her know what Frank said ... No, no delaying, I'll do it after I get the records!* She realized she was trying to put off her trip to the clinic's records department and chastised herself. Her phone buzzed, startling her, and she dropped the folder with her reports just as the elevator dinged its arrival. "Crap," she muttered, trying to simultaneously cram the phone into her pocket and reach down for the file that had spilled out.

"It's okay, I got it," a female voice said, and Justina looked to see a young woman with sandy-blond hair in light blue scrubs bending to pick up the files before she had a chance to.

"Oh, thank you … Kristy," Justina said, noting the girl's name and status as a resident on her badge.

"Sure, no problem," she said, and Justina noticed her looking for a badge. She knew there was a policy about wearing a badge, but her visitor's badge was back in her briefcase. "Sorry, I'm a visitor, my badge is in my bag. I'm just here on a project."

Kristy laughed. "That's fine, I don't care," she said, then asked, "Going down?" as she entered the elevator and pushed a button.

"Um, yes, to the clinic," Justina said.

"Oh, me too! Convenient," the girl commented. "What are you here for? Are you part of that audit?"

Justina looked to see if there was any sign of concern on

the girl's face, but nothing seemed out of the ordinary. "Yes, I am," she replied, not wanting to elaborate.

As they stepped out of the elevator, Kristy glanced around. "Let me know if I can be of any help," she said, her expression still neutral. "I work mostly for Dr. Al. I'm still learning—I'm in my first year—so if I'm doing anything wrong, I want to know."

"Okay, thanks," Justina said. "Right now, we are just reviewing claims and records, routine billing stuff."

The girl hesitated, as if trying to make a decision. "Um, can I ask you something?" Kristy looked up and down the hallway to make sure they weren't being observed.

"Of course."

"Okay, let's go around the corner, there's a conference room," Kristy said, leading the way.

She led Justina to a small conference room, barely bigger than an office, and shut the door. Standing with her back against it, the girl took a deep breath. "You know this is my first year," she began. "I was lucky to get in here, and if I screw up, I don't know if I can get another residency, especially if any of the physicians are unhappy with me." She shifted her weight, pausing.

Justina could see the girl hesitating, and she waited for a moment, practicing Frank's tactic, but it started looking to Justina like the girl was going to change her mind about talking. "So why wouldn't the physicians be happy with you?" she prompted.

"Well, we are supposed to be supervised, and given training. But that's not how it works, you know? Dr. Al has his third-year residents supervising and signing off on everything. They won't ever say a word of complaint; he pays them on the side, and they help him at his practice, too. I've heard they have a similar arrangement with Dr. Powers. We all know what happens if you blow a residency. I'm still learning the rules, but I can tell you ..." She paused, and Justina could see she was blinking hard trying to keep her emotions in check.

"Yes?" Justina nudged.

"I'm not getting properly trained, and I'm so scared I'm going to make a mistake and harm a patient!" This last blurted part came out with the tears she'd been trying to hold back.

"Oh my God," Justina said, feeling the enormity of the girl's anxiety. "Have you spoken with anyone? What about the other residents, the third years?" She was feeling at a loss for how to respond.

"Oh, no. Believe me, they are like the doctors' henchmen. The doctors will make sure they get great recommendations, and they are getting paid, like I said, for moonlighting at the doctors' practices. We work crazy hours, more than we are supposed to, and I'm so exhausted. They are breaking all the rules down there. And everyone is too afraid to say anything." Sniffling, she added, "After what happened to that compliance officer, we are more scared than ever. So much for nonretaliation!"

Justina knew she was out of her depth, and the girl's reference to the compliance officer as part of this was reinforcement of her own worst fears. "Kristy, I'm glad you told me. But I'm like you, I'm new to this and I'm not leading our review. Let me talk to Frank about what you've told me. I'm sure he will want to meet with you."

Kristy frowned but nodded. "I just need to be very careful. Those third years are like spies; they keep tabs on us and report anything we do wrong. Do you think you can help?" Her eyes were pleading. "I really need this residency to work, but I need to be properly trained. I can't keep doing this if I'm putting patients at risk," she said.

"Of course! I don't blame you," Justina said. "I'll let Frank know, and he will find a way to handle this, I'm sure. He's worked on many of these types of cases," she explained, trying to relieve the girl's anxiety.

She pulled out one of Frank's cards she had in her pocket. "Do you have a pen? Let me give you my phone number, too, just so you have it." She scribbled her cell number on the back. "Call me if you need to, okay? We'll take care of this!" she said with more confidence than she felt.

Kristy smiled, taking the card and wiping her eyes. "Thank you. Thank God you are here. I worry every day about our patients." Tucking the card in the pocket of her scrubs, she said, "I'm going to leave first, if that's okay. No offense, but I don't want anyone to see me with you," as she scooted out of the room.

Justina put her hand on her chest, which was tightening. *No pressure there,* she thought. *That poor girl! And the pa-*

tients! She forced herself to take a few deep breaths before heading out of the conference room.

Justina cracked the door to the clinic office open and peered in before entering. It appeared to be deserted. She had thought that at least one of the auditors would be there, or one of the office staff. As she deliberated what to do, Dr. Al came around the corner from the front desk. He looked at her coldly. “We are down staff today,” he stated. “Is there something I can help you with?”

24

JUSTINA

Justina massaged her rigid neck muscles as she rode the elevator back up to the conference room. Getting her hands on the complete medical records had been more difficult than it should have been. Dr. Al, predictably, demonstrated his skills at passive resistance, providing endless reasons why nobody could help her pull the records and trying to convince her, in an aggressive fashion, that she didn't really need the complete records and wasn't really qualified to be reviewing them anyhow. Finally, she gave up and found her way back to the medical records department, where her newfound friends were able to access most of what she needed and print them out for her. She also connected with Mark, the lead auditor, to let him know where things were at and to coordinate their work. He agreed to stop by and get the records.

When she arrived at the conference room, Frank was hunched over his laptop, his face hardened in concentration. Justina slipped in and sat down, stacking the medical records on the table. She wasn't even sure what to look for or how to find it, but at least she should be able to easily flag the ones where there were prescriptions. Or so she hoped. Frank glanced up and nodded to her but went right back to what he was doing. Justina spread out the report with the highlighted cases so she could make notes on what she found. After everything she went through to get the files, she was eager to see what they held but also felt very out of her depth. Not only that, but she also had a hard time focusing, still thinking about Kristy and the conversation in the meeting room.

She kept one eye on Frank, waiting for him to finish whatever he was doing so she could tell him about Kristy and the new information. Finally, he looked up, sighing, and stretched his neck.

"Frank, I had an interesting encounter with one of the residents," she began.

"About the clinic?"

"Yes, a first year. She told me that they are not getting adequate training or supervision. She said they are breaking all sorts of rules." She thought back to the disturbing conversation. "Frank, she is scared that patients could get hurt by her or one of the other first years, just because they don't know what they are doing! She said the third years are basically running things, but they are buddies with the doctors, and getting paid by them, so won't ever cross them. She's scared to death!"

Frank frowned and shook his head. "Is there anything good coming out of that clinic?" he asked, his voice weary. "I honestly don't know where this will end; every day it's a new problem we hear about. Although this is consistent with what the auditors saw in the records. Not good."

"I know, right?" Justina said. "You should have seen her. She was so scared, and she said she is so grateful we are here because somebody needs to stop it. I told her I would let you know, so we could help address it. I didn't know what to tell her. It kind of freaked me out, honestly, to think about the patients and what could happen, for instance if they prescribed a wrong medication."

"Oh, I agree," Frank said. "And just so you know, the residency programs are highly regulated. They can't work the residents beyond a certain number of hours, they need a specific amount of training and, of course, supervision. The third-year residents can do some supervision, but the physicians still need to be involved. And all that needs to be documented. Those are some of the core requirements for a legitimate residency program. So, we will need to talk to the residents about these issues and look at the documentation of training, schedules, all of that. I will also need to talk to Dr. Shoemaker," he said, rubbing his temples.

"She's not going to be happy," Justina commented, stating the obvious.

"No, she's not, and neither are the physicians running this operation." Frank stood, cracking his neck and stretching. "The hospital gets reimbursement for running residency programs, so this is also a financial issue, if they aren't meeting the requirements." He glanced at the clock. "I'm going to wander down to her office now," he said. "Just go ahead and take a look at those medical records, see what you can see. And we'll get them to the auditors to do the formal review. But it's good for you to get familiar with the charts, anyhow. I'll be back."

Eyeing the pile of records with trepidation, Justina dug in. There were a mixture of cases for Dr. Powers and Dr. Al, but in both cases even Justina could see that they weren't the ones seeing the patients for the most part; the residents were. Or at least it appeared that way: the signatures on the records didn't match the signature logs for the physicians. She still wasn't sure what the specific rules were about that, so she focused on the prescriptions. Sure enough, there were a majority of patients with vague pain complaints and prescriptions for painkillers. The patients with pain prescriptions also had very minimal notes in the charts compared to others who Justina presumed were legitimate patients that had documented injuries or illnesses.

Justina made notes for each case on the printed list so the auditors and Frank would be able to quickly see which was which and she put the records in the same order as the list. She felt like she was starting to get a feel for which cases were more appropriate than others and was writing up her notes when Mark poked his head in the door.

"Do you have the files for us to go through?" he asked.

Justina nodded, scooping up her notes and the pile of records. "Here you go. I made some notes, but I'm still learning. Let me know if I'm on track or not, okay?" She smiled as she handed over the records.

"Yeah, sure," he said, starting to turn to leave when Frank entered the room.

"Hey," Frank interjected. "Before you take those, can you make a copy for us? I'm waiting to get some data from Medical Records that will help us track which patients filled the prescriptions here in-house."

"Sure thing," Mark said.

When the auditor returned with the copies, Frank motioned to Justina. "Justina, can you hang on to these? I'll have you crossmatch the report from the hospital pharmacy when I get it so we can verify the actual scrips filled here versus the documented complaint and orders, okay?"

Justina nodded, taking the charts.

Once Mark had left, Frank sighed and shut his laptop.

"Dr. Shoemaker was, indeed, not a happy camper," Frank said. "Apparently, they had a recent survey of the residency program, and there were some problems, but she believed they were resolved. So, I doubt we'll find much in the documentation, if they already cleaned it up for surveyors."

"So, what's next? We interview the residents about this issue?"

"Yes. I think we should start with the one you spoke with, then the other first years, work our way up to the third-year residents. That way we will hear what's really going on before tackling the ones who won't want to talk." Frank's phone chirped, and he glanced at it. "Can you get Mina in here to help us set up meetings with those residents?" he asked. "I need to respond to this email real quick."

"No problem," Justina responded, looking through her files for the list of residents.

Mina wasn't at her desk, so Justina left her a note about scheduling the interviews and returned to the conference room. Frank was back at his laptop, and his face was serious.

"Looks like these guys are both making a ton of money off this hospital," Frank observed. "I've been going over their contracts. They get paid for seeing patients—who they mostly don't see—plus a flat rate as 'medical directors,' and then on top of that they make extra money for training and supervising residents. Plus, of course, they both have their own private practices and maybe arrangements with other hospitals. Not to mention it looks like they are siphoning off patients for their pharmacy across the street, to the hospital's detriment. If this is how the hospital rewards all its doctors, I'm surprised it makes any money at all."

"Is that legal? How can they actually do all those things? I mean, we know they aren't seeing the patients, and it doesn't look like they are here much providing training to the residents. Why does the hospital pay them so much?" She was shocked. She always knew that doctors made good money, and they should, after all the time they spent on their education and training. But this was something totally different.

"Well, the arrangements themselves are structured legally, but they could be problematic in terms of the rate of pay. The amounts do look pretty high to me. We prefer to see physicians getting paid a more 'average' amount, which is fair market value. If they get paid too much, it raises the question of why. As you know, it's not legal for them to get paid for referrals. I need to look at some data, but I'm thinking these guys are up at the ninety percent mark, if I had to guess." Frank paused, looking at his notes. "Dr. Shoemaker signed these contracts, and they have been renewed twice for Dr. Al, three times for Dr. Powers. In any event, they are doing something that the administration values. Probably bringing in a lot of patients."

Justina shook her head. "So they get paid based on seeing patients, who they don't see, and then training residents, who they don't seem to train, and to be medical directors, but they aren't on-site much. Nice work if you can get it, huh?"

Frank nodded. "Yes, it would seem so. We need to dig a bit deeper, though, to really validate their role in the teaching program and as medical directors. Those duties should be documented, so we can't assume they aren't doing them. And the supervision issue is often a challenge. The auditors will determine if there is adequate documentation to show that they are reviewing the cases and signing off appropriately. But now, with what we've heard … who knows what we may find. So we still have more digging to do; we can't presume this is all inappropriate without validation," he reminded her. "If you think it's ugly now, try accusing these guys of committing a crime when we haven't done a thorough review."

"I know, it just seems crazy to me. I had no idea this kind of stuff went on! How do we find that documentation?"

"We will need to talk to Dr. Shoemaker, again, because

she signed their contracts. We want to see the files she has, which should include documentation to support renewing the agreements, at least in theory. Then we will talk to the key residents and see what documentation we can get on how they are running that program. We'll get there. It's just a lot of different issues and records to look at. This project is going to take longer than we expected."

"It seems like everything we find leads to a whole bunch more we need to look at!" Justina said. "I can see why these things take so long—it's like peeling back the layers of an onion!"

"Yup, that's exactly what we are doing, and in this case I think there is more than one onion!"

Frank glanced down at the phone. "It looks like we've had enough fun for today, and I don't want to give our hospital president another headache. Let's wrap up for the day and I'll get us on her calendar for tomorrow."

Thank God, Justina thought, and hurried to bundle up her files and laptop.

25

THERESE

Therese fought back a wave of sadness that threatened to wash over her. The worst part of her job, and yet the most meaningful part, was working with grieving families. The family she had just spent time with had lost their five-year-old son to a rare cancer after battling it for two years. She knew it would be a long time before those ravaged parents' faces subsided from her thoughts. She had to believe that she had provided them with comfort and that she was doing God's work. Otherwise she couldn't keep going, especially on days like this.

She grabbed a cup of coffee and headed back to her office for a few minutes of quiet reflection before getting back to her regular pile of challenges. The first thing she saw, as always, was the picture of Mateo, and her heart felt broken once again. Her faith was strong, but she couldn't help wondering how life could be so unfair to take away her precious son, like the family downstairs, especially when other families didn't appreciate their own children. Far too many of those precious angels were neglected or abused. She saw it all the time, and it was a heavy burden to carry.

She closed her eyes and said a silent prayer for all of those suffering grief and losses.

A tap on her door disrupted her thoughts. Justina. She could immediately see how tired the girl was, and anxious. Even in her short time with Justina she could tell that she struggled with anxiety and a lack of confidence, although she seemed determined to get past it.

"Hey," Justina said in greeting. "Frank just released me for the day. Do you want to head home with me? Or do you have more work here to do?"

Therese looked at her blinking phone light. "I better stay. Your dad said he could pick me up, or I could catch an Uber later. I've had a lot of unexpected things to handle today, and I'm definitely behind. You go ahead, I'll be there later."

She could see the disappointment on Justina's face. "Are you okay?"

Justina nodded. "Just tired and overwhelmed. More stuff keeps coming up. It seems like instead of solving problems we keep finding more. And I don't know how they will get solved without anyone getting hurt somehow. It's just too much, I don't know. How do you handle it all the time, people coming to you, crying, and you feel powerless to really help?"

Therese wondered briefly what had happened to trigger that particular question at this moment. "It's not easy. But I feel that if I can take some burden off of them, I have done some good. Sometimes I can't. But when people trust you and come to you, that's a gift. And believe it or not, it makes you stronger."

Justina set down her laptop case, frowning. "I suppose, it's just that—" Justina was interrupted when the phone on Therese's desk rang.

Therese felt a flash of frustration. That phone never stopped ringing. "Honey, I need to get this, but let's talk tonight, okay? Why don't you scoot home and enjoy some time with the little guy? That should make you feel better."

"Sure, okay," Justina said, and reluctantly picked up her laptop case. "See you later."

Therese spent the rest of the afternoon returning phone calls and emails. *How do things get backed up so quickly?* At least she had a ride home, though. Victor was nearby and offered to pick her up. She found herself looking forward to that, a welcome break from the day's drama.

The ride back to Long Beach was a nice distraction. Therese found herself respecting Victor more and more as she got to know him and watched how he had taken his problems working for the senator and turned those challenges into his own campaign run. She also admired him for spending all those years as a single father and found herself relating to the unspoken grief she knew he carried.

When they got home, the house was quiet. They found Justina in the dining room, law books and laptop spread out all over the table. Justina looked frazzled, her usually sleek hair stuffed into a clip, her shoulders slumping over the books.

Victor spoke first. "M'ija. We're home. Are you okay?

Where is Jose?"

Justina's greeting was subdued. "Hey. Yes, I'm okay. Jose is upstairs."

Therese was puzzled. "I'm surprised he isn't down here jumping all over us," she commented.

"No. He got in trouble. I told him he had to stay in his room." Justina paused, sighed. "I'm going to flunk out of law school if I can't study, and he wouldn't leave me alone. I told him and told him, and he wouldn't give me a break. I pretty much snapped. I'm sure he's up there pouting."

Victor frowned, his lips tightened. "I'll go talk to him. I need to go up and get out of these clothes anyhow," he added, heading for the stairs.

"Great, now Papa is mad at me," Justina grumbled. "There is just too much going on; I can't handle Jose on top of it all. He just won't settle down. Ever."

Therese fought to keep a neutral tone. "Well, he's a little boy, Justina. You can't expect him to behave like an adult. And he is still new to this family and, in fact, this country. Having a child in the house is not easy, but it's a blessing."

Justina rolled her eyes. "Yes, I know. And I love him. I do. But he has to learn that he can't just run amok *all the time*!" She started putting tags on pages of her books, closing them up for the day with an exaggerated sigh.

Therese couldn't help herself, especially after the day she'd had. "Justina, I know you're tired. I get that. But that little boy just lost his mother and got taken halfway around the world from where he was born. He's learning a new language; he has a new family. You need to be patient with him. Do you know what I would give to have my little boy back, driving me nuts?"

Therese immediately regretted her words as she saw tears start to fill Justina's eyes. She stacked her books up, head down, and left the room.

"Lord, give me strength," Therese murmured to herself, as she heard Victor coming down the stairs.

Victor entered the room, with Jose riding on his shoulders piggyback. Therese was relieved to see the boy looked fine. *At least he recovers quickly,* she thought. When Victor set him down he ran to Therese, all smiles. "Hola, niño," she greeted him, and hefted him up.

Victor smiled at them, and Therese thought how much his smile lit up his face, especially when it was directed at Jose.

"You know what," Victor began. "Today was a very hard day for everyone. I think we should order pizza. Who wants to order pizza?" Therese cringed as Jose squealed in her ear.

"Okay, I think that's a yes vote," Victor said with a chuckle. "Jose, here's what I want you to do. Go find Justina, tell her you're sorry you gave her trouble, and tell her we're getting pizza so she needs to come help decide what to order. Okay?" Jose nodded, scampering off to find Justina, the earlier dispute forgotten.

"That was a good move, Victor," Therese commented. "I'm afraid I upset your daughter. I chastised her and said some things that were out of line."

"She'll get over it, don't worry. It's just a big adjustment for her, too. She's never had to worry about anything but herself, and suddenly she has this job and Jose on top of school. She's stronger than you think, and she has a good heart. She's just overwhelmed. Probably I am to blame, as well. She's been very sheltered; I have tried to protect her too much since her mother died."

"I'm understand. I just had one of those days, too, but it isn't my place—" She broke off when Justina entered the room, holding hands with Jose.

"It's okay, Therese," Justina said, her face mottled from a crying jag but a determined smile on her face. "Jose and I are fine, and I get what you said. And you're right. I need to do better. I'm just overwhelmed sometimes. But Jose is going to help me, right Jose?"

Jose bounced up and down. "Yes, Tina. Can we order pizza now?"

After everyone had eaten their fill, Therese and Justina worked on cleaning up the kitchen. Therese was still feeling an ache in the pit of her stomach over her comments to Justina. "Justina, I really am sorry for what I said earlier. It wasn't right. I was just very upset after counseling a family who lost their little boy to cancer today. It hit me harder than I would have expected."

Justina gave her a hug. "It's okay, really. And you are right, I'm not patient with him. I'm so worried about what's going on at the hospital and keeping up at school. But it isn't fair to Jose, it's not his fault, and I did tell Papa I would help. I need to do my part."

"Well, I can help some, too, you know. I don't mind working into the babysitting rotation if I need to, whenever I can. I don't have to be on-site at the hospital every minute. In fact, it would be nice to have a reason not to go, the way things are lately." As she said the words she realized it was the truth; she really didn't want to go to the hospital with so much drama going on, most of it unpleasant.

Justina smiled. "That would be great, maybe just now and then. So long as Papa doesn't think I talked you into it ..." She stopped short as her phone dinged with a message. "Now what?"

After reading the message she looked up, her eyes clouded with worry. "That was a message from one of the residents, one I talked to today. She was telling me some things going on in the residency program. She was really upset. Anyhow, she just texted me that she's being called in for performance counseling with Dr. Al."

26

JUSTINA

The meeting with Dr. Shoemaker the next morning did not go well.

"I've had a discussion with the board about this review," the CEO began, leaning forward in her black leather office chair, resting her elbows on the desk. Her previous friendly demeanor was completely absent as she peered directly at Frank over her reading glasses.

"The board is concerned about the disruptions to operations that this investigation is causing, as well as the cost. We understand, of course, the need to complete this review for compliance reasons, but the board has recommended that we conduct the audit using internal resources. They believe that we could get the same information without alienating our physicians and alarming staff . . ." She trailed off as she noted Frank shaking his head. Justina listened in disbelief, silent, waiting to see how Frank would respond.

"With all due respect to your board, I would recommend that we be allowed to complete this review. There are a variety of issues, beyond just billing questions, that really need to be examined now that we've uncovered possible problems. You have some potential whistleblowers here who could easily report concerns to the government if they think the hospital isn't properly evaluating the matters that have been reported. If that happened, the records would show that the hospital pulled the plug at a point where questions were being raised—that creates the appearance of a cover-up, which I know isn't what you intend. But it would look that way to regulators." Frank paused, watching her reaction.

Dr. Shoemaker shifted in her chair, leaning back. "You're right, of course. But you need to understand my position. I answer to the board, and they want this taken down a notch. There has been too much disruption."

Frank nodded. "Can you tell me who is on the board, and who staffs those meetings? Are Doctors Powers and Al-Basri in attendance?"

The hospital president grimaced. "Oh yes, Dr. Al is, and, of course, our chief medical officer, Dr. Pascale. It was very clear that Dr. P has been getting an earful and, of course, he sticks with his docs."

Frank was quiet for a moment, digesting the information. "It's not surprising, of course, that the doctors would feel this way. But the board has a fiduciary duty, they should understand the importance of an impartial review when there have been allegations such as these. And, quite frankly, internal staff have been the ones mostly engaged in pulling records and other data; we have not been disrupting operations. I would advise you, in my legal capacity, that it would be a mistake to stop this investigation midstream."

"I expected you to say that," Dr. Shoemaker admitted. "And, truthfully, I thought that your boss, Peter Hancock, who sits on the board, would also make that argument. And I suppose he would have, but he recused himself from the discussion due to conflict of interest. So the doctors pretty much ran the show."

Frank frowned. "And Dr. Al didn't point out his own conflict of interest? And neither did anyone else?" Frank's tone was a little testy, Justina noted with surprise.

Dr. Shoemaker again shifted in her chair and nibbled her lip before responding. "I don't think anyone was willing to call out Dr. Al," she admitted. "He started the meeting on offense, and he was very heated. I admit I was intimidated, and I don't scare easily. I'm not a voting board member, anyhow, but I should have spoken up. It was very awkward for me, since I called you in and everyone there knew it. I felt like I was being attacked, in part, so it was beyond difficult to respond by telling him to step aside. I'm sorry. It's wrong, but you know how the politics in a hospital can be." She cast her eyes down and fidgeted with a pen on her desk.

Frank didn't acknowledge her admission, but instead said, "How about this, by way of compromise, to keep your board happy and off your back, but also to protect you—we will continue through the end of next week and evaluate where we are, with a report to you and the board if they so choose. By that time we will have enough information to make preliminary recommendations and findings, at least for some matters, and can also outline any other areas needing further exploration. Will that work? You know I'm not trying to pad my bill here. I am trying to protect the hospital. I truly think it could be a very costly mistake to stop at this juncture."

Dr. Shoemaker toyed with her pen again, considering. "I think that's a reasonable solution. I'll explain the risks to them, and suggest that in two weeks, with your preliminary findings and recommendations, we can move this over to our in-house attorney, who will be back by then. They won't like it, because Dr. Al wants this shut down immediately, but I believe the board will agree with the approach."

Frank nodded. "Very well. So, while I have you here, I would like to discuss the contracts for Dr. Al and Dr. Powers. They have several different arrangements with the hospital, and the agreements are very lucrative, to say the least. Their compensation is definitely in the upper range of what I would expect to see. Do you have documentation to support how they fulfill the contractual obligations, particularly the medical directorships and teaching roles? Do you keep timesheets or other records? With that level of compensation, it's important to show how those salaries were determined and the duties performed, particularly when you've renewed these agreements."

The president frowned. "We don't keep timesheets. The doctors felt it was demeaning. The compliance officer raised this issue in the past, and I've never seen the Med Exec

Committee get so up in arms."

Frank sighed. "Yes, I'm not surprised. I've heard before, many times, that physicians don't like to keep track of their time. So how do you know they are meeting their obligations? What documentation shows they perform the duties under the contracts?"

"They are running the clinic! They hold meetings, they manage operations … What more do you need? I really think this is a bit much. These are well-respected physicians. It's insulting to suggest that they fill out timecards like a low-level employee." Her voice was raising, and Justina could see patches of pink starting to mottle her cheekbones.

"Okay, okay, let's talk about the teaching program. Is there someone who maintains records of the curriculum, the training sessions, and schedules for the residents? I am not trying to undermine anyone's professionalism, but it is my job here to identify any risks. I'm here to help. Who coordinates the residency program? We've heard some concerns in that quarter, as well, just so you know." Frank kept a calm tone but didn't miss a beat with his questions. Justina admired how he moved the discussion but persisted.

Dr. Shoemaker took a deep breath. "I'm sorry. This feels personal to me, too, as a physician, but I know we need to make sure our house is in order. Gabrielle O'Brien is down the hall; she is the coordinator for the program. She has all the records, which I'm sure are in order. There are strict requirements for residency programs, and she is very diligent."

Frank nodded. "That works for us, thank you."

Dr. Shoemaker glanced at her computer screen and then the clock on the wall. “I’m sorry, I am going to be late for a meeting, and it’s already been postponed twice. I will talk to the board about this approach, and Mina can direct you to our residency coordinator.” She stood, straightening her black blazer and gathering up a small pile of file folders on her desk. “Oh, and Frank? Keep me in the loop, okay? You can see how sensitive this is.”

“Certainly, of course. Thank you for your time.” Frank nodded to her as she gave them each a tight smile and left them in her office. They could hear her sending Mina in as she passed her assistant’s desk.

Justina and Frank exchanged glances and stepped out of the office as Mina approached. “Dr. Shoemaker asked me to take you to meet with Gabby? If you’re ready I can take you now,” Mina said.

Frank looked at Justina. “Do you need a break?”

“Nope, I’m good. Let’s go.”

“Okay,” Frank said, addressing Mina. “Let’s go meet our residency coordinator!”

27

JUSTINA

Justina eyed the text message from Therese, advising her that she had been able to get a rental car and had gotten a ride to pick it up. "See you at home," the message read. Justina was relieved things were back to normal with Therese. She still felt guilty and ashamed of herself over the incident with Jose the night before. She couldn't imagine Therese ever being as unable to handle a child as she was. *Time to let it go*, she scolded herself. Too much to do!

Today, however, had been especially intense, with so much happening in one short day. She felt a headache coming on as she thought about the day's events. First of all, the medical records with prescriptions for pain medications looked suspicious, even to her untrained eye. The lucrative contracts for the clinic physicians were another concern, and she realized how much she had to learn about the rules for physician compensation. On top of all that, the hospital president was trying to cancel the investigation, just as the list of issues was expanding! As if all that wasn't enough, the meeting with the residency program coordinator had reinforced her doubts about the residency program. When Frank had stepped out to take a phone call, Gabby had been very candid about her views of the two doctors in question, and the clinic in general, saying that the two physicians were rarely present and were having two third-year residents run everything. She told Justina that the residents worked more hours than what was allowed, but that they couldn't complain for fear of losing their positions.

Justina was learning that losing a residency spot was a professional death knell, and that the residents were practically held captive, which was why there were so many rules in place around things like scheduling and training requirements. The requirements were necessary to make sure the residents weren't just used to do all the work without getting their educational needs met. According to Gabby, however, the clinic rotation was known for being grueling to excess. *Just like Kristy had said*, Justina kept thinking.

Although Justina felt that the residency coordinator was being truthful, it also seemed that she was careful about how she said things, and she was very clear that their documents were all in order. Justina asked about the third-year residents doing the supervision, and she could see Gabby literally tense up.

"Well, it's normal for the third years to have more of a leadership role and help with oversight," Gabby said, sounding to Justina a bit defensive. Justina could tell she was getting into touchy territory.

"Oh, I'm sure!" she said. "I am still learning the rules, and I'm not trying to suggest anything. I just want to understand how it works and what the requirements are, that's all." She figured playing the inexperience card would work in her favor here.

"No, that's okay," Gabby said, and leaned forward, speaking in a quiet voice. "They do supervise more than they are supposed to. Of course I don't officially know that, because all the documentation they give me looks fine. But they complain to me sometimes. I know that they also see patients over at both private practices. I don't know how they stay on their feet; I can't imagine they are getting any rest. In fact …" She stopped talking as they heard footsteps in the hall. In a normal voice, Gabby said, "Just let me know if you need anything else, okay? I think you will find all our records are well organized. We just went through survey."

Taking her cue, Justina said, "Okay, great. Thanks."

Keeping in mind Frank's comments about verifying what activities were actually getting done, Justina gave Gabby her cell phone number and email address and asked her to forward over the training schedules, who led them, and attendance. Even though Gabby said it was all in order, she wanted to see for herself. She felt she was starting to get the hang of how Frank was gathering documentation, now that she knew what issues he was looking at. She hoped she was on the right track. She felt she had done well with Gabby, in Frank's absence, and was eager to get to the bottom of all that was happening. Frank's experience was amazing, but Justina was impatient and wanted to push forward with more urgency. The dead compliance officer and threats to Therese were never far from her thoughts.

The day ran later than it was supposed to, especially since Frank had left her on her own to wrap up with the residency coordinator. Since they didn't get a chance to debrief, Justina had all sorts of questions running through her mind:

— *Have any of the residents been getting adequately trained? How long has this gone on?*

— *Who was really prescribing the pain medications, if the doctors were rarely around? Had the physicians actually told the residents to do that? How were they getting those patients?*

— *How much did Dr. Shoemaker know, or suspect? She seemed innocent, but was clearly controlled by the doctors to a large degree.*

— *Did the other residents believe things were not being done correctly, as Kristy thought?*

— *How could those doctors manage their own practices with so much time commitment at the hospital? Were they really allowing residents to work in their own practices, unsupervised?*

— *Would the board take action against the physicians if they were caught in wrongdoing, or were they totally controlled by the doctors?*

And the questions that seemed most important to Justina: *Were the doctors making a profit by writing or approving phony prescriptions? Were they both in on it? Who else was involved? Were they paying the guy in the van to go find fake patients? Where did he find them? Were the patients also getting paid, or were they paying for the access to the drugs?*

— *Lastly, was there any explanation that would render all of these issues moot, some rational justification that would put it all to rest? Was that even possible?*

So many questions, and no Frank to hash over them. Justina knew enough to know that a lot of this was probably easily answered by someone with experience, but to her it was overwhelming in its complexity.

As she drove home, or, more accurately, sat in traffic on the way home, she mulled over possible next steps. The investigation had to be fast-tracked, so she felt a sense of urgency to get answers. She found herself completely absorbed in this job and wanted to impress Frank by coming up with a plan, not just more questions (although she had many of those, to be sure). To her, a few things had to get done quickly:

— *Touch base with the auditors to get their input on the documentation and prescriptions. Was there overbilling, and were the scrips appropriately signed, etc.?*

— *Interview the residents. Tricky, with the third years,*

because they would probably be afraid of what could happen to them for talking. Find out what they were being asked to do, including anything related to prescriptions, signing records, working for the doctors offsite, or seeing "fake" patients.

— *Verify where the prescriptions were being filled: find out if the in-house pharmacy was being used. Frank had just emailed her the report that would show that. Were they all going across the street? Who is getting paid, and how is that whole activity set up?*

Justina wasn't sure how to get to the root of that matter. She made a mental note to ask Frank.

As she pulled into the driveway, she was glad to see a strange car in front of the house. *Good, Therese is already home! I can see what her thoughts are on some of this stuff. The sooner we can figure this out, the sooner we can be sure that she is safe.*

When she got in the door, however, it was clear that something else was already going on. Jose came running downstairs to meet her, as always, but instead of his usual random chattering about his day, his eyes were wide as he dramatically whispered, "Papa had a bad day! Need to be very quiet!"

"What?" Justina asked him. "Are you in trouble?"

"No! Not me! Some lawyers took Papa's money. Mother told me to be very quiet and watch TV upstairs!" His face was solemn and his eyes wide. "You should be very quiet, too," he advised.

Justina tried to imagine what new drama was unfolding. "Okay, I will go see what's wrong. Thank you for the warning, Jose. You go back upstairs like you were told, okay? I'll check on Papa." The boy nodded, his face very serious. He scooped up Hercules, who was winding around Justina's legs, and crept up the stairs in an exaggerated tiptoe fashion, whispering to the cat about being quiet.

What in the world is going on? she wondered as she headed toward the voices in the kitchen.

As she rounded the corner, it was clear that Jose had not been mistaken about a serious situation. Victor's face was set in tense lines, and Therese was stirring a pot on the stove but was looking at Victor with her brow furrowed in concern.

"M'ija, I'm glad you are home safely," Victor greeted her. "We have a problem, all of us, and I don't think you should continue working for the law firm."

28

JUSTINA

"What? Why? What are you talking about, Papa?" Justina was stunned by Victor's greeting.

"Your law firm pulled funding from your father's campaign," Therese interjected. "He's worried that maybe it's because they are too aligned with the hospital and all the issues going on there." Justina noticed the two of them exchanging glances as she tried to process this new information. Therese continued, "It's because of me that this is happening. I should never have come here, I brought this to your doorstep. I don't think Justina's role would have put this family on the radar. If that's even what is happening."

"Wait, what?" Justina demanded, looking back and forth at the two others.

"No"—her father ignored her, responding to Therese—"This isn't your fault. But I'm afraid there are some bad people involved here, and I don't want my daughter in the middle of it."

"Well, that is between you two, but I need to move out of

here so they will leave this family alone. This started with me and has followed me here." Therese turned to go, but Victor grabbed her arm.

"No, I won't have you leave here and be unprotected," Victor insisted. "We are all in this now, we stick together."

Therese looked at him, eyebrows raised. "You're telling me what I have to do?" she asked.

He released her arm. "Sorry. But I'm worried about your safety. My campaign issues are just about money, and we will deal with it. We don't even know if it's related. But we do know you have been threatened. I think it would be a much better idea if you and Justina just stayed put at the house while the law firm and hospital sorts all of this out. If there is something big going on here, there is no reason for the two of you to be in harm's way. Why don't you take some time off, and Justina can quit her internship. Then they will leave you alone."

"Hello, I'm right here," Justina exclaimed. "I'm not quitting my internship. I am learning so much, and it would leave a bad mark on my record to walk away in the middle of a case. No." She paused. "We don't know if any of these incidents relate to the hospital issues; the only thing we know for sure is that someone threw a rock through Therese's window. The rest of this is just speculation. And I am certain that even if something very bad is happening at the hospital, the law firm is not part of it! I'm not going to wreck my career because you are overprotective, Papa!" She could feel the heat rising in her cheeks. She wasn't about to let her father go back to treating her like a child. This was a sharp reminder of why she had moved out in the first place.

Victor started to respond, but Therese cut him off. "Look, I appreciate your concern, Victor. Truly. But Justina is right that we don't know what is really happening. It could all be coincidence. If you really want me to continue staying here, I will, just for a little while longer. I admit I am not eager to go back to my house. But I won't take time off from my job and hang around here all day. I have a lot going on at work, and the security office is watching out for me. I won't let them win. Really, I've taken care of myself this long, I will be fine."

Victor smiled wryly. "I can see I'm outnumbered here by the women. You are a good pair, both stubborn. M'ija, I really don't like you so involved at the hospital. I really don't. Can't you do some work from home? Just until this gets resolved? That lawyer you work with shouldn't let you be in danger …"

"Papa, it won't last much longer. The board is going to pull the plug at the end of next week. They claim they don't like the disruptions and expense. The doctors got to them, and to the hospital president. I didn't get a chance to tell you yet, with all this drama." She waved her arm around, gesturing broadly. "They want to continue the review 'internally.' Probably so they can just sweep it all under the rug." The idea of that sort of cover-up made her furious, but so did her father's chronic bossiness.

"See, that just goes to show you how serious this is, if they are pushing that hard," her father began, but Justina interrupted.

"Papa, we are very close to getting finished, at least as much as we're allowed. If it looks like there is a drug diversion issue, Frank will have to refer it to the feds. And I think that may be where it is headed, on top of a bunch of other issues. The other problems, like inappropriate billing, can be handled mostly by Frank and the hospital, internally. But if the doctors have some sort of drug ring operating, that will go to law enforcement, probably the DEA and Department of Justice, I think. So that should make you feel better."

"Oh, well, yes, I'm sure the hospital will be thrilled if you call in the feds," her father noted sarcastically. "Don't you see how dangerous this could be? Those drug rings don't mess around. It's all starting to make sense now. In addition to whatever issues they have with the two of you, I'm running a campaign with a strong message about cracking down on the opioid overprescribers and drug cartels. I couldn't figure out why they would pull funding for my campaign … now I see it."

Justina saw her opening. "See! This isn't about me. It sounds like you should be focused on your campaign, not on me. And I don't believe my law firm is in cahoots with drug rings. Seriously, Papa?" Sometimes he was so ridiculous!

Victor frowned, continuing as if she hadn't said a word. "And, of course, they are also funding Jefferson, and he's been starting with the smear campaign … probably not related, but all of it put together …"

"Papa, again, I don't believe the law firm is in support of

drug rings. What makes you think they pulled your funding because of the hospital issue? Or because of Jefferson? They have lots of clients, it doesn't make sense." Justina was stunned at her father's suggestion. "You don't usually jump to conclusions like this."

"Well, there are a few things I've found out. After we learned about the funding, I told Marci just a little about your work there. Nothing too much, of course. But you know how tenacious she is. She did some digging, and it turns out there are plenty of connections between your law firm and that hospital. For instance, Dr. Al's wife works directly for Peter Hancock."

"What?" Therese interjected. "Dr. Al's wife works for Justina's law firm?" Therese looked as stunned as Justina felt.

"Yes, and one of the other senior partners has a son who is trying to get a residency at the hospital. There are a number of connections here. None of that means anything wrong, by itself, of course. But it does suggest that the hospital and law firm are, shall we say, looking out for each other?" Victor sighed. "And the timing, with Jefferson starting some ugly rumors about me at the same time as the funding got pulled—it just doesn't feel random to me."

Seeing his daughter's shocked face, he continued. "I'm not saying the firm is knowingly supporting illegal activities, Justina. But they are in bed with the hospital in a variety of ways and could be influenced. You even said yourself how cozy the hospital president is with Peter Hancock. And he's on the hospital board, which just shut down your investigation."

"Yes, but he recused himself due to conflict of interest," Justina explained. "So he didn't vote to stop the investigation."

"Hmmm." Victor pondered. "But don't you see, if the doctors on the board wanted it stopped, and he recused himself, it's the same as voting for it, except his hands are clean. He didn't make the physicians recuse themselves, did he?"

"Wow, good point. As an attorney on the board, he probably should have suggested that, shouldn't he? I don't know how boards work ..."

"I've been to several of the hospital's board meetings," Therese offered. "They seem to be a rather passive group, very conflict averse, and physicians are overrepresented, in my opinion. The board chair is very ethical, but I've seen him get outmaneuvered. I think if there was a strong voice or two the others would go along. So if Hancock didn't speak up, for whatever reason, I would not be surprised if Dr. Al or one of his colleagues was able to push their agenda. Not surprised at all."

"So now what?" Justina asked. "I don't feel like I can go to Frank with all this. Peter Hancock is his boss ... and our client contact is the hospital president, who reports to the board. And it is, really, all still a coincidence, although I don't believe that. What a mess!"

"Well, the campaign funding technically isn't related, at least that we can prove, so no reason to go to Frank about any of this anyhow. It would just put him in an awkward position. I think it's a good thing they want to wrap this up. It's one area where I agree with the hospital!" Victor said. "If there are a lot of dirty dealings going on, I hope that Frank does hand it over to the feds quickly. And hopefully he won't have an 'unfortunate accident' before that happens!"

"Papa! Don't even say that, it isn't funny!" Justina exclaimed.

"I know it isn't, m'ija, and I'm not joking. I understand how ruthless these drug rings can be, if that's what this is. I know a bit about these types of criminals, and you know that. Fortunately, from what you've said, he has been around these sorts of cases enough to watch himself. It's you I worry about."

"I know it's none of my business," Therese began.

"No, go ahead," Victor encouraged.

"The more we talk the more I am starting to agree with your father, Justina. Do you think you could tell Frank you don't feel safe and would like to help but work offsite somehow?"

Frustrated, Justina found herself glaring at both of them. "Really? I'm the only one here who hasn't had some sort of suspicious incident. Nobody has bothered me. The physicians just think I'm a pesky student running errands for the boss." She looked at her father pointedly. "I'm not a little child anymore, Papa. I thought you had finally understood that!" Arms crossed, she waited for the response.

29

JUSTINA

On her drive into the hospital the next day, Justina felt like her head was going to explode. Her father was so bossy, and Therese even siding with him, that was too much! She worried about her father, though. It was obvious that in addition to his worries about her he was also having troubles with his campaign. She'd seen some of the smears from Jefferson on social media that morning and the press were having a field day. Anonymous sources, of course, suggesting he had a history of sexually harassing women, among other unsavory accusations. She was so outraged for him. Her father had always been very appropriate with women, surprisingly so, given how many had chased him over the years. Any relationships he'd had were never serious enough that Justina knew about them directly. So for anyone to accuse him … it was outrageous.

She pushed her thoughts aside as she neared the hospital. *Time to refocus,* she chastised herself, mentally pulling up her list of to-dos and questions for Frank. She was startled, however, to literally run into him as she started to enter the elevator.

"Whoa!" she exclaimed, stepping back to let him out, letting the door close behind him.

"What's going on?"

Glancing around, Frank put his hand under her elbow, steering her away from the elevators and over to a deserted hallway.

"We are officially off the case," Frank said quietly. "Dr. Shoemaker has just resigned as CEO, effective immediately. All nonessential activities are on hold. Including us."

"What? Why? Did you talk to her?" Justina couldn't believe what she was hearing. "How does the CEO just leave?"

Frank shook his head. "I don't know more than that. I was just advised by my boss, Peter, who is on the board. They called an emergency meeting last night. Now she is gone. The CFO is acting as interim, reporting to the board."

"Is this because of us? The audit? I thought we were okay to finish out at the end of next week and make recommendations? Why did she agree to that if she was leaving?" Justina asked incredulously. "It makes no sense."

"Well, she agreed with our suggestion, but I suspect the board did not. And I doubt she just suddenly resigned on her own. That's not how it usually works. It may have had to do with our investigation, but it might have been any number of things. I wasn't given any insight."

"It must have had to do with us!" Justina said. "I may be new at this, but executives don't just walk away. And we know they were pressuring her. How can they just tell us to drop this?"

"I know," Frank said. "But there's nothing we can do about it. Anyhow, you've been working a lot of hours on this, you might want to take a little time to get caught up with school and your life. I will hopefully learn more when I get back to the office; we are having a quarterly meeting this afternoon to go over case statuses. I was told for you to take the rest of the week off and check in on Friday if you don't hear anything before that." He paused, noting her frustrated expression.

She couldn't contain herself. "We are just starting to unravel what's going on here and they pull the plug? How can they just do that? There are clearly some issues here!" Unbelievable. They were going to get away with it!

"I understand how you feel. There is definitely something going on, something that some people want kept hidden. It's very concerning to be called off. But you've done an outstanding job, and I've passed that along." He smiled. "We may well get to come back and finish up. Sometimes things like this are just a chance for an organization to hit the reset button, and we'll get back to business soon. We have to hope they will want this open item resolved," he said, without a lot of conviction, it seemed to Justina. "I will have to debrief Peter, since we do have open issues that I can't in good conscience ignore."

Justina shook her head and wanted to question Frank about Peter Hancock's trustworthiness, but knew she couldn't. She and her father had discussed and agreed on that issue, at least for now. "I don't know what to say … All right. It really stinks that they got away with this," she said, then added when Frank started to object, "Yes, I know, we don't know that's what happened. But we do, right? Dr. Shoemaker got bullied, and when she tried to stand firm, she got disappeared. Just like we heard about others here." She thought for a minute, then asked, "I still have boxes of files. Should I bring them back here?"

"Why don't you bring them to the firm when it's convenient, and I can bring everything back all at once? And don't forget to turn in your visitor's badge," Frank reminded her. His phone buzzed, and he pulled it from his pocket, glanced at it, grimaced, and switched it off. "I need to run. Thank you again for your help on this case—you've done a fantastic job. I enjoyed working with you." Frank smiled, and turned, leaving Justina standing alone in the hallway, feeling like the rug had been pulled out from under her.

30

JUSTINA

I guess I better let Therese know, Justina mused, and she considered heading to the reverend mother's office. No, maybe best to just text her … Her stomach rumbled, helping her decide her next move.

"Hey, heading to cafeteria for a bite and coffee, can you join me? I have news," she texted before heading to find something to eat.

Her phone chirped back immediately. "5 minutes will be there."

The cafeteria was crowded, with a cluster of blue and green scrubs clumped around the coffee dispensers. *Must be a shift change,* Justina thought, and she walked back out to the little coffee-and-pastry stand outside the lunchroom to get a blueberry muffin and a latte. Clutching her little white bag, she ventured back into the cafeteria to meet Therese, navigating the clusters of staff in scrubs who were sharing stories about patients without any apparent awareness of the patients' families also making use of the cafeteria.

"You should have seen the size of that thing, once we got finally got it out of the guy," a chubby young man in green scrubs was telling his avid listeners at the table. The storyteller's tablemates all laughed, and Justina groaned inwardly.

So much for confidentiality, she thought.

Winding her way between tables she finally found a booth back in the corner that offered some degree of privacy for a conversation, as well as a bit lower volume. As she pulled the top off the muffin and started eating, she saw Mark, the auditor, enter the cafeteria. He craned his neck, looking over the busy lunchroom before spotting her and heading over.

He plopped down across from her, sliding his black canvas laptop case onto the seat. "Hey, I was hoping to find you. I went up to the conference room, but you weren't there, and nobody was talking," he said, a question in his voice.

Justina hesitated, not sure how much to say. Mark wasn't a hospital employee, and Frank had been in charge of bringing the auditors in, after all. "Um, yes, looks like we are doing some offsite work. I expect you will hear from Frank or the firm," she said vaguely.

"Sure, okay. Well, let me just give these files to you, then, and you or Frank can let me know what you need next. We are done for now here. Oh, and looks like your notes were pretty much on target, as you'll see in my comments on the spreadsheets. I'm still working on a formal report, which I will send to Frank, but I didn't want to be carrying these around." He unzipped his bag, pulling out a thick packet and glancing up at the clock. "I gotta go, the team is waiting for me. There is an early draft of the report in there, as well. It's very rough, kind of a working document, but I figured it was better to hand it over to the attorneys rather than leave it here to get discovered somehow. You know, attorney privilege and all that. We wouldn't want things getting into the wrong hands," he said with a wink, zipping up his case.

"Oh, yeah, of course, thanks," Justina said, taking the bulky beige envelope. "Thanks for the fast turnaround," she added as he smiled and left.

She looked down at the packet, indecision weighing heavy on her mind. *I know I should hand these over to someone here,* she told herself. *But who? These are confidential, and Frank was leading the work, hired by Dr. Shoemaker ... But now she's gone. And he's gone. So what is the process?*

"Hey, you." Justina's thoughts were interrupted by Therese, who plunked down across from Justina with an extra large to-go cup of coffee. "What's the big news?"

Justina looked around to make sure nobody was close enough to hear them. "Dr. Shoemaker is out. And so are we!" she said in a loud whisper.

Therese stopped in the middle of a sip of coffee. "What? What do you mean 'out'? As in gone? And who is 'we'?"

Justina nodded. "Apparently it just happened, she supposedly 'resigned' and is gone effective now. And so, of course, are we. Frank and I."

Therese frowned. "How can I not have heard that? I'm on the exec team! And how did you hear it first? Are you sure?"

Justina nodded. "Well, you know Frank's boss is on the

board here at the hospital, so he got it straight from the source, so to speak. And the first thing they decided was to stop all the 'extra' projects until they get it sorted. Or at least that's the excuse. They wasted no time in pulling the plug on us."

"Wow. I don't even know what to say. I'm shocked." She paused. "Well, one good thing: it will get your dad off your back!" she said with a little smirk. "Maybe the timing, for you, is a good thing!? But Dr. Shoemaker … I can't believe that!" Her face reflected the shock that Justina was still trying to manage.

"Yeah, well, sure, Papa will be thrilled. But I don't like it. They are getting away with whatever it is they are doing. And it looks to me like the doctors are making all the decisions here to protect themselves. How can this be allowed? How do we just walk away when we know all this?" Justina tapped the remaining muffin crumbs into her hand and popped them into her mouth, following with a sip of coffee. "It just feels very wrong, and unfinished. I don't know. Someone dies, others get threatened, people leave suddenly, and apparently that's all fine—don't go looking too close!" Justina felt herself getting angry as she thought about everything that had happened.

Therese nodded. "I agree. I'm still stunned that Dr. Shoemaker is out just like that. A CEO. Never saw that one coming. Everyone thought she was doing a great job, although she was kind of an outsider. Not one of the good old boys. But the staff liked her." She shook her head. "Terrible."

"That's why I wonder if it has to do with our investigation. We pushed her to keep the audit going, and she said the board, and specifically the doctors, had wanted it stopped. Seems like a pretty big coincidence, don't you think? Or am I just paranoid?" Justina couldn't shake her uneasy feeling.

"At this point, I can't call you paranoid," Therese said in a half-joking tone. "I'm the one who thinks I'm being followed, remember?"

"Well, how do we know that you weren't? I mean, a lot of weird things have happened since this began. It wouldn't be the first time—" She stopped midsentence, looking over Therese's shoulder, as she saw Dr. Al enter the cafeteria and scan the room. Quickly she grabbed the envelope of records and set it down on the seat beside her, under her laptop case.

"What the—" Therese demanded, looking around just in time to see Dr. Al corner a young man in scrubs and appear to berate him. They watched as the physician wagged his finger in the face of the younger man, who was almost cowering by the time the reprimand ended and Dr. Al stormed out of the lunchroom.

"Wow, poor guy," Therese commented, her attention returning to her companion. "And what are you hiding, Justina?"

Justina hesitated before admitting in a whisper, "I have the audit records and the draft report … You know, the ones Frank had outside auditors doing—looking at the chart notes, prescriptions, and bills? I don't think I'm supposed to have them, but the auditor didn't know and he gave them to me." She grimaced. "This was Frank's investigation, and

Dr. Shoemaker's, But I don't feel I can hand these over to the foxes who are guarding the henhouse. And I sure don't like having them in my possession. If Dr. Al knew …" She trailed off, the concern obvious.

"I would agree, although I shouldn't be saying that as an executive here at the hospital. But it would be better to give them to Frank. He will know what to do."

Justina nodded. "Agreed. That's what I'll do. I just don't like being in the middle of this, with everything going on. It's kind of scary. You know, I don't want to admit this, but I think my dad was maybe right. But if you tell him I will deny it!" she said, not totally joking.

Therese laughed and glanced up at the clock. "Well, I have a meeting to go to, so I better scoot. You stay away from the bad guys, okay?" She smiled and reached over, patting Justina's hand. "I'll see you tonight."

Justina gathered up her garbage and stuffed the packet of records in her bag as her phone chirped. She frowned, looking at the caller ID. St. Matthew's Hospital. *What???*

She answered warily, "This is Justina."

A vaguely familiar female voice responded, "Oh good, so glad I got you. This is Gabby, you met me the other day? The residency coordinator." She sounded breathless, speaking quickly but in a rather hushed tone.

"Oh, yes, hello. How can I help you?"

"I have a resident here who wants to talk to you guys. She heard about your audit. Apparently Kristy, one of our first years, told her who you were, and she came to me to help connect her with you. She's, um, pretty upset. When I called the other attorney's cell, it went to voice mail. I wasn't sure what else to do. She's been in here crying."

"Oh, no." Justina's mind raced. She wasn't even supposed to still be there, and Frank wasn't responding … but didn't she have a duty to help the girl? She couldn't just say no. Without much hesitation, Justina asked, "Is she in your office now? I'm still here, getting ready to leave. Frank isn't on-site right now."

"No. She doesn't want to meet here at the hospital; she is very afraid. Justina, you need to hear what she has to say. She is devastated. She says it's her job, her ethics—she feels like everything has been violated." Gabby sounded like she herself was on the verge of tears, her voice shaky. "Can I give her your number to meet somewhere? I told her she could trust you. I think she is off her shift soon."

"Yes, of course. Have her call me." Justina grimaced inwardly as she said it.

"Thank you. I didn't know what else to do! This poor girl. Those doctors are so horrible. I didn't want to say much before, but seeing her so upset, I don't want to protect them. The truth needs to come out … Oh, no, gotta go. Bye." Gabby hung up abruptly.

Now what do I do? Justina fretted. *Try Frank, that's it,* she told herself, pulling up his number on her cell. The call went straight to voice mail. *Crap!*

"Hi, Frank, I have a question. If you could call me, um, as soon as possible." She stopped there, not wanting to say anything more in voice mail.

She stuffed the phone in the side pocket of her bag and quickly headed out of the cafeteria. *I don't think I should be seen around here at this point,* she decided, her only thought being to get to her car and out of the facility before running into any of the doctors from the clinic. She headed toward the back entrance but stopped short when she spotted Dr. Powers and another man in scrubs standing and talking at the elevator. She darted back around the corner before he could see her, heart pounding. She tried to calm her reaction, telling herself she was being ridiculous, but the pounding adrenaline didn't subside until she had doubled back and exited out the front entrance.

No sooner had she launched herself into her car than her phone sounded again. Another unknown local number, but this time she had an idea of what to expect.

A shaky voice greeted her as she answered the phone. "Hi, my name is Ramona Diaz. Gabby gave me your number to call? I'm one of the residents at St. Matthew's … Is it okay to talk?"

"Yes, yes, of course," Justina confirmed. "Gabby said you would like to meet somewhere to discuss some issues you've been having?" *What am I doing?* Justina asked herself. *I should totally not be doing this!*

"Thank you, yes, thank you so much. I don't know where to go at this point, I am so scared. But I can't talk here. Are you able to meet now?"

"Yes, I can meet you. Why don't you pick a place you

feel comfortable, okay?" Justina responded, hoping she was handling this correctly, or at least as correctly as possible, considering she shouldn't be involved at all. But she couldn't abandon this girl without knowing what was wrong. Maybe she could help.

A deep sigh on the other end of the phone. "Sure, yes, thank you so much. I will text you an address, I know a diner where nobody around here goes. It's not very nice, we won't see any of our doctors or fancy people there. I don't know what would happen if anyone knew I was doing this, and I can't lose this residency!"

Justina swallowed hard. "It's okay, we'll talk through this and see what we can do, all right?" She didn't know what she could offer the girl, other than an ear. *You shouldn't even be doing that,* her inner voice reminded her.

Signing off, Justina's phone immediately pinged with a text, containing the address.

Well, here goes nothing! she thought, feeling anxiety gnawing at her stomach.

31

THERESE

Finally, a moment's peace, Therese thought as she stuffed her file folders into the drawer. *Maybe now I can look over that budget ...*

She pulled up the spreadsheet and was just getting focused on her least favorite part of management when there was a knock at her door. "Come in," she called, not totally dismayed at the interruption. She really hated budgets.

Gabby entered the office and shut the door behind her, all in one motion. "Do you have a minute?" she asked.

"Of course," Therese answered, noticing the dark circles under the other woman's bright blue eyes. "What's going on?"

"I don't really know where to begin," Gabby said, shifting her weight until Therese motioned her to a chair.

"Start at the beginning," Therese said, her antennae picking up anxiety in Gabby's body language.

"Well, okay. You know I was promoted last year to be the residency coordinator, right?" Therese nodded.

"You probably also know that when they made Dr. Powers the program director, Dr. Al was not happy because he thought he should have gotten the job."

"Yes, I do recall that," Therese said, remembering the stories she had heard about Dr. Al publicly stating his opinion on the matter and making not-so-subtle accusations of discrimination.

"Dr. Al can be the biggest jerk on the planet, for sure," Gabby said. "But he did have a point about the director job. Anyhow, Dr. Al had been the one to recommend me for the promotion. Dr. Powers had someone else in mind. I'm not sure what kind of deal was worked out, but I ended up getting the job."

Therese nodded, unsure of where this was going.

"So, anyhow, Dr. Powers was really nice to me in the beginning, and very patient with me because I was learning. When we had the surveyors come in, he pulled a couple people to help me. I thought he was good with me at that point." She paused then, crossing her legs and looking down, fidgeting with her badge. Therese waited.

"Well, we had a problem with the survey, some training records that weren't up to standards. Dr. Al and Dr. Powers were all over me like white on rice about it. Dr. Al was ready to write me up, even though he isn't the director. He's still one of the main attendings I deal with for the residents. Anyhow, Dr. Powers came to my office late, when I was working on cleaning up the records ..." She paused, chewing on her lip.

Therese had a sudden sense of where the story was headed. "What did he do, Gabby?" she asked, knowing in her gut what was next.

"Dr. Powers said he would get Dr. Al off my back and make the reprimand go away … if I, um, made it worth his while."

"Oh, Gabby. Why didn't you tell someone?"

Gabby shook her head. "You know how long I've worked to get a decent position here? I have two kids and barely make my bills as it is. This is a good job. But I told him no, very respectfully. I tried to work around it, appeal to him as a professional, all that."

"And?"

"He did back off when he saw I wouldn't give in. But he's been watching my every move, and Dr. Al, of course, does that anyhow. He used to actually kind of like me, Dr. Al, that is, but since Dr. Powers took over, nothing is ever good enough. I have the residents crying in my office all the time, and I try to be a go-between to take some of the heat off them. They are already too tired and stressed out."

"So what's going on now? Has something else happened?"

Gabby nodded, refusing to meet Therese's eyes. "Yeah."

32

JUSTINA

Justina pulled up to the address on her phone. The diner was, indeed, not a place that the status-conscious doctors or hospital leaders would frequent, she could tell immediately. The outside had some peeling paint, and the landscaping was choked with weeds, the flowers all gone to seed and leaves turning brown. Glancing around, she decided to go in and wait, since she didn't see any youngish females hanging around the entrance.

As she entered, the heavyset, fortyish waitress in a stained brown polyester dress immediately approached. "Just one for you, hon?" she asked, looking less than interested in the answer.

"Um, no, I'm expecting a friend. Can I get a booth?"

The waitress gestured broadly. "Take your pick. What does he look like? I will tell him you're here when he comes in," she added with a jaded smile.

"No, it's a she, and I don't know, but she will be looking for me."

The waitress shrugged. “Okay, whatever. Pick what you want.”

Justina found a booth in a corner, avoiding the friendly smiles from a couple of men wearing flannel plaid jackets and work boots at the counter. When the same waitress approached to take her order, she asked for a coffee and pulled her phone out to watch for any messages.

Her phone immediately pinged. It was Ramona. “Are you here?” it said.

“Yes, back corner, red jacket,” Justina answered.

Within a minute a nervous-looking young woman entered, her scrubs partially covered by a knee-length beige trench coat. She spotted Justina immediately and hurried to the corner booth.

“Hi,” she said, dropping a scuffed-up green canvas tote bag on the seat and making eye contact but then quickly looking away. “Thank you so much for meeting me. I didn’t know who I could talk to, but I’m so scared …” She trailed off as the waitress approached.

“Um, can I just get a coffee, black, for now,” Ramona said, smiling tightly.

The waitress sighed. “Sure, hon, one more coffee coming right up.”

Ramona watched her walk away. “I shouldn’t be meeting with you. But I’m getting scared. Gabby said I could talk to you. Are you working at the hospital still?”

Justina hesitated. “Yes and no. I’ve been working on a privileged investigation, so I can’t tell you details. But I will do what I can to help you. Why are you scared?" She felt bad for her less-than-truthful answer but couldn't turn her back on the girl.

"Okay, well, I wasn't sure what was going on—everyone is in a tizzy today, people coming and going …" Ramona looked around and smoothed a stray lock of black hair behind her ear. "I'm a third-year resident," she began. "I work in the clinic much of the time, and it is my job to manage the other residents and to see patients."

Justina processed this, thinking about what she had heard before. "Okay. So is that not what you should be doing?" She didn't feel she knew enough about the residents' requirements to proffer an opinion, so she hoped the girl would just keep talking until she could figure it out. She felt her anxiety level rise as she pretended to be able to help this nervous resident.

Ramona shook her head. "No, it's okay for a third year to lead the residents. But what we are doing is fraud!" She looked around again and paused as the waitress appeared with the coffee.

"Thank you," Justina said to the waitress, hoping she would go away before Ramona either shut down or started crying.

"Fraud? How so?" Justina asked, once the waitress left. *Frank, where are you?* she thought, trying to focus. *What am I supposed to do with this?*

"We aren't supervised," she began. "We aren't supposed to be seeing patients and prescribing, writing orders, with no supervision. And we have virtually none. I am in charge, so I'm afraid for my career. We have to play the game … The PG-1 and 2's, you know, the 1st and 2nd year residents, they hate us, I think, but what am I supposed to do? I spent so many years, and have so many loans …" She trailed off, her eyes filling and voice cracking. "We have been threatened, we've been told what to do … This is confidential, right? You can't share it with the hospital?" Her wide eyes were focused on Justina, glassy and anxious. "I should have asked you that first, I'm such an idiot." She started chewing on her thumbnail, peering at Justina with wide eyes.

Justina felt panic rising, unsure how to respond. "Um, I'm working under a law firm, that's who I work for," she hedged. "So my boss is the attorney who was hired; I don't report to the hospital. I share what I learn with my boss, who is a very good attorney, very ethical, and understands these types of cases."

Ramona leaned forward, her eyes boring into Justina's. "So, you know they are firing everyone, right? The doctors can get to anyone. That's the problem. If you get in their way, well, you're done. One way or the other."

Justina swallowed. "I know some people are no longer there." She struggled to appear informed without giving away any information. *Jeez, how did I get in this mess,* she thought frantically. *What do I tell this girl now?*

Ramona leaned back. "Look, I know you are new, like me. We have our jobs and our futures to consider. I need help. Can you help me or not?" Desperation shone through the tears in her eyes, but also determination. Justina admired her for that.

Justina felt her stomach clench, but her commitment to help this girl was stronger than her anxiety. "Yes, I'm still learning, too, you're right. But I will do whatever it takes to help you. The firm I work for is very ethical. They will help keep you protected, I will make sure of that." She hoped she was right, but she did believe the firm would stand behind her if she brought a big case or witness forward. They would probably be grateful! *You better hope so,* her niggling inner voice reminded her.

Ramona smiled uncertainly. "Okay, so we are in this together. We could both get screwed. But I have nowhere else to turn; my so-called leaders are owned by the doctors, and the doctors own my career, too. So …" She reached down and rummaged in her bag on the seat beside her. "I brought you some records. I should have never taken these off campus, and I shouldn't share them, due to privacy rules, on top of everything else. But I didn't know what else to do, and since you already work for the hospital … well, sort of … anyhow, these show the doctors are committing fraud."

With that she wrestled a packet of documents, rolled up and rubber-banded together, out of her canvas tote bag.

"What is that?" Justina asked in disbelief. *This girl actually stole medical records from the hospital!*

"These are records of forgery. Forgery by residents at St. Matthews's clinic. Where we ordered tests and prescribed narcotic medication without any supervision whatsoever, which we were told to do by the clinic's medical directors."

33

JUSTINA

Justina washed down a couple of Tylenol with the last swallow of warm water that had been in her car for who knows how long. She massaged her temples, closing her eyes and trying to calm herself. She wished, not for the first time, that she still had a Xanax prescription. She felt the familiar pressure in her chest from the anxiety of not only what has happening but also the fact that she was totally operating outside the boundaries. The "smoking gun" documents from Ramona were in the seat beside her, lying on top of her bag with the other contraband papers from the auditor. Their mere presence pushed her stress to fever pitch. As she was getting ready to start the car, her phone pinged. *Frank. Thank God.*

"Frank, I am so glad to hear from you. What happened to you? I've been calling …" Justina began, still feeling adrenaline pumping through her body, now accompanied by waves of relief.

"I'm sorry," Frank replied. "As soon as I got pulled off of

St. Matthew's we got a request from our Seattle office. They have a client in Alaska, of all places. It's an issue where I have specific experience, so …" He sighed. "Anyhow, I got your messages, and I'm sorry you've ended up in this situation. However, I do want you to know that I discussed this with my contact at the Department of Justice. Turns out they already are looking into the pharmacy and the clinic! So they will be contacting you and taking it from there. Okay?"

"Oh, okay. I have a lot of documents, Frank. The auditors gave me all the records back, and their draft report, then a resident made copies of some materials and told me that they've been committing forgery and bogus prescriptions. This is getting out of control!" She took a breath. "Does the firm know you referred it? Never mind, of course they do." She was struggling to think of all the questions she had for Frank, which wasn't easy in her agitated state. "So, am I allowed to share this information with the feds? I mean, attorney-client privilege. I can't think the hospital will—"

"No, it's fine," Frank interrupted. "The hospital had yet another emergency board conference call last night, without certain physicians, of course. We explained to them that the government expects cooperation, and that their choice is to cooperate or be seen as participating in this scheme. They do not want the legal or public relations crisis that would be created if they tried to protect any sort of drug or fraud scams. They agreed that we would cooperate and share our information but requested absolute confidentiality from us beyond that."

"Seriously? They fired Dr. Shoemaker but now they want to cooperate? I don't get it!"

Frank cleared his throat. "At the end of the day, they will want to be painted as working on the side of law enforcement, even though, in many respects, they were negligent in letting this go unchecked for so long. The warning signs were all there. But anyhow, you got the green light to share everything from our investigation, so make sure you share your interview notes and the material from this latest meeting with the resident, as well as the audit records and the compliance officer's documents. Okay? I'm sorry I didn't get to you sooner. I got no warning on this case and had to get a flight."

"Oh, okay, good. I wasn't sure ..."

"So, Justina, without getting into too much detail here ... this case has served to identify some serious conflicts of interest with one of our partners at the firm. I want to be clear, there is no proof yet that he took part in anything illegal, but he was influenced by his relations with certain people at the hospital. As a result, Peter has taken some time off and has recused himself from the St. Matthew's board. None of this reflects on the work you've done. Everyone knows that you got thrown into the middle of something very ugly and complicated. Your internship there is secure, but you can report to Carmen for now. Okay?"

Justina swallowed. "Sure, yes, that's fine. Wow. So I will be getting a call from someone at the Justice Department? I will be glad to hand all these records over at this point. I've been very nervous having all this information."

"Yes, that's right, and I understand completely. It will probably be a couple days before you hear from the DOJ, so just sit tight." Frank paused. "Okay, well, I am at the SeaTac airport and my flight is getting ready to board for Alaska. I'm sorry I didn't get back to you sooner, I've been on an airplane or running to change planes for most of the day. But if you do need to reach me, just be aware there's four hours' time difference, and I may not be able to take your call right away. Better to call Carmen. She's been briefed on everything and should be able to answer any general questions you have. I need to go now; they just called my flight. But I've enjoyed working with you and will give you a good reference if you ever need it."

Justina could hear the muffled flight announcements on the other end of the phone. Reluctantly, she ended the call, wishing she could have had a better debriefing with the experienced attorney.

34

THERESE

The sun finally broke out from the cloud cover as Therese pulled into the driveway. After her conversation with Gabby, she had to get out of that hospital. She was worried because several residents were in the hallway when Gabby left her office, but nothing she could do about that.

Dr. Powers is a sexual predator! she thought, still trying to absorb the story she had just heard. *Lord give me strength. Now I'll need to tell someone about this ... The chief medical officer is the appropriate person. That will make me popular,* she thought. *I'll probably get fired on the spot.* She told herself she would report it first thing the next morning, after a good night's sleep to formulate her plan. She had to make sure that Gabby wouldn't be fired for exposing the issue. With that resolution, she hauled her bag out of the car.

As she turned the key in the front door and opened it, Jose hurled himself at her, almost making her lose her balance. "Whoa. Jose! You're going to knock me right down, big guy!"

"Look, Mother, it's summer now! Can we go to the beach? Papa won't take me. He says he's working," Jose said, pursing his lips in a dramatic pout.

"Jeez, the sun just came out two minutes ago, kid!" Therese said, laughing at the child's energy. "And it's not really summer yet, you know ..."

"Pleeeeeeaaase!" he begged.

Therese thought about what she ought to be doing rather than going to the beach. Her work held no appeal, especially after the day she had experienced already. "Okay. Give me five minutes to change clothes, okay?"

"Yeeahhhh!" Jose yelled, running off presumably to tell Victor about his triumph.

After changing into jeans and a lightweight sweatshirt, Therese gathered up her phone, a towel to sit on, and a pair of sunglasses. Jose was hopping up and down by the front door. "Did you tell Papa where we are going?" Therese asked, not seeing Victor anywhere.

From upstairs she heard Victor call out. "Yes, I heard. Jose, you behave, understand?"

"Yes, Papa," Jose said, reaching for her hand to pull her out the door.

The beach was more crowded than Therese would have expected. *I guess everyone needed a mental health break today,* she thought. And it was unseasonably warm, a perfect beach day.

She found a spot and settled on her towel. "Are you going to build a sandcastle?" she asked, hoping the child would be content to stay close by. She really didn't feel like an active walk.

"I'm going swimming!" Jose announced, taking off his sandals.

"No, you're not. You don't even know how to swim!"

"I do! I went swimming at school. They took us to a pool." Jose started taking off his T-shirt.

"Jose, you're not going out in that water. It is dangerous. No," Therese said, wishing that for once the boy would go along without an argument.

Pouting, Jose said, "Can I just put my feet in? Pleeeease?"

Giving up, Therese agreed. "Okay. Just your feet. And stay right here in front of me. If I see you go in the water, I'm yanking you out and taking you home. And I will tell Papa. Do you understand?"

"Yes, yes!" he said, and raced off toward the surf, squealing.

Therese watched him jumping in the shallow waves, where he turned and waved to her every couple of minutes, shrieking when a cold wave hit him.

At least he's doing what I said, she thought. *What a handful that child is!*

She breathed in the brisk, salty air, enjoying the sound of the surf and kids playing. The warmth of the sun felt so good on her face. *Life really IS a beach!* she thought. Her phone rang from inside her jacket pocket. Ugh! It was an unknown number.

Answering it, she could barely hear the male voice on the

other end. She turned, covering one ear to block the noise of the surf and people. "Hello? Can you hear me?" she asked. The connection wasn't very good, but at least it didn't sound like a marketer.

"Is this Therese Devereaux?"

The voice was deep, with an accent she didn't recognize. "Hello? Yes, this is Therese Devereaux. Who is this?"

"Hello, my name is Thomas. I am calling you about an internship at St. Matthew's Hospital in the Pastoral Services Department. Are you accepting new interns now?"

"Thank you for reaching out, Thomas. We are in the middle of our quarter right now, but you can come in to apply for next quarter."

"Can you tell me the requirements for an intern?" the caller asked.

Tucking her head down to better talk without the background noise, she explained the criteria and the process for choosing the interns. When she finished explaining, the caller abruptly thanked her and hung up.

Well, that was weird, she thought, tucking her phone back in her jacket. She looked up, to check on Jose. But Jose was nowhere in sight.

35

JUSTINA

Justina pondered what she should do next as she sat in her car in the diner parking lot, practicing deep breathing and hoping the Tylenol would kick in soon to relieve her stress headache. She thought about what Ramona had told her about the forgeries. If the residents had been told to forge signatures, then the physicians weren't on-site at those times. But how to prove the records were forged, other than one resident's statement? One resident's testimony wouldn't mean much up against two powerful doctors and their colleagues, she reasoned.

The schedules. If the records were signed and dated but the physicians weren't even there that day ... Yes, that's it! Deciding, she turned the ignition and headed to the hospital.

She parked behind the hospital and headed to the back door to avoid the security desk at the main entrance. She didn't want anyone documenting her presence at this point. She was grateful she had forgotten to drop off her visitor's badge as the lock clicked open when she swiped her card.

Whew, good thing they are not too good on security! she thought as she slid in the door. They should have turned off her access once her project was canceled.

The clinic was at the opposite end of the building, so she hoped that she could avoid running into anyone who would know she wasn't supposed to be there. She made it onto the elevator without incident, breathing a sigh of relief as the doors closed.

Once she reached her floor, she glanced both ways down the long hallway before exiting the elevator and heading for the residency coordinator's office. She was pretty certain that Gabby would have all the schedules and recalled her previous conversations with the woman. *I bet she will be more than cooperative* ... She had seemed willing to talk and had sent Ramona to her. Justina was starting to understand the dynamics here, and who was on which side, although she still wasn't sure of all the residents, since she hadn't met them all and wouldn't be able to recognize most of them on sight.

Gabby's door was partially open when Justina tapped lightly. "Come in," Gabby responded, in a subdued voice.

Justina stopped short when she saw Gabby putting some framed pictures in a white cardboard file box. "Gabby! What's going on?"

Gabby turned to her, and Justina could see from her mottled skin and damp eyes that the woman had been crying. "I'm getting my stuff together," she said, then motioned. "Shut the door, please."

Justina shut the door and sat down across the desk from Gabby. "I don't know if Mother Marie told you," she began, and Justina shook her head.

"No, I haven't spoken to her."

"Well, there are some sexual harassment issues going on here, and I can't keep quiet about it anymore. Mother Marie is going to help me, but I don't see how I can stay here. There is no way the hospital will get rid of Dr. Powers and keep me, no matter what the 'right thing' to do is …" Her eyes started filling with tears. "I loved this job, and I worked so hard to get it." She stopped and wiped her eyes. "I know that if I report it, officially, then I'm history. If I don't report it, then it will keep happening. Probably will anyhow. But not to me, not anymore. I don't see any option here."

Stunned, Justina didn't know what to say. She had expected anything but this. "Oh my God, Gabby! What are you going to do? Dr. Powers?"

Sniffling, Gabby nodded. "Yes, he's the worst one, although not the only one. I spoke with Mother Marie. She told me to sit tight; she wants to think through the best channel for reporting this, given that our attorney is out, no CEO, no compliance officer … Probably it will go to the head of medical staff, Dr. Pascale. We all know what *that* will do … nothing." Gabby fidgeted with a highlighter pen on her desk. "Thing is, even if Dr. Powers gets a reprimand, they stick together, and he will make my life hell. And so will other attendings as well as some of the residents. I know how it goes around here. You shut up and play the game or you're out." She shook her head. "I'm getting my stuff out of here today so if things go south I don't have to come back."

"But they can't retaliate against you for reporting—" Justina began, then stopped, seeing the look of disbelief on Gabby's face.

"Seriously?" she said, her tone bitter. "If they can get rid of a hospital president overnight, do you really think a residency coordinator is protected?" She paused, then added, "What do you think happened to our nursing director? Our compliance officer? Dr. Shoemaker, even? They all had totally sudden life-changing personal emergencies that required quitting jobs they had worked years to get?" She snorted. "Honey, you have no idea. It's like the mob. And they take care of each other, at any cost." She tucked a stray blond curl behind her ear distractedly, her mouth set in a grim line and her eyes sad.

What in the world am I supposed to do with this? On top of everything she had just learned in her meeting with Ramona-it seemed insurmountable. She had to make sure all the evidence got into the right hands so that something could be done to stop all of this before others got hurt. It struck her that she was the only one who could do it. She had all the information and wasn't part of the hospital. In fact, everyone thought she was long gone, so in theory she had the benefit of not being on anyone's radar. Or so she hoped.

"Gabby, just between us, I'm going to be turning a lot of information over to the DOJ," she began, and at Gabby's puzzled face, she clarified, "The Department of Justice. But one thing I don't have is schedules of the residents and the physicians in the clinic. Do you have that? Like for the past six months?"

Gabby nodded. "Sure. Tell me anything you need, and I'll get it for you. There is too much going on here, it needs to stop. I'm probably out of here either way, so I might as well." She turned her attention to her computer, tapping away at the keyboard. The printer behind her started humming and spitting out sheets of paper. "Here you go," she said, once it had printed out. "Let me know what else you need."

"Well, there is one more thing-I heard there was a period last fall, early November, when Dr. Powers and Dr. Al were both out, at a conference in Florida. But the clinic was still billing under them. Do you know if they really were in Florida?" That would be definitive proof!

Gabby snorted. "Oh yeah. And it wasn't the only time. In fact, I remember it well because Dr. Al yelled at me about his flight back. It was sooner than he wanted. I had made the reservations based on the conference dates, silly me. Those guys like to stay a couple extra days, play some golf, enjoy time away from their wives, kids, and work. So I got reamed for actually assuming he would come back after the conference." She shook her head. "I have the email. You want it?"

"Sure! And their reservations, too. That'll show for sure they were both out of town." Justina felt like she had struck gold. "You said there were other times?"

"Oh yeah. They went on some cruise for a few days, sponsored, of course, by some pharmaceutical company.

That was like …" She frowned as she thought about it. "Early February. No, midmonth. I told Dr. Powers he could take his wife and they could enjoy Valentine's Day together on the cruise. He laughed at me. That was before all this other stuff happened. Now I understand. Why would he want his wife there to get in his way?" She started scrolling on her computer. "Yes, here it is. The request to book them on this boondoggle." She hit print and the printer started humming. "And here are the reservations …" The printer continued spitting out pages, Justina grabbing them as fast as they came out.

"What else?" Gabby asked. "In for a penny, in for a pound, as my gramma used to say."

"Is there anything else that would show they weren't here for times they should have been? Like for the residency program, I don't know …" Justina probed her mind for other things Frank had said the physicians were supposed to be doing.

"I'll have to think about that and see. I'm sure there is. You want me to forward anything else? Can I have your email?"

Justina scribbled it down on a Post-it Note and handed it over.

There was a knock on the door and before Gabby could respond, the door opened. "Well, what are YOU still doing here?" Dr. Powers demanded.

36

THERESE

Jumping to her feet, Therese scanned the surf in both directions. Racing to the water's edge, she yelled for Jose, first in one direction and then the other. There were only a few people in the water so it was easy to see Jose was not just wading in the surf. She looked farther out, in case he had decided to go swimming. There was nobody out there except a couple of surfers. Where could he be? She raced along the shore, calling for him, and stopping a few times to ask people if they had seen him. Nobody had.

Heart pounding, she told herself not to panic. *He's done this before,* she reminded herself. But the fear in her gut was undeniable, and her instincts told her this was not the same. She didn't know where to look, which way to turn. After running up and down the beach in both directions, it was clear: Jose was not there.

Panting from running, she dug out her cell phone and called Victor, who told her to call the police and that he was on his way. She could hear the fear in his voice, matched only by her own. *How could I look away, even for a minute? What was I thinking?*

She kept looking, scanning the surf, the beach, the water, until she saw a police car pulling up at the beach parking strip.

Racing up the beach, Therese continued looking in every direction, stumbling at one point in a hole near a sandcastle that she hadn't noticed in her rush. Her ankle twisted, pain shooting up her leg, but she kept going, barely noticing.

Out of breath, she gave the police her story and Jose's description as fast as she could. "Please," she said, willing them to miraculously find the boy. "He was in the water, but he was being very good to stay in the surf. I looked away only to take a phone call, I couldn't hear—" She stopped short. The phone call. Was it a setup? The caller seemed to want to keep her talking, but then abruptly ended the call. Were they watching? Did someone take Jose? Thoughts racing, she implored the police. "Please find him! I'm afraid someone grabbed him!"

The police gave her the usual assurances and told her they would have the search-and-rescue team coming to check the water. The officers headed down to the beach to talk to potential witnesses just as Victor's car pulled up.

"Oh my God, Victor," Therese cried, struggling to slow her breathing while her heart felt like it was going to explode. "The police and rescue teams are looking …" She could see Victor was feeling the same panic she was, as his jaw was set and his eyes roved up and down the beach. He took his jacket off and threw it in the back seat of his car.

"I'm going to go down and look, too," he said. "Where was he when you last saw him?"

Therese pointed. "That blue towel, it's the one I was sitting on, he was right in front of me. Playing just in the surf." She blinked to hold back the tears and swallowed hard. "Victor, I had a weird phone call, and I turned my head because I couldn't hear. I think it was a setup! When I turned around Jose was gone. So fast, like two minutes! And he was being very good, staying right there in front of me." She shook her head, trying to stay rational. "I just don't think he went out in the water or just took off. Not this time." She was crying now and looking at Victor as if he could magically make it better. "What do we do? I think someone snatched him!" Saying it out loud, to Victor, made it real, and she felt another sob rise out of her chest.

Victor frowned. "Did you tell the police that?"

Therese shook her head. "No, I didn't think of it at first, I mean, about the phone call. And I just wanted them to go find him! But then I thought about it and I really think … I mean, it was a very odd phone call, and then for Jose to be gone, right then …" She swallowed hard, again, trying to focus.

Victor grabbed her hand. "Come on, let's go see if anyone saw anything."

Therese nodded and cried out in pain as she put weight on the twisted ankle. At Victor's questioning look, she said, "I'm okay, I just twisted it on the beach. Let's go."

They could see the officers talking to people on the beach,

so they went the other direction, hoping to talk to anyone who might have seen something. Therese could feel her ankle swelling up and leaned on Victor as they walked, trying to take weight off it. She almost welcomed the pain—it was her punishment for letting that little boy out of her sight. She couldn't believe nobody had seen anything, and she said a silent prayer that the police were having more luck than they were.

She saw the search-and-rescue boat already just off the shore, with divers looking in the water. Victor saw it, too, and she could see the grief and worry stamping his face with lines that hadn't been there earlier. "Victor, I am so sorry," Therese began, knowing that nothing she said would help at this point.

Victor stopped walking and turned to look at her directly. "Therese, this was not your fault. I agree with you, I think someone grabbed Jose. And if so, they were just waiting and watching. They created a situation where you would be distracted. There is no way you could have predicted this and probably could not have prevented it. But we need to tell the police. Everything." He paused, scanning the beach. "Looks like they are heading up to the parking lot. Let's go tell them the rest of the story."

Nodding, Therese grabbed Victor's arm again and they trudged up the beach.

37

JUSTINA

Justina willed her trembling legs to carry her out the back door of the hospital and to her car. She clutched her bag with a death grip, knowing now more than ever that she had dangerous and contraband records in her possession. She just prayed that nobody else had figured it out. Her hands shook as she tried to fish her keys out of the pouch in her laptop case.

Finally getting into the car, she heaved a sigh of relief, clicking the car locks. *What in the hell do you do now?* she asked herself, trying to take deep breaths and think calmly. The run-in with Dr. Powers had not been overtly hostile, so he was apparently trying to still maintain some appearance of normalcy. He did know, however, that she was no longer supposed to be there, so she had to fabricate an excuse on the fly about returning some documents to Gabby. Justina thought of how Gabby had reacted when Dr. Powers came into the office; she had never seen a more panicked person in her life. If she had ever doubted Gabby's story about Dr.

Powers, she sure didn't now after seeing that reaction.

And then, of course, Justina couldn't leave the office so long as the doctor was in there with Gabby. No way. So she had lingered around, pretending to just be chatting as Gabby gathered up her purse to leave for the day. Whatever pretext Dr. Powers had for coming to see the residency coordinator was never revealed when he was faced with both of them instead of just Gabby. Justina felt good about helping Gabby get out of there, but she knew it was just a temporary respite.

She pulled her phone out to call Frank, then stopped. Frank had pretty much told her to go to Carmen, not him, since he was so far away and tied up. Frank had told her Carmen was briefed on the case. She deliberated, knowing that Carmen was pals with Peter, who had just stepped away due to the conflicts with the hospital. And who knew what else he was involved in! Could Carmen be trusted? She would never have imagined that all the types of people she had always admired could be so dishonest and even dangerous. Doctors and lawyers, the pillars of society. This whole thing had been so disillusioning. Now she didn't know what to believe. *Am I being paranoid? Who do I even call?*

Therese. Gabby had spoken with Therese already. Justina tried to remember the other woman's schedule for today, but her brain was so overloaded she couldn't recall. She dialed, and Therese picked up on the first ring. "Justina. Where are you?"

"What? I'm at the hospital, leaving now ..."

"You need to get home. Someone took Jose." Barely pausing, Therese added, "we told the police everything. We had to. You need to get back here."

"Oh my God. I'm on my way!" Justina hung up and turned the ignition, feeling the earlier panic and adrenaline pumping back up to disabling levels. Someone took Jose? How could that happen? Maybe it was another false alarm … But no, Therese and her father would not have exposed the whole story to the police unless they were sure it was necessary. Especially since it could put them all in danger once the wrong people found out. *Oh my God,* she kept thinking.

Getting back to Long Beach was a nightmare, as usual, but this time was different: every car behind her or alongside seemed threatening, and Justina felt trapped in the traffic. If someone wanted to do something to her, she had nowhere to escape … The thoughts kept circling in her head, tormenting her. She had always struggled with claustrophobia, but usually traffic didn't faze her. She was a New York girl, after all. But today was different; it felt menacing. Justina focused on her breathing. *It won't do Jose any good if I flip out and get in an accident,* she scolded herself.

By the time she reached Long Beach her hands ached from clenching the wheel and her headache was back, worse than ever.

When she got to the house, she was surprised to see several vehicles out front. She realized quickly that one of them was local news. Oh no, now what? As she parked and got out, she was immediately accosted by a thin young man with sandy-blond hair. "Ms. Gonzalez, we heard that the boy from Mexico, Jose, has been kidnapped, is that correct?" He shoved a microphone in her face as the camera rolled. Looking around for her father, she felt a wave of panic. "No!" she exclaimed. "I don't know what's going on, okay? Please leave us alone!" She tucked her laptop case under her arm, making a quick dash for the house. Once in she slammed the door and leaned against it, her chest heaving. *Where are Papa and Therese?* The rental car was in the driveway, but Therese was not there, and her father's car was gone. *Must be out looking for Jose.*

She dialed her father, but the phone went to voice mail. Therese, however, answered on the first ring. Justina could hear a cacophony of voices in the background. "Justina … are you home?" Therese asked, practically shouting over the noise.

"Yes, I'm here, where are you?"

"We are at the beach, that's where Jose disappeared. We have the police here, rescue team … and plenty of reporters." Her voice sounded strained almost beyond recognition, and Justina could hear her father in the background but couldn't understand what he was saying.

"Do you need me there?" Justina asked, torn between wanting to help find Jose and wanting to be home in case he miraculously appeared, as he had before.

"No, there is no need. You stay home and keep an eye out, just in case," Therese said. "There is no reason for you to get involved in this circus. The police are doing the best they can.

They found a potential witness, so they are working on that. And I'm sure by now Jose's picture is all over local news and social media, so that's one good thing about your father being a public figure. Everybody knows the story of Jose."

"Yes, okay … Oh, and Therese? Just so you know. Reporters are here, too. Just a couple, but they appear to be camped out."

"Great, that's all we need. Thanks. I think we will be home soon. We'll give you the whole story then."

Therese signed off and Justina put the phone down, her mind whirling with everything going on. So much adrenaline but nothing to do but sit there and wait. She paced the house, her mind racing over recent events. They all must fit together somehow. Unzipping her laptop case, she pulled out the various stacks of papers. There was no way she could focus on that right now, she realized, setting them aside. But why would someone take Jose? And who?

Her mind flashed to Ramona, reporting the fraud going on in the clinic. Kristy, with her concerns about lack of training and supervision, and, of course, now Gabby with not only sexual harassment issues but all the other information in the schedules and other documents that would show that the attending physicians were not even on-site when patients were being seen in their clinic and prescribed narcotics. *But would any of these issues lead someone to snatch Jose? How does this all tie back to us?*

Therese, obviously, had been a target from the beginning because she reported the complaints to the hospital president. Dr. Al knew she was staying with them. Dr. Powers had chatted her up and gotten a lot of personal information out of her, too, she realized. He knew who her father was. And her father, the champion of stopping drug crimes, had just gotten his campaign funding stopped abruptly by the law firm, which was in bed with the doctors, who owned a pharmacy and were probably at a minimum self-dealing … Everything went back to the clinic and those two physicians. And now her father had told the story to the police, it sounded like. How long before the police go to the hospital, and everything blows up? Frank had alerted the feds already, but he had said they would take a couple days to get to her.

She recalled Frank coaching her about the drug rings and how they operated. Her father telling her how dangerous the drug cartels were, with millions of dollars at stake, not to mention jail time. She thought of her father's story of his younger years in Guatemala, how the drug lords had run everything and killed or disappeared anyone who got in their way. "*Oh my God*," she murmured to herself, raking her fingers through her hair and absently tying it into a loose knot as she paced.

Her thoughts were interrupted by the chirping of her cell phone. Running back to the living room, she grabbed it, noting an unknown local number.

A familiar but shaky voice came over the line. Kristy. "Justina. I'm so sorry to bother you, but the police are here and all hell is breaking loose!" She sounded breathless, but trying to talk quietly. "I didn't know who else to call. Do you know what's happening? Dr. Al is in a rage, Dr. Powers is nowhere to be found!"

Justina felt like her brain froze, unsure what to say. "Are you still at the hospital? Who are they talking to?" She paused, trying to organize her thoughts. "I'm not sure what's going on, to be honest. I just got home."

"They were talking to Dr. Al. He started yelling, that's when I scooted out. I'm in the lunchroom. I don't know what to do!"

Justina focused on taking a deep breath. "Stay out of the line of fire, I guess," she said. "I really don't know …" She was interrupted by a key turning in the front door lock. "Kristy, keep your head down but let me know what you find out, okay? I gotta go now, we have a problem here, too," she said, clicking off the phone as her father and Therese came through the door, her father admonishing the reporters before he shut it.

"Any news?" Justina asked, desperate to hear something hopeful.

"No," Victor said. "The police did find a couple who saw a man talking to Jose. But the guy was wearing a blue baseball hat and a baggy football jersey, so the witnesses could only say that they thought he *might be* Latino. Dark-skinned, anyhow. The husband thought he was, the wife didn't agree; she thought he might have been Indian or Middle Eastern. But they didn't think anything of it when the man took Jose, they figured they were together. And they said there was no ruckus, the boy went with him."

"Oh my God!" Justina said, aghast. "What now?"

"The police are following up on what we've told them as well as canvassing the beach and neighborhood. They will also be here shortly to look through the house. It's standard procedure," he added, before Justina could ask. "Hopefully someone else at the beach or parking area saw them get into a car. Maybe some of the condos down there have cameras in their parking lots." Victor raked his fingers through his hair. "I'm going to make a couple phone calls and get the word out, before the police get here."

Turning to Therese, Justina asked what had happened. Therese looked awful, her eyes red and hair in wild disarray from the wind. Justina realized the woman was hurt, too, as she eased herself down on the couch, trying to put no weight on one leg.

After hearing the story, Justina got a couple of ibuprofens and a glass of water for Therese. She couldn't wrap her brain around someone kidnapping Jose. It was too awful to be real.

"Should we just be sitting here?" Justina asked. "I can't stand this!"

Therese nodded. "Yes, in case someone tries to contact us, or he somehow makes it back here. The police have a massive hunt underway. And thanks to your father being so well known, it's going to be all over the news. It would be very hard for anyone to hide that boy for long, at least around here." A pained look crossed her face. "So long as he *is* nearby. Who knows what these people might do! You hear all the time about human traffickers …" Tears returned to Therese's eyes, and she tried to blink them back. "This whole thing is because of me, and I will never forgive myself."

She was interrupted by the doorbell ringing. Justina ran to answer it, ushering in two Long Beach police officers. They explained the need to search the house as a standard protocol and Justina told them where Jose's room was, trying to stay out of the way.

When the police were done going through the house and yard, they laid out the process, including the creation of a command post nearby at the police station and having an officer at the house. Justina felt overwhelmed; she just nodded to show she was listening, but let her father do the talking. She had no words left. The magnitude of everything happening had left her stunned.

Hearing the officers refer to Jose as an "endangered" child sparked a whole new crying jag for Therese, and Justina understood that response as she tried her best to stay focused. When they explained about notifying the National Center for Missing and Exploited Children, the whole nightmare became even more real. Justina watched her father, who had switched into crisis mode and was being very businesslike, while she could see the gray pallor in his face and deep lines around his mouth that weren't there earlier as he asked the officers procedural questions.

Justina's phone chirped and she jumped up to grab it. It was an unfamiliar number, which she soon discovered belonged to one of the agents, Andy Yang, from the Drug Enforcement Agency, calling to set up an interview with her.

"Oh, thank God," Justina told him. "We have another problem. Jose, a boy we brought here from Mexico recently, has been kidnapped! We think it's related," she added. She saw Therese motioning at her and turned. Therese handed her a card.

"Police officer on the case," she whispered.

Justina gave the agent the police officer's information and agreed to meet with them first thing the next morning unless something happened in the meantime.

Hanging up, she told Therese, "That was one of the DEA agents that Frank contacted. They are going to touch base with the police and meet with us tomorrow. Thank God they called. Now we will have all the people involved who can help."

Therese nodded. "We can only pray it's enough."

38

JUSTINA

Justina slouched down the stairs after a restless night of not sleeping. She knew she had slept some, because she had nightmares about being lost and then drowning. She hadn't had many nightmares for years and remembered now why they had disrupted her life so much when she was younger. She was exhausted.

Her brain went down dark paths about Jose as she made coffee, and she fought the persistent gloomy thoughts. The house was too quiet. One of their assigned police officers was out front; she could hear him talking on the phone outside when she came downstairs. *If Jose were here, he would be out there pestering that officer,* Justine thought. How many times had she chastised the child for getting up too early? It was really just because she couldn't cope with his energy before she had some caffeine in her system. *Why was I so selfish?* she asked herself, watching the painfully slow dripping of the coffee.

She heard a door close upstairs and soon Therese appeared, looking as haggard as Justina felt.

"Coffee?" Therese asked, totally bypassing her usual perky morning greetings.

"Almost," Justina responded, also not in the mood for chitchat.

Once they both had their coffee in hand, Therese asked, "I don't suppose there has been any news?"

"Only what we heard last night, that they didn't find him in the water," Justina answered, adding some more sugar to her coffee. Today she needed it. "Our officer is out front. I think he must have gotten rid of the media. It's very quiet. Too quiet."

Therese acknowledged the last comment with a sad grimace, then added, "Hopefully someone had a camera set up in the parking lot. Or found another witness they are tracking down. Or maybe someone will recognize him after the Amber Alert."

"Yes. And the DEA guy is coming today, so maybe they can help put the pieces together," Justina added. "I'm sure they've already talked with the police." She was so tired she couldn't face interviews with the federal agents, but at the same time desperate to help locate Jose. There was no telling what clue might lead the agents to find him. She drank deeply from the coffee mug, praying for Jose to be home soon.

Hearing footsteps on the stairs, Justina turned to see her father coming around the corner. He looked exhausted, too, with dark trenches under his eyes. But he was freshly showered. Justina had noticed that her father had made it a habit to get showered before coming downstairs in the morning ever since Therese had started staying there. She had thought it was kind of cute, but today her mind was elsewhere.

"Any updates, Papa?" she asked, hoping that by some miracle her father had received good news.

He shook his head no. "But we have the police working on it, and they are involving the FBI, so this will be a coordinated effort. Let's just pray there are results soon."

"Don't forget we have the DOJ and DEA here this morning, too, Papa," Justina added. "Hopefully they can all coordinate the different pieces and figure out how to get Jose back."

The doorbell rang, and her father jumped up off the kitchen stool. "That may be them, I'll get it," he said.

Justina looked at Therese. "You want to shower first, or should I? Looks like we're going to have a full house today."

"You can go, you need to get ready for the agents. And I'm glad we have so much help, from so many people." She stopped as her father returned to the kitchen with Marci in tow.

"Hey," Marci greeted them. "I just came by to see how I can help. This is so horrible." Her face was creased in worry. "I just love that little boy. They've got to find him!"

Marci's pregnancy was obvious in the thin t-shirt she was wearing, and it reminded Justina how Marci had come to be involved in her father's campaign. "Hi. Yes, none of us have slept. We're just going crazy, waiting for the news. The police have issued an Amber Alert and they are bringing in the FBI." She looked at Marci's protruding belly. "But, Marci, you're not supposed to have stress. I don't know if you should be here. I can't think of anything more stressful than this house right now."

"I know, I know," Marci agreed, her usual perky demeanor shrouded in worry lines. "But you guys are like family to me, so it's more stressful to sit at home not knowing or helping. What can I do?"

Victor shook his head. "Marci, Justina is right. But I know you're going to do what you want. Like all the other women around here," he said, making an attempt at humor. "Maybe you can go to the store and pick up some snacks and bottled water, something to have here for all the law enforcement people who are apparently moving in?"

Marci smiled. "That is definitely something I can do. And you let me know if you want me to handle the press outside—they are still lurking. You know I'm more than happy to deal with those vultures," she said. "Looks like that cop sent them back out of your yard, but they are hanging around."

Victor nodded, smiling for the first time. "Marci, I would love for you to do what you do so well. But the police said they need to handle the media."

Marci's face dropped. "Okay, all right then. I'll at least go get some doughnuts … and other stuff."

Victor's phone rang and they all jumped, eager for it to be good news. Justina watched her father's face as he listened to the caller, and she could tell right away it wasn't news. As he clicked the phone off, he told them, "The FBI are on their way. They will be interviewing all of us."

Justina jumped out of her chair. "Okay, I'm going to get cleaned up. I need to get ready for the DOJ agents, too." She could barely think about the issues at the hospital, with Jose missing. But maybe that information would somehow lead them to the boy. She prayed that would be the case.

* * *

Agents Tim Stanford and Andy Yang showed up promptly at 10:00, as promised. Tim looked like everything a DOJ agent would be expected to be: tall and broad shouldered, with close-cut brown hair and a square jaw. Andy worked for the Drug Enforcement Agency and could have easily passed as a college student with his youthful, smooth face and spiky black hair. It was clear right away, however, that both of these agents were deadly serious about their jobs and the case at hand as they wasted no time on chitchat.

Justina ushered them into the formal dining room so that they could have some privacy and also spread out her materials for their review. Both agents set up their laptops and accepted a bottle of water.

She told them everything she could about Jose's disappearance, and they explained they had spoken with local police and were aware of the FBI coordination as well. "We are hoping we can help tie all this together," Tim confirmed for her. "We will be working with the FBI, local police, everyone we need to. This case just became top priority. And I know how frantic you must be, but let's try to go through what you have from St. Matthew's, since it may well be useful in finding Jose. Okay?"

Justina nodded, trying to hold back the tears at the mention of Jose. Every time she thought about him getting taken, she felt like breaking down. "I'm ready," she said, trying to sound strong. "Everything is here. Let's do it."

"Okay, but before we get started, we need to let you know. We talked to the local police after they went to the hospital. They didn't learn anything about the kidnapping. Those officers were advised not to reveal the scope of the entire investigation in order to buy us some time, but they said everyone there, including the physicians, seemed genuinely shocked. Although one physician I guess was pretty agitated at having the police come and ask about him about it."

"Oh yes, I know," Justina said, picturing Dr. Al and his temper. "He doesn't like anyone in *his* clinic poking around."

"Yes, well, he started making noises about harassment and calling his lawyer. From everything our police colleagues reported, it really doesn't sound like he knows anything but rather that he's just a hothead," Tim said with a grimace. "But it doesn't make sense that this was random, so obviously we're going to keep after it. It most likely does all fit together somehow. That's what we need to figure out."

Justina felt a flash of despair, which was becoming familiar. She had hoped that if they nailed the bad guys at the hospital that Jose would be home safe. But what if not? She couldn't stand it. She forced the thought aside, trying to help the agents, which, hopefully, would lead them somehow to Jose. "Okay, I see," she said. "Let's get through this part, then."

Tim started the interview, after outlining their role and confidentiality requirements, by asking Justina to summarize her history with the case. By the time she had shared what she had, she was surprised by their apparent knowledge already of the chain of events and issues she related, finally asking, "Did Frank already give you all of this information? I feel like you aren't getting much new from me."

Andy cleared his throat, taking a sip of water. "Well, actually, Frank did give us a good summary, but we've been watching the pharmacy for a while. The quantity of Schedule II drugs going out of that place, OxyContin in particular, is way off the charts. And the documentation doesn't add up, in terms of what they are buying versus what we know they are distributing, and then, of course what they are reporting. But we've been trying to figure out their scam before we tip our hand. The information about the vanloads of patients is very helpful. We are getting very close to tying this whole thing up." He frowned. "We are still trying to identify their sources of drugs and a potential silent partner or some other supplier. There is a piece here we are still trying to nail. How could they be selling more than they are buying? But we are getting much closer."

Tim spoke up while looking at his notes. "The information and documentation from the resident, um, Ramona, is also huge. It's great that you were able to get that from her."

Justina recalled the meeting with Ramona. "You don't know how scared I was. I wasn't supposed to be working the case at that point. I was totally on my own with that. When I heard she wanted to talk to me, though, I couldn't say no. Those people at the hospital really have nowhere else to go at this point. When she pulled out those documents, I about had a heart attack!"

"I'm sure. But you did great," Tim stated. "We will need to talk to her, of course. We want to make sure we get all our facts straight, dot our i's and all that, before we make a move. But as Andy said, we are just about there, and this is more urgent now, of course."

"I am so glad to have you guys here," Justina said. "We are desperate to get Jose back. And this case has taken over my life, even before Jose was nabbed." She refocused her thoughts, which went sideways every time she thought about Jose. "How does this sort of scam work? I still don't really know how it all fits together or why anyone has bothered with us."

The agents looked at each other, and Tim nodded as Andy continued. "In general, what happens is that a physician will have an arrangement with a pharmacy and with someone who will produce 'patients,' some sort of a 'runner.' The runner will recruit patients from soup kitchens, homeless shelters, bus stations, or even outside a detox facility when patients are released."

"A detox facility? And they recruit them to go get drugs?

That's awful!" Justina said, shocked.

Andy nodded. "Yes, it is. A lot of times they will offer the patients something, a payment, a gift card, or some other incentive. These are desperate people they recruit, so they don't usually have to offer much. The so-called patient goes in and sees the doctor or, in this case, usually the resident. That's a piece that's a bit different here. Anyhow, the patient says they have severe headaches, or a back problem, and they get a prescription for narcotics. Part of their job, then, is to go to the pharmacy that they are directed to, get the prescription filled, and turn the drugs over to the runner. The runner pays the patient whatever was agreed and then takes them back to wherever they found them. The runner, the pharmacist, or the doctor then sells the drugs on the illegal market. That's just one scenario, which is what we see here. Some arrangements are simpler, but this is a more layered laundering scheme. With more layers it's harder to identify the key players."

"I see. So this pharmacy is owned by Dr. Al-Basri and Dr. Powers. They are both involved in this, right?" Justina still had a hard time believing Dr. Powers could be involved, but the ownership records were clear. And he was apparently a sexual predator, so his perfect image was long gone in her mind. She was really starting to question her own judgment of people. Dr. Powers had really fooled her.

"We don't think so," Tim interjected. "One of them is using the residents and having them bill it under the other physician most of the time, so if anyone catches the billing issue it will point to the other physician. Since both of these guys bill for seeing patients, and neither is consistently on-site at the clinic, it has gone undetected. The hospital gets lots of billable visits, the doctors look good and keep their hospital income secured, so nobody asks the question."

Justina smiled. "So it was just Dr. Al! I knew it!" she stated. Maybe she wasn't as blind as she had started to believe!

Andy shook his head. "No, we think it was the other way around. Dr. Powers was having certain residents put most of the drug patients under Dr. Al-Basri. From what I've heard, Dr. Al is very defensive and protective over his records, he intimidates anyone who tries to take a look. So, Dr. Powers didn't have to worry that he would get caught, first because billing records would point to Dr. Al, and then if anyone did have the nerve to ask, he knew Dr. Al would pull strings to make it stop."

Justina was silent for a moment as she processed this, then she asked, "But the resident told me that Dr. Al instructed them to forge his signature, not Dr. Powers. Are you sure about this?"

Tim smiled. "Oh, Dr. Al is not clean either! He isn't involved, that we are aware of, in the drug scheme, but he's scamming the hospital. He has his own practice, and so he sees patients there most of the time, billing those patients, while he has the residents seeing patients unsupervised and signing off on the charts for him at the hospital clinic. The hospital is paying him to see patients and supervise the residents, and it appears that he is very productive, supervising all those residents, running the clinic, and reviewing charts. In a nutshell, he's double dipping. We think that Dr. Powers quickly realized this and took advantage of it."

"So, they are both crooks, but in different ways," Justina observed.

"Yup," Andy confirmed. "Dr. Powers is more than happy to appear to have fewer patients because of what he's taking in on the drug operation, and the volume at the clinic is high so his contract is secure. And he does pad his bills by up-coding—he bills for more complex visits when the patient is just in for a sprained wrist or ear infection, things that are simple to diagnose. In that way he's contributing his share to the clinic's revenue stream. But each one probably knows the other is dirty, and working the system, too, so it's like they have leverage over each other. Dr. Powers just plays the game a whole lot better."

"So, they both were billing while they were out of town or offsite, right? I mean, you saw the schedules. You don't believe they are collaborating at all?" Justina couldn't believe both doctors were that unaware.

Tim nodded. "We'll find out. What I suspect is that they had some level of agreement around the use of the residents when they were offsite, since they both used them at their private practices as well as at the clinic. They must have agreed on some of the more, shall we say, garden variety billing fraud. That's also an incentive for them to both co-operate. Each had some leverage over their colleague."

"Wow. I'm still trying to wrap my brain around this. Plus,

as I mentioned, there have been some threatening incidents with Therese, before Jose disappeared. She is the one who got that first complaint. So, who is responsible, do you know? It sounds like it could be either of them." Justina was now trying to piece it together, realizing that her assumptions about Dr. Al had been very wrong.

"We don't know yet," Tim admitted. "We didn't know about any of this until we spoke with Frank, and that was before the child was taken. He was worried about all of you and asked us to get to the bottom of it quickly. That's why we are here, to get all the info we can about what has happened." He paused, and she could tell he was trying to be sympathetic because of her anxiety.

"Thank you," Justina said. "This whole thing is a nightmare. And I do believe they killed that compliance officer. If that's the case, who knows what they might do to Jose." She couldn't stand it and felt like she was close to losing control every time she thought about Jose. Which was constantly. She was trying to stay focused, but that was getting harder and harder with each passing minute.

"If it helps any, we do agree this is all related, despite what law enforcement observed at the hospital. Which at least means we may be very close to finding Jose," Andy said. "Most kidnappings by strangers don't have so many clues to follow right from the get-go."

Justina found his words reassuring, even though she knew he was mostly just trying to calm her. She forced her mind back to the issues at the hospital, which were hopefully a good trail of breadcrumbs for the agents to follow.

"Well, you have the audit reports, and those look pretty bad, as far as I can tell. Not much documentation, but lots of prescriptions. That was the auditors' bottom line. And the documents from the resident who gave me examples of the forgery in the clinic. That resident is so scared. I'm worried about what will happen to her if they find out she was talking to me." Justina chewed on her lip as she stacked the various documents back into one bundle and pushed the pile of records across the table to the agents.

"Well, according to Frank, the board has been instructed to keep this entire thing totally under wraps, and obviously that includes not telling the physicians. If the hospital has managed to maintain confidentiality, they should believe that the CEO and the attorneys who were the source of their worries are all gone. We were hoping that they would relax a bit, although after the police visit, they probably realize we've put it all together. However, there are no guarantees, especially if that resident you spoke with tells anyone. It wouldn't be hard to imagine someone wanting to be in good graces with one of those two doctors, especially another resident who thinks it will protect their career …" Tim paused. "We will talk to Ramona and will help protect her. We need to be ready within a day, two at the most, to raid the pharmacy and bring in these two physicians."

Justina nodded. "Oh yes, I understand. The only person from the hospital who knows about this part of it"—she waved her hand toward the pile of files—"is Therese. She's been staying here since the rock-throwing incident. But she is very worried, since she's been a target, so she's certainly not talking to anyone. And Jose was with her, of course, when he was snatched, so she's a basket case now."

Andy said, "I'm sure. We will want to talk to her before we go, as well. You never know when some minor detail can be a make-or-break piece of the case."

"Yes, she's here today. I'll get her when we are done," Justina said.

Justina handed over the various documents that were in the compliance officer's boxes, as well, and sent her notes to them electronically. She felt so relieved to be giving all of those materials to the agents. She hadn't realized the weight she felt just from being in sole possession of all those damaging records. Especially now, since they could cost Jose his life. They felt poisonous to her.

As they bundled up all the records, placing them into a white file box, Andy asked, "How is your father's campaign going? I've been following it. He has a good message about going after corruption and drug dealers; obviously that is something I would like to see more of in our politicians."

Justina smiled. She could tell he was trying to refocus her thoughts. "He's doing well, mostly. His opponent seems to be collaborating with the press to smear him, so I guess he must be moving up in the polls and considered a threat. He's still working on getting more donors, but he has a good person helping him, so I think he will be ready to take it up a notch as we get closer. And fight the smear campaign.

Although right now … who knows. We can't even think about that."

Tim interjected, "Of course, understandable. You know, we do believe there is a connection between that pharmacy and the cartels. The supply of drugs going out of that pharmacy doesn't match the records of their documented purchases. They clearly have a hidden source, which we are looking into. That's another possible reason these criminals targeted your family. They tend to try and shut down anyone who gets in their way, and your father has taken a pretty strong stand against the drug cartels and is doing well in the polls, so he could be seen as a threat."

Justina felt another stab of anxiety. "Well, the law firm who was a big donor did just quit funding Papa's campaign," she said. "That firm has a lot of connections to the hospital and the physicians at the clinic. The woman helping my father's campaign did some digging and found that out. But there's no reason to think the firm and the hospital are connected to drug cartels."

"Which law firm?" Tim asked.

"McIntyre, Jones, and Hancock," Justina responded, watching them closely. "Same one who hired me as an intern."

The agents exchanged looks. "Okay. Well, thanks for telling us. There are many moving parts here we are looking at," Andy said, clearly not willing to say more.

Justina couldn't shrug it off. "Wait. Is my law firm involved? Please. I need to know; I work for those people.

I know there was an issue with one of the partners, but I thought he was innocent of breaking any laws."

"We are looking," Tim said. "That's all I can say right now. Just be patient while we focus on finding Jose, then hopefully these other pieces will all come together quickly."

"Yes. Please find Jose. That's all that really matters to my family," Justina said. "Are you ready to talk to Therese?"

At the agents' nods she went to find Therese, who was hovering in the kitchen, at loose ends. Bags of bagels and sandwich rolls were piled on the counter, along with a case of bottled water and a twelve-pack of cola. "I don't know what to do with all this stuff," she commented, and Justina could tell she was still trying to busy herself, now with the mountain of food and drinks Marci had procured.

"The agents want to talk to you now," Justina told her. "I'll organize this stuff."

Therese took a deep breath and exhaled. "Okay. The FBI just had me, now the DOJ … They're talking to your dad now. Nice folks, but I'm fried already. I hope this helps. Seems like a lot of time talking, when they should be out looking." She smiled. "I know, it's a process. Marci is out there entertaining our officer. She's nervous as a cat in a room full of rocking chairs, can't sit still."

Justina smiled. "Yes, I know. She's that way on a normal day, so I'm sure she's going crazy. I'll go check on her and our officer."

The meeting with Therese was only a half hour, then the agents took their leave, after giving Justina and Therese each of their business cards. As a parting message, Tim said, "Don't hesitate to call either of us if you have any incidents, phone calls from the hospital, anything, okay? We want everyone to stay safe and secure while we wrap this up. And let us know immediately if there is any news on Jose."

Watching them go, Therese breathed a heavy sigh. "Whew. Glad that's over with! I bet you are, too. Good to see all that stuff go out of the house and into their hands!"

Justina agreed, but her thoughts were elsewhere. "Let's just hope it helps bring Jose back home. That's all I care about at this point." The tightness in her chest was almost unbearable, and now there was nothing for her to do but wait.

39

JUSTINA

Justina rolled over on her side to look at her bedside clock. She groaned as she saw it was almost four in the afternoon. It was hard to tell, with her blinds drawn, leaving her room dark and gloomy. Perfect for an extended nap, but not what she should have been doing today! After the agents left, she found a Xanax left over from her old prescription and took it, forgetting how those pills had knocked her out. She couldn't believe she had fallen asleep, with Jose missing and everything else going on. But she couldn't remember her last solid night of sleep, so it wasn't all that surprising. Still. She shouldn't have done it, impending panic attack notwithstanding.

Sitting up and brushing the stray hair off her face, she reached for her phone, its LED blinking insistently to indicate missed calls. She held it, staring at the blank screen for a full minute before powering it on. *Please don't let this be more drama,* she pleaded silently. *I need some good news!*

Two voice mail messages. *Ugh!* Now fully awake, Justina hit play.

The first one started with a lot of rustling noise, like papers being shuffled right next to the phone. Then a familiar voice: "Justina? This is Gabby, at the hospital? The resident coordinator. I'm hoping you get this message soon. I am very worried about Ramona and maybe you, too. Dr. Al found out about Ramona talking to you and he is pissed! Especially after the police were here. He went storming out of here. Please call me!" More rustling and then the call ended.

"Oh crap!" Justina said aloud. She tried dialing the number back, waiting while it rang once, twice, three times, and Gabby's voice mail came on. "Of course, it's after four. She probably leaves at four," Justina mumbled to herself. She left a generic message for Gabby to call her back, just in case.

After switching on her bedside light, Justina pulled up the second voice mail message. It was from an unfamiliar local number.

"Justina. This is Ramona. I wanted to warn you. Dr. Al found out I spoke with you and he came to track me down. He actually came to my house! My boyfriend was home and sent him packing. Tony doesn't scare too easy! But I don't know where he is going now. Hope you get this message." The message paused, then resumed. "Oh, and this is my mom's phone. I'm staying at her house in Queens right now. I talked to one of those agents, he suggested I stay somewhere else. You can reach me on this number or my cell. Call me."

Justina swallowed, trying to tamp down the anxiety rising in her stomach and throat. *How did I get in the middle of all this?* she asked herself before hitting the number to call Ramona back.

Ramona answered on the first ring. "Justina. Thank God you're okay. You are okay, right?" The girl sounded out of breath and anxious, speaking quickly. "Have you heard from Dr. Al? He was *so* pissed I went to you! And then the police showed up. I know he thinks it's all my fault." She paused, taking an audible deep breath.

"He hasn't been here," Justina answered, standing up and sliding her feet into a pair of slippers. "At least I don't think so, I fell asleep …"

There was silence on the line before Ramona answered. "I think one of the other residents overheard me talking to Gabby. I came out of her office, and he was walking away, fast, like he didn't want me to see him. Jorge. He is Dr. Al's right hand and is tight with Dr. Powers, too. I didn't tell you because I was hoping I was wrong. I didn't want to create any unnecessary drama." She paused. "I'm sorry. Gabby and I were both being very careful, but I think maybe the docs told him to keep ears and eyes on all of us since you've been here."

"Not your fault. And we were afraid of what would happen after the police showed up. But we had no choice."

"Yes, about the police. Why did you send them to the hospital? What's going on? Everyone here is in an uproar!" Ramona's voice sounded accusatory, and Justina couldn't blame her.

"Jose, the boy we brought back from Mexico, was kidnapped," Justina explained. "They grabbed him when he was at the beach with Therese. We felt we had to tell the police everything that's been going on. At this point it could be life or death. I'm sure if you go online, you'll see the story. We've had reporters here ever since it happened."

"Oh my God!" Ramona exclaimed. "That's horrible!"

"Yeah. So we have police stationed here, the FBI is involved. It's all one big nightmare. I really need to get back downstairs and see if there's been any news. But first, tell me real quick, what did Dr. Al say? Did he threaten you?" Trying to think what questions she should be asking the girl as her mind raced to keep up with her adrenaline.

"No, I mean I don't know, not really," Ramona babbled. "Tony isn't the best at details, you know? He said that this doctor showed up, demanding to see me, said he worked with me at the hospital. Tony told him I wasn't there and that he shouldn't be coming to our home unannounced. Tony is a real big guy, you know? Nobody would mess with him. But he did say that Dr. Al told him to tell me he was looking for me. And that he looked really mad."

"Are you sure it was Dr. Al?" Justina asked, thinking about her recent discussion with the agents.

"Oh, yes. Tony described him perfectly. Those two doctors, him and Dr. Powers, they don't look at all alike, you know? But what should I do?" Ramona asked, her voice starting to rise. "Those agents said they could protect me, but I wasn't sure if I should call them; I wanted to talk to you first."

Justina's mind raced. She was worried about Ramona but more worried about Jose and couldn't believe she had passed out for a couple of hours. She needed to get back downstairs and see what was happening. She should never have taken that pill! "Just stay there at your mom's, okay? Does he know your mom's address?"

"No, I don't think so. I mean, it is probably somewhere in my file when I applied for residency. But he would have to get that out of the coordinator's office, and she locks up at four."

Justina nodded, thinking. "Okay. I'll tell you what. I need to see what's going on here. Why don't you go ahead and call the agents and let them know, okay? And keep me posted. This was all supposed to be wrapped up soon, but now with Jose missing, I don't know." She felt that familiar tightness in her chest and tried to will it away with a deep breath.

Ramona agreed and they signed off. Justina stuffed her phone in her pocket and rushed downstairs, which was strangely quiet even though the lights were on. She could smell onions cooking and headed into the kitchen.

Her father was sitting at the counter, his face set in grim lines as he looked at something on his laptop. Therese was cooking, and Justina could tell from both their body language and the silence in the room that there had not been any positive updates.

"Anything?" she asked, hoping.

Her father shook his head no. "Nothing." He closed his laptop, then added, "They are monitoring the Amber Alert and other notices on the news and social media." His eyes were sunken and hollow, and Justina thought he looked ten years older than he had just a few weeks earlier.

Therese covered her pan and adjusted the burner. When she turned, Justina could see she'd been crying recently. Or perhaps still.

"I can't stand this," Therese burst out. "I keep thinking of that little angel and wondering where he is, if he's scared or hurt …" She stifled a sob and grabbed a paper towel. "I'm sorry. I just can't …" She mopped her eyes and blew her nose. "There is not much worse than your child getting killed … but when you just don't know, and can't do anything …" She shook her head. "It's almost worse."

Justina could feel the tears starting to burn the back of her eyes, too, and went to hug Therese. "We have to believe the police will find him and he's fine," she said, not really believing her own words. Everything felt so immense and overwhelming, and she felt powerless.

"It's been twenty-four hours," her father observed, frowning. "More than that, actually. That's not good." He stood, pushing back the stool. "I'm going to go out front and check in with the officer, in case there are any developments."

"Good idea," Justina said, letting go of Therese and going to grab a bottle of water out of the fridge. Therese looked so bereft, it broke Justina's heart and pumped up her own level of fear and anxiety.

"What are you cooking?" she asked, hoping to distract them both, even if only for a minute.

Therese glanced at the stove. "Oh, I thought I'd make a

chicken stew; it's an easy dish. Mostly I just needed something to do. I'm going crazy just sitting here." She paused, then added, "I'll finish putting it together so it can cook for a bit. Not that I'm hungry. Did you get some rest?"

"Yes, that Xanax totally knocked me out. I shouldn't have taken it. But we do have some other troubles. Dr. Al is on a rampage. He went looking for Ramona because he found out she was talking to me. Plus, of course, the police were at the hospital. So, he's furious. She called, and so did Gabby. They were worried he would come here."

"Are you serious? How did he find out? I thought it was all very secret squirrel?"

"It was supposed to be. We're not sure. The residency coordinator at the hospital left a message to alert me but didn't say much more than that. Ramona thinks one of the other residents was spying on her for Dr. Al. Anyway, the cat's out of the bag now. Ramona is staying at her mom's and was going to let the agents know about Al showing up at her house. Her boyfriend got rid of him pretty quickly, apparently."

The front door slammed, and Victor emerged with Marci following right behind. "Look who I found lurking outside," Victor said.

"Lurking? Hmmm," Marci said. "You should be nice to me. I've been doing a lot of research and I think you will be interested in what I found out. Looks like for sure all these guys are in bed together. Including your lawyer friends, Justina."

40

THERESE

Therese forgot the throbbing in her leg as Marci waved a file of papers in the air. She had been unable to focus on anything since Jose's disappearance; her heart hurt even more than her ankle, and she had been unable to distract herself so far. Her primary activity had been talking with law enforcement of various stripes and playing hostess to the various officers and agents who were trooping in and out of the house as a matter of routine.

She hobbled over to the kitchen counter to hear what Marci had found, seeing worry on Justina's face and hope on Victor's.

"My lawyers?" Justina asked, disbelief in her voice.

"Well, maybe. Here's what I found." Marci spread the manila folder open and pulled out a printed page from the secretary of state website.

"What's that?" Therese asked, seeing the name of an unfamiliar corporation.

"This, my friends, is the missing link!" Marci announced

with her usual flair for the dramatic. "Well, I hope it is, anyhow," she qualified.

"This corporation, Top Trust Medical LLC, is owned by our favorite attorney, Peter Hancock."

"Yeah, so?" Victor asked.

"Well, Top Trust Medical is a management service company. And guess what they specialize in?"

Therese wasn't in the mood for guessing games. "Come on, Marci," Therese complained. "What did you find?"

Marci pulled out a page and read from her file. "This company provides 'supply chain management and other contracted services for its pharmacy clients, including procurement contracts, data analysis, and inventory management.' It's registered as a group purchasing organization, or GPO. Anybody want to guess who is supporting our friendly neighborhood drug-dealing pharmacy?"

Therese looked more closely at the printout. "Wait a minute. It lists a Sheila Masterson as the principal, not Peter Hancock?"

"Yes. That is Hancock's wife," Marci responded. "That's her maiden name. I'm sure they figured it would keep this from showing up so easily for anyone looking at it, at least on the surface." Marci looked around the group. "I missed my calling. I should be on the FBI team," she stated with a smile.

"Wow!" Justina said, pushing her hair back behind her ear as she leaned over to look closer. "But we don't know if they have anything to do with our pharmacy …"

"Well, sometimes the truth is hiding in plain sight," Marci said triumphantly. She shuffled through the papers and pulled out another printed page.

"GPOs are required by law to report money paid to physicians and teaching hospitals," she said. "It's a requirement under the Sunshine Act." She looked at Justina. "See, you're not the only one studying health law."

"I see that," Justina responded as she examined the page. "It says here that Top Trust Medical gave a variety of funds to Dr. Powers … consulting fees, meals … and here is a conference in Acapulco!" Justina shook her head. "So, they can't say they never dealt with Dr. Powers!"

"It gets better," Marci said, thumbing through her folder again and producing a grainy photo. "Sorry about my home printer, it's not good for this. But you can see who we have here."

Justina gasped. "That's Dr. Powers with Peter Hancock!" They all leaned in, and Therese could see the photo was taken at an exotic resort, with the two men sitting at a pool bar.

"Yes, they are together at a drug conference of all things," Marci confirmed. "This photo was buried on the conference center's website. No proof without pictures, right?" Turning to Victor, she said, "We are definitely in the wrong line of work!"

"Okay, so let me see if I get this straight," Justina said, still trying to piece it together. "This company, which is owned by Peter Hancock, is supplying and managing the pharmacy owned by Dr. Al and Dr. Powers, right? So that company is supplying the drugs to the pharmacy.". Her frown deepened. "This was the question the DEA had, about where the pharmacy is getting its drug supply. It's pretty unlikely that Peter Hancock has no idea what's going on here."

Marci nodded. "Right." Shuffling papers back into the folder, she added, "This is in addition to all the connections between the hospital and the law firm. But most of that looks like it's Peter Hancock, so it may well just be him. Although, of course, Dr. Al's wife works at the firm with him."

Victor spoke up. "M'ija, you need to call the DEA agent and make sure they are aware of all this. Chances are that they are not, at least not based on what they've told us so far. I think this is a totally different direction than they have been looking. Right now we need to get Jose back, and if any of this helps them with that …" Therese could see that Victor was thinking about the missing child rather than the details Marci was sharing, and who could blame him?

"Exactly what I was thinking," Justina said, pulling out her phone. "I'll go right now and call them."

"Good job, Marci. Thanks," Victor said, and Therese thought the strain on his face seemed to be a permanent look for him ever since Jose's kidnapping. She wished there was something she could do to ease his misery. Losing a child was the worst kind of pain.

Marci's face became more serious as she looked at Victor, probably noticing the same new grim lines. "Victor, I hate to tell you this, but there is more. And it's ugly."

"What now?" Victor asked, his voice weary.

"Well, I don't know for sure, but one of my reporter sources said that your opponent is accusing you of setting this whole kidnapping thing up for sympathy and free press."

"What?" Therese exclaimed. "Are you serious? How cruel can anyone possibly be?" She couldn't believe what she was hearing. "That man needs to be exposed for the creep that he is!"

Victor appeared stunned, raking his hands through his hair. "Unbelievable. And I suppose this is going to be all over the news. That won't be good for us finding Jose, if people believe it's a hoax. Goddamn it!" Victor cursed, something Therese had never heard him do.

Marci put her hand on his arm, concern all over her face. "Victor, let me talk to the law enforcement folks about this, okay? This type of dirty trick is in my bailiwick. I can make sure they understand it's just politics."

Victor nodded. "Yes, that's fine. I'm sure they will want to talk to me, depending on what story is put out there. But if you want to prime the pump, that would be great. It's better they hear it from us." Marci pulled out her phone.

Victor reached out for her before she could turn to leave. "Marci, remember how I said I didn't want to play dirty with all that information you got about Jefferson's sexual harassment cases?" Marci nodded. "Well, I've now officially changed my mind."

Marci nodded again and gave Victor a salute. "Yes, sir. I am on it. With pleasure. But first let's find Jose!"

"Of course, no question. But this guy should never hold elected office. It's not about me. This is despicable."

"Agreed. I will enjoy taking him down." She reached over and gave Victor a hug. "We'll find your boy and stop all these bad guys. Wait and see. I'm going to get on it right now."

After Marci left, Therese watched Victor checking his phone for messages, his face drawn. It broke her heart seeing how devastated he was, and the latest news only compounded the agony. She went to Victor and put her arms around him without saying a word. There was really nothing to say.

She only hoped that it wasn't going to get worse.

41

JUSTINA

Another rough night. Justina would have thought she hadn't slept at all, except that she had nightmares bad enough that she woke up crying. She splashed some cold water on her face and stumbled downstairs, her feelings a mixture of hope and dread over what the day might bring. Hopefully Jose.

Her father was already up and talking to the officer on duty. She could hear their voices as she slipped into the kitchen for some coffee. She could smell it as she rounded the corner, and Therese was already there, setting out the sugar.

"I guess you didn't sleep either," Therese observed, taking note of Justina's messy hair and blotchy face.

"I slept enough to have nightmares," Justina clarified. "I don't suppose there is any news?"

"No news so far," Therese confirmed. "Your father has already been on the phone with the FBI this morning. This is driving him crazy, not being able to do anything."

Justina could see that Therese wasn't faring much better;

she looked haggard compared to her usual glow.

"Well, they should be going after the pharmacy and doctors very soon," Justina offered. "We have to believe that we'll get to the bottom of it then. I know they've fast-tracked it."

"Let's just hope that helps us find Jose! I mean, what if it doesn't? Then we've all been chasing down the wrong rabbit hole." Therese frowned, worry lines creasing her face. "You know, we've been assuming that as soon as they nail these guys that everything will fall into place. But what if it doesn't? I'm just saying. What if we've all wasted time looking in the wrong direction?"

The front door slammed, and Victor came into the kitchen in time to hear the last comment. "The police say they think they have some footage of the vehicle Jose was taken in. It was a black SUV, which doesn't narrow it down much. And they say that usually a rental car is used in cases like this, anyhow, to keep anyone from tracking them down by their vehicle. Not only that, but they couldn't see the license plate in the video, it was blocked by a truck parked in front. But at least it's a starting point. Maybe." He looked at Therese. "I can't think of anyone besides the crooks at the clinic and pharmacy who would have any reason to grab Jose. Who else would have a reason? We don't have a ransom request, nothing."

"I don't know," Therese said, then added, "I just have a feeling. But I'm probably just tired. My head isn't very clear at this point."

Justina felt her anxiety level shoot upward. Therese was

right: What if this wasn't the right direction to be looking? But it didn't help to say any more along those lines; everyone's nerves were already frazzled. They just had to believe that the police and FBI were getting close to wrapping up the case at the hospital and that would produce answers.

Her phone rang. Tim. Briefly he let her know that they had nearly everything to raid the pharmacy. Probably first thing the following morning, he told her, to catch them as they came in for the day. Justina let him know about the black SUV.

"We'll keep a lookout, Justina," he assured her. "But a lot of times these types of criminals have hired guns and they often use rental cars or other vehicles that are hard to trace. We'll keep it in mind, though. I know the police are doing their part to track that vehicle down. They've been keeping us in the loop."

Justina sighed, knowing what he said was true but still hoping. "It's so hard not doing anything," she said, but Tim had no answers for her other than to hang in there and let them get through the process.

The day dragged on with no development, and everyone's patience was short. Victor wanted to be doing something, but there was nothing he could do, so he was short with everyone. Therese was nervous, trying to find little tasks to keep her hands busy. Justina tried to stay out of her father's way, given his mood, but Therese's nervous energy only made her more anxious. Late in the afternoon Marci showed up. Justina could hear her outside talking to the officer stationed out front before she blew into the house at full speed. Justina was on her phone, monitoring various social media sites that had posted the picture and news about Jose, hoping someone would put up a comment that might be helpful.

"Justina, where's your father?" Marci went right to the point, skipping pleasantries.

Justina looked up, noting the tension in Marci's voice. "I think he's in the dining room," she said. "Why, what's going on? Is there news?"

Marci shook her head. "There's news, but not about Jose." She raked her hair back in an agitated gesture and threw her purse on the couch. "We have other sorts of problems. That's why I need to speak with Victor."

Justina followed her into the dining room where her father was on his laptop. Justina saw the Amber Alert on his screen and the grim set of his mouth.

"Hey, Victor," Marci said, plopping herself down in a chair across from him. "We officially have a problem with the media."

Victor closed his laptop. "What could be worse than what we're dealing with now, Marci?" he asked, his voice rough.

"One of my sources told me that the *New York Times* is 'breaking' the story that Jefferson's camp has 'leaked,' about how the kidnapping is probably a hoax. And suggesting that your campaign is behind it." She held up her hand as Victor started to speak. "I already told the police that this nasty story might be coming, and just now I warned them it was definitely going to print. Jefferson's camp is clearly doing this because they want to make sure you're not getting any sympathy from voters. They want to bring you down, Victor. And they clearly don't care who they hurt."

Justina was mortified. How could anyone do this? If people didn't think the kidnapping was real, they would be much less likely to provide any tips or information. And if law enforcement bought into the story, would they treat her father as a criminal instead of a victim? It was too awful to comprehend.

Justina's horror was reflected on her father's face. "When is this coming out?" he demanded. "If the police quit working this case, we'll never find Jose."

"I know," Marci agreed. "But I did tell the officers and they seem to understand. But you will want to reach out to the FBI contact and the others."

Victor stood. "I'll go talk to them myself. Isn't there anything we can do to stop it?"

Marci shook her head; her body language was rigid, and her face flushed and mottled. "No, this is too juicy. You know the media. We will issue a denial and try to turn the tables on Jefferson for his dirty tricks. I'll work on that right now. This is an outrage!" Justina had never seen Marci so angry.

Justina watched in dismay as her father stormed out of the room with Marci on his heels and buried her face in her hands. Why was all this happening? Her father had never done a dishonest thing in his life. It was so unfair! And none of this was helping find Jose. It was all a major distraction. She felt fury boiling up, threatening to explode. Anger at the ones she knew were causing them harm as well as the unknown thugs who were undoubtedly involved. How can people just wreck other people's lives for money or politics? She felt so impotent and unable to do anything with all that anger.

This is not helping anything, she thought. *I can't just sit here!*

Deciding, she went upstairs and put her shoes on. Her father and Marci had gone outside, but she found Therese in the kitchen, cleaning the oven. She gave Therese the latest awful update and headed out, hoping that a bit of exercise and fresh air would give her some renewed energy to deal with all that was happening to her family. Sitting in the house wasn't helping anyone.

She found herself drawn subconsciously to the spot where Jose had disappeared. The beach looked normal, families clustered along the shore with kids playing in the surf or building sandcastles. Justina watched, trying to understand how life could go on as usual while her universe was upside down. It seemed so unfair. To be living in a world where that kind of evil exists, alongside regular people just trying to live their lives, and nobody recognizes it until it's too late.

"This isn't helping," she muttered to herself, tearing her view away from the happy families on the beach and setting out to walk along the boardwalk. The boardwalk always reminded her of the days following Hurricane Sandy, when she and Daniel had come to see the damage and were horrified that their boardwalk was smashed to bits. It was now rebuilt, and the usual foot traffic was in full force.

She walked all the way to the end of the boardwalk and back, her stride fast and purposeful, hoping to burn away that ball of fury and helplessness in her chest. She was tempted to find a bench and just sit there indefinitely, letting the ocean breeze purge her dark thoughts, but she didn't want to be gone that long, in case anything was happening, and she was too agitated to sit still, anyhow.

As she got back to the house her problems quickly resurfaced as several vans were parked out front and clumps of reporters were broadcasting in front of her house. "Oh my God, seriously?" Justina muttered to herself. The police were preventing the reporters from going right up to the front door, but that didn't stop them from descending on her like a flock of buzzards when they spotted her crossing the street. Although she tried to circumvent the media frenzy by heading around to the back of the house, she wasn't quick enough.

"Justina! Is it true that your father engineered this kidnapping for voter sympathy?" one woman shouted at her in a shrill voice.

"Where is Jose?" a male reporter yelled.

The reporters as a group started converging on her, microphones thrust forward and cameras rolling.

"No! This was a setup!" she responded, feeling her rage return. She stopped in her tracks, momentarily forgetting any instructions about dealing with the media. "This whole story is manufactured by Jefferson's campaign. Why don't you go ask them?" As they started clamoring again, she shook her head at them. "You are jeopardizing this child's safety! You should be ashamed!" She was so angry, she felt tears of frustration burn the back of her eyes. She wanted to say more, but one of the police officers approached and pushed the reporters back, so she darted around them and ran up the front stairs, slamming the door behind her once she got in the house.

42

JUSTINA

Nobody was very hungry, but they sat at the kitchen counter, dutifully picking at the sandwiches and salads that Marci had bought at the deli earlier. They weren't even using the dining room anymore, leaving that as a space for the various law enforcement officers and agents to work. Justina watched her father monitor his phone, noticing the way his mouth formed a grim line every now and again, letting her know that there was no good coverage or positive news. Her father's tense face had become his new normal, and Justina wished she knew how to fix the situation. It was beyond frustrating.

She hadn't mentioned the run-in with the press earlier to her father. There was no point in it, he was already so upset. Her comments had not gone unnoticed, however.

The back door slammed, and they all looked up to see Marci, who had quit using the front door once she realized she could come in the back and avoid the press. Justina thought how ironic it was, since Marci was usually trying to get in front of the media. Nothing was funny right now, though, and she felt it was about to get worse.

Without preamble, Marci addressed Justina. "Did you tell the press that Jefferson made up this story about Jose?" she demanded.

Justina felt a flash of panic. "Yes, I said something like that," she said, and as she saw her father and Marci look at each other, she added, "They pounced on me right outside! What was I supposed to say? It's true!"

"You're not supposed to say anything," Marci said, her voice shrill. "Now Jefferson's office is threatening a lawsuit for defamation. I swear to God!" Marci huffed, throwing her purse onto the counter in frustration.

Her father stood up, looming over her. "Justina. Why didn't you tell me about this?"

Feeling cornered, Justina looked around at Marci, her father, and Therese. Therese looked concerned, but her father and Marci were scowling in unison.

"I was upset, okay? I'm sorry. I wasn't thinking. They chased me down right in front of my own house, and they are pushing these lies! What if we never find Jose because of this?" She fought back the tears, which seemed to be a regular thing these days.

Marci just shook her head and pulled her phone out of her pocket.

Therese stood and came around the counter to give Justina a hug. "I know, honey," she said, clearly responding to Justina's tears, which were starting to form puddles in her eyes. She was afraid to blink for fear they would start gushing down her face. At least Therese understood.

The front door slammed and Officer Wilson, who had also become part of their daily routine, called out as he entered. "We're in the kitchen," Victor called to him.

"Sir, just to let you know, we're bringing in some additional support outside. These reporters are growing in number, and now we have some other people gathering, too. I'm afraid it could get out of hand."

"Oh my God," Justina exclaimed. Didn't these people know they were having a personal emergency? How could they be so cruel? "What is wrong with these people?" she began, before Marci cut her off.

"Justina, just let them handle it. You've done enough," she advised in a weary tone, while rubbing her temples. Justina clamped her mouth shut, feeling chastised but no less furious.

Turning to Victor, Marci said, "We need to give them a statement, Victor. Maybe we can defuse this." She did not sound confident.

"Yes, you're right. Let's go in the living room, where it's quiet, and figure it out," he said, and nodded to the cop. "Thank you, Officer. We appreciate your help. Hopefully this dies down quickly."

* * *

After conferring with the various law enforcement officers, Victor prepared to give a statement to the press. By the time Marci and Victor had written the speech there was a very large crowd gathered. Additional media and nonmedia people had shown up once they got word of the coming press conference. It was clearly not an overly friendly crowd; Justina noted how much the tone had changed since the accusations had been made against her father and had a very hard time keeping her mouth shut. She knew politics was dirty, but this was her family, and she couldn't believe how evil people could be. Her father and Marci had long ago mastered the art of keeping a neutral expression on their faces, but Justina knew she would struggle with that in front of the camera. She clenched her jaw tight, focused on keeping her mouth shut. How could they reprimand her for stating what everyone knew was true? And, if that wasn't awful enough, putting Jose in more danger while everyone wasted valuable time on this ridiculous drama! The total injustice of it made her feel like she would explode.

They set up a spot in front of the house, and Justina, Marci, and Victor went outside after going over the speech. They all agreed it was better for Therese to stay inside, since she wasn't family, and it could raise unnecessary questions or discussion that could be a distraction.

Marci started off, introducing Victor, and handing it off to him. Despite being aggravated with him for reprimanding her, Justina watched her father with pride and hope. He was so good at this. If it were any other circumstance, she would have really enjoyed seeing her father do what he did best. But instead, she was seething at the reporters and the Jefferson campaign and, generally, anyone who bought the awful story being told. She reminded herself, if anyone could turn this around, it was her father. She had total faith in him.

Victor cleared his throat and looked out over the gathered crowd.

"Thank you all for being here," he began. "As you all know, we are in the midst of trying to locate a child who has been kidnapped." He held up a photo of Jose, in a bright blue SpongeBob T-shirt and with the cat at his feet. Justina loved that picture and was glad it was the one that they chose.

"You may recall that Jose is a survivor of the devastating earthquake in Mexico City. We were fortunate to be able to bring him here after he was orphaned. I am Jose's legal guardian. Jose is a wonderful child and has become a well-loved part of our family."

When he paused, several reporters started yelling out questions, but Victor held up his hand to silence them and miraculously it worked.

"We are desperate to find Jose. We are asking everyone to keep an eye out for this child. He has already been through so much in his short life, and this kidnapping is the worst form of cruelty. We have no idea why someone would want to commit such a heinous act against an innocent child; we've received no communication from the kidnappers, so all we can do is ask for everyone's help. Jose was taken from the beach, right here in Long Beach. Someone must have seen something, and the police and FBI have been chasing every lead."

Justina watched her father with admiration. She never got tired of seeing him handle crowds and reporters. Something in his demeanor always seemed to connect. If anything would get the press back on their side, it would be this speech.

"Now, I want to address the accusation that I somehow engineered this kidnapping as a ploy for sympathy or votes. I can't tell you how appalling this fabricated story is for me and my family. Let me be clear; we love Jose and would never put him in harm's way or resort to the sort of devious hoax which is being alleged. I'm not sure who came up with that story, but let me just state, for the record, that not only is it a total lie, but it could also jeopardize this investigation. It is unforgivable to put a child in danger for any purpose. I'm calling on my friends, neighbors, the public, and the press in particular to assist us in locating our child and not engage in this disgusting distraction which could threaten our chance to recover Jose safely."

He scanned the crowd, which had somehow grown in the short time he had been speaking but was riveted by his speech. A couple of homemade signs demanding "Where is Jose?" were brandished.

"I would also ask for some privacy and respect for our family as we are going through something that I would not wish on anyone. There is nothing more important than bringing Jose home. Political mudslinging can wait. A child's safety is at stake. Please help us find Jose. That is all I have to say for now."

The press started clamoring and shouting questions. One

young female reporter, who was right up front, managed to shout out over the others. "What about your accusation that Jefferson's campaign was behind this story?" she asked. "Your daughter told us outright that it was Jefferson. His campaign denies any involvement and is threatening legal action. What do you say to that? Do you have evidence it was Jefferson's camp who made this accusation?"

Justina fought to maintain a neutral face while feeling like she was getting kicked in the stomach. She was mortified her father was having to answer for her, and she started to better understand why Marci and Victor had both been so unhappy with her. She should have known better.

Victor frowned at the group, his already-serious expression becoming even harsher. "My daughter is devastated by these recent events," he began. "Our family has not been sleeping, we've not been eating, and we are being hounded in our own home. Justina, like the rest of us, is trying to make sense of a senseless situation. She is not a politician; she is a private citizen who made an unfortunate remark due to anxiety and exhaustion. We don't know why anyone would do this to our family; she regrets the comment, but we would expect Jefferson to recognize the extreme stress we are under and to be understanding rather than threaten us with litigation at a time like this. I am apologizing to Jefferson on behalf of my daughter, assuming that her comment was inaccurate."

Victor's last statement caused another eruption among the press, but Victor held his hand up. "I have nothing else to say. We again ask for help in locating Jose. We are devastated and exhausted, and desperate to find our boy. That is the only thing that matters right now. The FBI has set up a tip line, and a link to it is on their website. Thank you for your attention."

With that Victor nodded to the press and herded Justina and Marci back toward the house, ignoring the clamoring reporters.

Once inside, Justina noticed Marci immediately sat down and looked pale. "Marci, are you okay?" she asked, which drew her father and Therese's attention.

Marci nodded. "Yes, I'm just a little dizzy headache. It was a bit warm out there is all. I'm fine."

"Let me get you some water," Therese said, and hustled off to the kitchen.

Victor sat down next to Marci and looked at her closely. "Marci, I think this is too much stress for you. I've said that before. Why don't you call your doctor? And you can lie down here for a bit. There is no way we can let this drama harm you or the baby."

"I really think I'm fine, Victor. Seriously," Marci said, and Justina could tell she was forcing herself to sound positive. Therese handed her a glass of ice water, looking closely at the pregnant woman.

"This is too much, Marci," Therese said. "Nothing is worth you losing your child. Nothing."

Marci took a deep swallow of the water. "Well, maybe I should go home and rest a bit," she conceded. "I do think

I'm fine, but you did a great job with those vultures outside. I think we did all we can for now."

Justina felt a wave of alarm. If Marci was willing to go home right now, she must be feeling bad, regardless of what she said. "Do you want me to drive you home, Marci?" she asked. "If you're dizzy you shouldn't drive."

Victor nodded. "Yes, Justina is right. You shouldn't drive. Let me get one of our officers to take you home. Justina, I think it's better if you stay in the house until this crowd disperses a bit."

Marci pursed her lips into a pout. "I hate to bother them; they have their hands full right now with all those idiots outside. Maybe I'll just relax a bit and go when things settle down. Or John can come get me."

Victor stood. "No, let's get you home now. I think we have half of the Long Beach Police Department outside; they can spare one officer." He turned and headed to the door.

Marci wiped her hand across her forehead, and Justina could see she was sweating. "You do need to call your doctor," Justina admonished.

Therese agreed. "Marci, you need to take this seriously. Call your doctor and get checked right away. Trust me, you don't want to lose your baby."

"I'll call when I get home," Marci promised. "I don't want to cause any more drama here. You all have enough to worry about, and I'm sure I'm fine. Those animals outside have been fed; hopefully now you can have a bit of peace and quiet. I'm sure they are done harassing you for a minute or two while they get their stories out there."

Justina craned her neck to look out the front window. "I only hope you're right," she said, noting the crowd, which seemed to have only grown. "Anyhow, I don't see how it could get any worse."

43

JUSTINA

Victor returned with Officer Wilson. He was a very young officer; Justina thought he looked to be about her age. He was very friendly and supportive, but equally determined to help protect the family and find Jose. The whole family had become very fond of him in short order.

He went right to Marci and asked her if she was ready to go, lines of concern marking his otherwise smooth and freckled baby face.

He held his hand out to help her up when she confirmed it was time to go and took her arm when she swayed slightly. "Still dizzy?" he asked, and she nodded.

"Just a little. I just need to get home and lie down."

"Okay, we'll get you there right away. We'll go out the back; my patrol car is in the alley."

"I think you should go to the hospital and get checked out," Justina told her. The dizziness and sweating could not be good signs, and her father and Therese both nodded in agreement. Marci scowled at her and shook her head even as she gripped Officer Wilson's arm.

Justina followed closely on their heels to the back door, watching Marci's gait from the window as they walked into the back yard to make sure she was steady, even with Officer Wilson's arm supporting her.

The next series of events happened so fast Justina could barely register it from her window viewpoint.

A man in a black baseball hat and camouflage jacket was in their backyard and darted behind the shed when the back door opened. Officer Wilson let go of Marci and ran after him.

Startled, Justina shouted for her father as she yanked the door open and found Marci on the ground, breathing heavily and holding her pregnant belly. She could hear Officer Wilson behind the shed; based on the shouting it sounded like he had the intruder in custody. She plopped down next to Marci.

"Marci! Are you okay?" she asked, panicking. Clearly Marci wasn't okay!

Marci's eyes appeared unfocused and sweat blanketed her forehead and upper lip. She tried sitting up but stopped, drawing her legs up and closing her eyes. "It hurts," she whimpered.

Victor burst out the back door, Therese right on his heels, with his phone in hand. "I'm calling 911," he said. "Therese, get her some water."

Two more officers came around the house to assist Wilson and the next thing Justina saw was the young man in a baseball cap and baggy jeans being led to the patrol car in handcuffs.

While the other two officers took the suspect to the car, Officer Wilson came back to check on Marci. Victor told him they'd already called 911, and Therese appeared with a bottle of water. Marci tried to sit up to drink but then shook her head. "I can't," she said weakly.

"Marci! Who is your doctor?" Therese asked. "We need to call and let them know you're coming in!"

Marci mumbled something Justina couldn't hear, but Therese ran back to the house, presumably to make a phone call.

Justina turned to Wilson. "What happened? What was that guy doing?"

"He was trying to get some pictures, looks like. He says he's a 'journalist,' doing a blog. He was just trying to spy on you guys, probably sneak up and get some photos through the back window so he could post them on social media. We see that a lot these days. Anything for a click. But we'll be taking him in and grilling him to be sure. This sort of thing brings them to the surface. Chief told me to stay here with you and my partner will get started processing him. Along with the FBI. That ought to scare him straight."

"Oh my God," Justina exclaimed. "I can't believe this. I ..." She stopped short as Marci whimpered and curled up into a tighter fetal position. As she rolled onto her side, Justina could see she was bleeding.

Victor crouched down. "Marci. What's going on?"

"I'm … cramping," she said. "The baby …"

They could hear a siren, and Justina felt a wave of relief. Marci looked awful, pale and sweating, and fear in her wide blue eyes.

"I'll go flag them down," Wilson said, before heading toward the front. "We'll need to get those people out of here now so the ambulance can get in!"

Minutes felt like hours to Justina as she stroked Marci's hair, feeling helpless. Even her father, who usually knew how to handle anything, looked worried as he squatted next to Marci and held her hand, trying to reassure her.

The team of medics arrived with a stretcher, and after asking her a few questions and taking her vitals they loaded her onto it. Therese went and spoke to them, probably telling them she had alerted Marci's physician. Justina could barely hear their discussion, as the medics had asked her and her father to move back, but she could tell Marci's blood pressure was high from the commentary she could hear, and, even worse, she was still bleeding. Justina said a silent prayer: *Please, God, let Marci be okay and her baby, too …*

"Call Jon for me" was Marci's last request as the medics lifted her up.

"Of course," Victor said as the medics whisked her away. Justina could hear her moaning as she went, although the medics appeared to be carrying her as smoothly as possible.

Justina looked at her father and Therese, none of them saying a word. Justina fought back tears, and she could see that Therese was as well. She didn't know how much more they could take, first Jose and now Marci, plus all the media and now even someone trying to spy on them to get some clicks! And no idea why or who would want to do this to her family. Was the kidnapping related to the hospital case? Jefferson's hate campaign against her father? A random crazy person? It felt like someone had rammed an ice pick into the back of her skull.

She could hear the cops shouting as they held off reporters and others who were trying to breach the boundary set by the police. "We should get inside," she murmured, and they went back into the house, where they would continue a vigil that had just expanded.

44

JUSTINA

Justina, sleepless, watched her clock as it moved through the 3 o'clock hour to 4, then 5. Finally giving up, she got up and washed the stale tear tracks and blotches off her face with cold water. Her eyes were bloodshot and even her hair looked dull. She gave it three strokes with the brush, mostly out of habit, and willed her tired body down the stairs in the hopes that coffee would somehow improve her mental and physical condition.

Within minutes of getting the coffee started, her father appeared. He looked better than she felt, for sure, although he still looked worn out. "Any news?" she asked. "Marci? Jose? Anything?"

"Ah, coffee," he murmured, and then he smiled for the first time in days. "Yes, good news on the Marci front. They were able to do a C-section and get the baby, even though he's very premature. Between the stress, and then Marci falling, they had to get him out. I guess there was some sort of damage from the fall, and her blood pressure. Anyhow, Marci and the baby should both be fine, thank God. Of course, the baby is very premature, but the prognosis is good so far." He closed his eyes and took a long sip of coffee, then said, "I could never have forgiven myself if anything happened to either of them because of me."

Relief flooded Justina. "Thank God! And you know I'm the one who shot off my mouth to the reporters and created that drama. I never would have gotten over it, either." She added some more sugar to her coffee, hoping it would give her an extra boost of energy. "When did you find out? You should have told me!"

"It was very late, m'ija. Like three a.m. by the time Jon called me. I told him to call me any time, as soon as there was news. He was beside himself, poor man. I imagine having Marci for a wife would be challenging on a good day, but this … I think it almost destroyed him when he thought he might lose both his wife and his baby. The baby will have to stay at the hospital awhile, he was premature, of course, but he is healthy, and the doctors think he will be fine."

Hearing Therese on the stairs, Justina poured another cup of coffee.

"Isn't that great about Marci and the baby?" Therese asked with a smile, accepting the coffee. "Our prayers were answered." Taking a sip, she made a face. "Too hot, needs some more milk," she said.

Puzzled, Justina looked at Therese and then her father. "I thought Jon called you like at three?" she said, wondering how Therese knew about it and she didn't.

The two exchanged glances before her father answered. "Therese was still up, her light was on," he explained.

"Well, I was awake all damn night!" Justina began, when her phone vibrated. It was Tim, from the DEA. It was a brief text.

"Just fyi. We are at the pharmacy. Waiting for pharmacist. Will let you know."

Justina typed a brief "thanks," so he would know she was up and on her phone, and felt a glimmer of hope for the day. "They are getting ready to raid the pharmacy," she told her father and Therese. "Hopefully today we will get answers and get Jose back!"

"That's excellent!" Victor said and Therese nodded agreement.

"Ours prayers for Marci were answered. Maybe today is the day that all the rest of our prayers are answered!" Therese said, her voice sounding positive for the first time in days.

Victor chuckled. "Well, if you have an inside track on that, see what you can do," he teased her. "But seriously, we are getting close, I feel it. This many days without a peep, without any requests from kidnappers, and no evidence that they've hurt him … We have to hope that this is about to wrap up. In a good way." He took another long drink from his coffee mug. "Therese is right. We need to stay positive and have faith. Something I sometimes forget to do." He smiled at Therese, and Justina noticed another look pass between them but didn't really have time to think about it before there was a tap at the back door.

Justina was closest to the window and peeked out. "It's Jordan," she announced, moving to open the door.

"Good morning, folks," said Agent Jordan, one of the FBI agents who had been practically in residence since the kidnapping. "I saw your light on and thought you might like an update."

"Come in! Yes!" Justina exclaimed, feeling a surge of energy, fear, and hope. "You want some coffee?"

"No thanks, I've already had too much." He smiled. "So, I'm not sure this is helpful, except to rule out some possibilities. But we went to have a visit with your friend Jefferson last night. Given the drama yesterday, and the likelihood that he pushed that story out, we wanted to talk to him. We had to make sure he was not somehow involved."

"And?" Her father beat her to the question.

"Well, we had an interesting conversation ..."

"What?" Justina demanded. Her earlier fatigue was forgotten.

The agent smiled. "Jefferson was actually very gracious. I have to say, he seemed truly mortified about Jose's kidnapping. There is no indication he knew anything. And it seems that whatever implications may have come out of his camp didn't come from him. He has a pretty aggressive campaign manager, and some other overzealous staff. He said he would put a stop to it and get a retraction out today if he found out who did it. He didn't seem convinced it was one of his people, of course, although I don't know. Oh, and he said he's not looking to sue you for defamation, said he was just very upset when he heard about the accusations." The agent smiled at Justina. "You shouldn't have said that."

"I know, I know," Justina said, relieved that her outburst wasn't going to create even more problems for them. The good news about Marci had given her a positive lift, too, so she didn't mind so much that Agent Jordan was also correcting her.

Victor set his coffee down, frowning. "You don't think there is any chance that Jefferson's people had any role in Jose's disappearance? Are you sure of that?"

"Pretty sure, but we will follow up with his staff today. We are pretty good at getting people to talk," he said with a slight smile. "If there is anything there, I'm confident we will find it."

Justina felt some small relief that they had maybe eliminated one possibility, but it wasn't getting them any closer to Jose. Not really. But the other agents were at the pharmacy, so hopefully that would yield some results.

"Are you in contact with the DEA and DOJ agents?" she asked. "They are at the pharmacy this morning. We are hoping that they can get something out of that."

Agent Jordan nodded. "Yes, we are all in contact. We are going to get to the bottom of all of it soon, I am confident." He paused, then added, "I know how hard this is. But we are following every lead, and I do think that by the end of today we may have some answers. We're going to be talking to a lot of people who have some explaining to do and some who will be facing charges."

More waiting. Justina felt like she was going to have a heart attack with all the waiting and no answers. Therese sighed heavily, showing her frustration as well.

"Don't give up. We are starting to unravel all this. If someone is trying to send you all these warnings, but hasn't hurt you, I don't think they will harm the child." Agent Jordan was clearly trying to keep their spirits up, but it had gone on too long.

"But what do they WANT?" Justina exploded. "How can we cooperate with them when we don't know why this is happening?"

"Exactly," Therese agreed, putting her arm around Justina's shoulders. "We don't know if we're doing anything to make it worse."

"Just lie low, like you are. I know it's hard. But I do think we are close."

"What happened with that black SUV you guys saw on the camera?" Victor asked. "Anything come of it?" Justina could see her father's patience waiting for answers was also wearing thin.

The agent shook his head. "Just not enough to go on. We couldn't see the plates, and the camera at the causeway was down for a while after the last storm."

"Of course it was," Justina huffed. So typical.

The agent continued, ignoring her comment. "All we really have at this point is the connection to the hospital. But that will likely go down today, depending on the cooperation at the pharmacy. Worst case, we bring in the two doctors who own the pharmacy for questioning, regardless. But we really don't have anything tying them to Jose's disappearance yet. What we are hoping is that the pharmacist will spill to give us a stronger case to bring in the bigger fish." He paused, looking around at them and then focusing on Justina, adding, "Which will likely include Peter Hancock."

Victor spoke up. "So the information Marci found was useful?"

"Yes, it was helpful. We would have gotten there eventually, but she did a masterful job at unraveling the relationships between Hancock and Dr. Powers. I see why she is so good at opposition research. She should think about an FBI career! How is she doing, by the way?"

"She's going to be okay, it looks like," Victor responded, providing an update on Marci's status. "He paused, then said again, "Thank God. I would never have forgiven myself …"

"Or me, neither" Justina added, feeling the enormity of what could have happened. But still … Jose.

"Do you actually still think we'll find Jose?" she asked. "I mean, I know after this much time?" She tried not to cry every time she thought about it, and she could see on Therese's face the same feeling.

Agent Jordan's face was solemn, which gave her a sick feeling. But his answer was "In a typical case that would be true. But in this instance, with no communication from them, and, to be frank, no body that we've found or even clothing, nothing to suggest violence, we are tending to still think this is either political or related to the hospital case. You and your family have been involved in a lot of things that some people may not be happy about. We're still not sure why you haven't gotten any threats or requests, though. It's very odd."

They all nodded in unison.

"Just lie low," he advised them, looking pointedly at Justina. She met his eyes and nodded. She had learned her lesson. "We don't know what triggered these people … and we will keep you posted."

* * *

Justina couldn't stand it anymore. All the waiting. No news from anyone, which she tried to convince herself was a good thing. Yes, the DEA and DOJ were busy with the pharmacy raid and getting lots of leads, which they were busy chasing—she had to believe that. But meanwhile, it was painful sitting in the house with nothing really to do. And it was so quiet, too quiet, without Jose. Even the cat seemed restless.

Her father had retreated with his laptop, which was typical for him when he was upset. Therese had started pacing once she had finished organizing every cabinet in the kitchen. Glancing at the clock, she told Justina she was going to the hospital.

"I've not been at my desk in ages, it seems like," she explained. "And I can't just sit here."

A trip to the hospital sounded like a wonderful reprieve to Justina. "Can I ride along?" she asked. "I won't bug you. I want to go see Marci and the baby anyhow!"

Therese looked skeptical. "We are supposed to be lying low …," she began.

"I'm not going to mouth off to any more reporters!" Justina exclaimed. "We can sneak in the hospital's back door. Nobody will even know I'm there! And I'll drive! My car is out back."

Relenting, Therese agreed, with a caveat. "You go tell your father. And you make sure he knows it wasn't my idea!"

Her father, of course, didn't want her to go but seemed to understand he couldn't make her stay home. "Keep away from reporters and the group at the hospital clinic," he said sternly. "We don't need one more bit of drama." Justina agreed. At this point she would agree to anything to escape the confines of the house.

The drive to the hospital was a quick one, after they had skirted reporters by using the back door and shrubbery in their subterfuge. The crowd had largely dissipated, however, after her father's speech. In the car, Therese confessed that she was mostly just worried about Marci.

"I know the baby is fine," she told Justina as they crossed the causeway that connected Long Beach to the mainland. "But everyone knows she works with your father, and she's been publicly seen with us. It makes me nervous. I will just feel better when I see her."

Justina felt a flash of panic. "Oh my God. I hadn't even

thought of that!" She pictured Marci, alone in a hospital room, vulnerable. "Now I'm worried too. I was so busy thinking about Jose …" She stepped on the gas as soon as the toll gate lifted.

She pulled into the emergency physician's parking area. So what if they ticketed her? She wasn't feeling particularly charitable toward St. Matthew's physicians at that point in time. Or at least a couple of them.

They snuck in the back door and Therese led the way up the stairwell to the maternity ward. The woman at the nurse's station gave them the room number and directions to see Marci. Justina didn't like the fact that the woman hadn't even asked them who they were, but then realized the nurse probably recognized Therese.

Marci's room was at the end of the hall. The door was open, but the room was empty.

"Where is she?" Justina asked nobody in particular, feeling her panic-state return. It was obvious the room was inhabited: the bed was unmade and there was a toothbrush by the sink, a food tray on the side table.

"I'll go find out," Therese said and headed through the door.

Pacing, Justina looked out the window, wondering if she could see the pharmacy and DME store from there. A wing of the hospital blocked her view. Surely the raid was done. Were they still questioning the pharmacist? Maybe they had already brought the physicians in to question. It was so hard not knowing.

She went out to the hall but didn't see Therese.

When she was almost to the nurse's station, she heard her name and turned to see Therese pushing Marci in a wheelchair. "Look who I found!" Therese exclaimed. Justina was relieved to see Marci looking healthy, radiant in fact, in her fluffy pink robe and red hospital socks.

Justina rushed over and bent to hug Marci. "I was so worried about you!" she said. "I was afraid some of our bad guys found you!"

Marci laughed. "No, I was seeing my bambino!" she said. "He's so tiny … but he's doing well! Even though he was so premature. But they have are taking great care of him and they say he's doing exceptionally well." Marci said, beaming.

"He's a beautiful baby," Therese confirmed with a smile, turning Marci's wheelchair toward her room.

As they got her settled back in her room, Marci gave them all the details of her delivery and the baby's condition.

"I have to go see him before we leave!" Justina told them both, and Therese nodded. It was a blessing that something good had happened during this awful time.

"How about you hang out here for a bit while I go check my desk, make sure there's nothing going on that I need to take care of. Okay?" Therese asked, glancing up at the clock on the wall. "Then we'll both go down so you can meet Mr. Jonathan Junior!"

Justina nodded as Therese scurried out of the room.

"So, what's going on?" Marci demanded. "Last thing I recall that cop took off after someone … Things are hazy after that. Did they catch the person? Any news on Jose?"

Justina laughed, happy to see Marci was back to her usual high-energy self, even in the hospital.

She had just started giving the run down when her phone rang. Unknown number, but local. Hmmm.

The voice on the other end was immediately recognizable. Ramona. The third-year resident who had given her all the forged records.

"Justina! Where are you right now?" she asked, and without waiting for an answer, continued, "Can you come meet me? I think I've found Jose!"

45

JUSTINA

Stunned, Justina's mind raced. "Of course! Where are you?"

"Hold on," Ramona said, her voice suddenly almost a whisper. There was a rustling, and the sound of a car starting.

After a minute or two Ramona returned. "I overheard something when I was at Dr. Power's practice," she said. "He had a visitor in his office, they didn't know I was there, but they were talking about 'the kid'! Dr. Powers was furious. I couldn't hear all of it, but he told the guy to 'take care of the situation.'" She took a breath. "I followed him. There was no time to do anything else! The house is on Beach 44th Street, in Far Rockaway. I'm across the street right now, but I think they just saw me, so I have to go. I'm not sure Jose is here, but there are two guys going in and out, loading up a van. I think they are getting ready to leave."

"Oh my God. Did you call the police?" Justina asked, grabbing her bag off the chair while mouthing to a wide-eyed Marci that she had to go.

"No, I just got here, and I don't think there is time. The cops don't come so quick around here, in this neighborhood. I figured your FBI guys might be faster."

Striding past the nurse's station, Justina said, "Okay, I'm on my way. I'll call them from the car. Do you know the address?"

The response was muffled. "I can't see the house number from here. It's a two-story brick and white house with a for rent sign out front. There are apartments just past, so you'll know if you go too far. It has a driveway alongside. That's where they are loading up a white van … I gotta go." The call ended abruptly.

Racing out of the hospital, Justina was grateful for her earlier illegal parking, which so far had gone unpunished. Of course, she hit every red light, but used the opportunity to call Agent Jordan, who had insisted she program his number into her phone.

Repeating the information she had from Ramona, Justina gave directions the best she could, also explaining that it sounded like the men were packing up. "If it is them, we don't have much time," she emphasized, stomping on the gas pedal as the light changed.

"Don't do anything!" the agent warned. "Stay away from the house and we will handle it. I'm on my way right now, and I'll call the local PD."

The very next light turned yellow as she approached. Cursing, Justina gassed it and raced through the light. A few miles never seemed so far.

Finally, Beach 44th. She hung a left, punching the gas pedal as the light turned green rather than wait for the oncoming stream of cars to pass. She had only gone a block and a half when she spotted the house with the for rent sign out front. It was right in the middle of the block, with not even a tree in the yard to block her from their view. Damn! She wondered if they knew her car. Probably so.

She slowed to a crawl as she drove past, craning her neck to see any sign of Jose or the men who may have taken him. As she watched, a screen door on the side of the house, by the driveway, was opened from the inside. She could see the backside of someone slowly pushing it out, as if carrying something heavy. She slowed down further, watching. A horn blared behind her, causing her to jump and reflexively stomp on the gas pedal. Damn it! She pulled forward, turning into the nearby apartment building's parking lot.

The pumping of her heart and the adrenaline were too much—she could barely think. She couldn't let them leave if they had Jose! Turning around in the parking lot, she pulled out and turned left on Beach 44th, back toward the house. She didn't really have a plan but couldn't let them get away. Who knew what they might do to Jose if they escaped? She said a quick prayer that Agent Jordan would get there quickly.

She pulled up across the street, behind an old blue pickup truck that looked like it had been in a nasty wreck. The good news was that she would be able to see if anyone left the house, and her car wouldn't be visible from the driveway or van; the bad news was that she was far enough down the block that she couldn't see the back door of the house or the whole van and couldn't tell what was happening.

She vacillated about what to do. Agent Jordan had been very clear to stay away, and she knew it was dangerous. But she couldn't let them get away with Jose. No matter what. This might be the only chance to save him.

Her thoughts were interrupted by the sound of three car doors slamming. She couldn't see anything except the rear bumper of the van. Justina scanned the other homes nearby. Nobody else getting in or out of cars—it had to be the van doors she heard slamming. No sooner had she come to that conclusion than the brake lights flashed on the van as the engine started. *Shit!* Without thinking she started her car and backed up. No way were they going to get out of there with Jose!

Without even consciously deciding what to do, she pulled out and swung into the driveway, blocking the van.

46

THERESE

It seemed to Therese like she had been away from work for weeks instead of days. She felt alien, out of place, as people scurried about doing their normal work. It was hard to realize the world was going along like usual when her entire universe was upside down and backward. Walking down the hallway toward her office, she watched for any sign of trouble. She didn't even know anymore who might be dangerous. Unbelievable. She wondered if she would ever feel the same sense of belonging and safety here that she had when she took the job.

As she unlocked her office door, she realized that even her office seemed foreign to her, although nothing was out of place. Her house and now her office had been rendered unwelcoming after all of this, she realized with a pang.

Her phone was blinking red, even though she had been checking messages from home. Funny how the Gonzalez house now felt like home, she randomly thought as she checked the messages. Her voice mail said there were three messages, but the first two were hang-ups. The third one was Gabby and was spoken almost in a whisper. "Mother Marie, it's Gabby. Just a heads up: Dr. Pascale and Dr. Al are both looking for you. Dr. Al is livid. Something to do with the pharmacy across the street. I gotta go. Just watch your back." The message ended abruptly.

According to her voice mail system, the call had just come in. Therese stood and looked down the hallway, which had felt mildly threatening a few minutes earlier. Now it felt sinister, especially since it was unusually quiet. She thought about going down to the clinic and confronting the physicians, but the idea went against every instinct. Running through the analysis in her mind, she concluded it was better to stay put. *The police told us to lie low,* she rationalized. She closed her office door and turned the lock. "I need to do what I came here for," she mumbled to herself, struggling to think about anything other than the message and facing an angry Dr. Al. Closing her eyes, she said a brief prayer for strength and looked at her picture of Mateo. She never tired of the picture, and although it made her sad, in an odd way she felt that they were still connected. It calmed her somehow when she was anxious. She took a deep breath, then another. *Okay, we got this,* she thought, and pulled her black plastic inbox to the center of the desk to see what her assistant had dropped in.

Flyers for conferences, advertisements, junk mail … and at the bottom a plain white letter-sized envelope with her name on it. No postmark, no address. Someone had been here and dropped it off—someone other than her assistant, who always opened her mail to make sure she didn't miss anything important. It was somehow left in her office. A chill washed over her body, accompanied by a strong sense of foreboding.

The uneasy feeling clutched her stomach as she ripped it open. It was very brief and to the point.

"If you want the kid back, you tell your friend Dr. Powers to do the right thing. If he doesn't? Hasta la vista Jose."

No signature.

Paralyzed, she stared at the block letters. How long had this been here? It was at the bottom of the inbox pile. Probably the same day they grabbed Jose, because that was the last day she was in the office. Was this the missing piece, the kidnapper's demands? But what did it mean? She fished her phone out of her bag, then realized she didn't have any of the agents' phone numbers. But Justina did, she recalled. She dialed Justina but got no response. Grabbing the note and her bag she headed back down toward Marci's room. This piece of paper had to be the key!

47

JUSTINA

Justina slammed her car into park just as the van started backing out. Brake lights flashed, the van jerked to a stop, and the driver's door slammed open. Too late Justina tried to recall if she had her Taser in the glove box.

A slim man in a navy-blue baseball hat and bulky camouflage jacket stormed to her car window. Panicked, Justina kept the window up, but wasn't about to move her vehicle.

"Move your goddamn car," he shouted through the window. He had one hand in his pocket, and Justina was certain he had a gun or some other sort of weapon in his hand. The other hand was on the roof of her car as he leaned in close, his face right up against the window.

"I want Jose!" she yelled back, trying to sound forceful and consciously not pulling away from the window. The man's angry face was way too close.

His dark skin was sweaty, and she could see he was either enraged or panicking, flipped out somehow. But she had come this far, she wasn't giving up. The cops would be here any minute, she told herself.

He gestured at her with the hand in the pocket, and she felt more certain than ever that he had a gun, pointed right at her. "Bitch, move your ass or you won't have to worry about that kid anymore!"

He does have Jose! Her resolve cemented, she fired back. "Give him to me and I will go away. No problems from me! I don't care who you are. Just give me Jose."

The man's eyes darted around, and she suddenly wondered if he was on drugs or, perhaps, had some mental problem. His eyes were dilated, and he looked very anxious. She lowered her window just a tiny bit, so she could talk to him. Just a crack, not enough for him to stick a gun in her face!

"Look. I don't know what your situation is. But that little boy didn't cause you any trouble. If you hurt him, it will only be worse for you. Please."

She could tell he was wavering, unsure. She felt she was gaining some leverage and opened her mouth to say more when the passenger-side van door opened, and another man came around her car. He had unnaturally black hair and pasty white skin that was covered in sores.

"What the hell is going on here?" he demanded, and the other guy flinched.

"This bitch won't move her car," the first guy answered. "She wants the kid."

"I am fucking done with this whole thing," he shouted, spittle hitting the car window. "You were supposed to get this taken care of days ago!"

"It's not my fault," the baseball hat guy said, but he was visibly backing away from his partner. "Maybe you should have had a better plan!"

"Yeah, well maybe you shouldn't have grabbed the kid before I had time …"

Justina watched in horror as the two men shouted at each other. Where are the cops? Where is Agent Jordan? The longer this went on the better, it seemed to her, so she could buy time. But they both seemed very agitated and very unstable. Anything could happen.

Then, to her dismay, the first guy pulled out a pistol and waved it at his partner. "I think we just dump this kid and go," he said. "We're for sure only getting half of what we want … Powers might make it right if we end this," he said.

"Are you fucking crazy? After all this? We need to get the hell out of here and hold out for the rest," he shouted, appearing unfazed by the gun being waved around. Justina tried to slide down in her seat, hoping they would forget about her while there was a gun in play. She had nowhere to go.

A movement behind the men caught her eye. Jordan! And he wasn't alone. She looked around and saw several uniforms and another agent converging. Unfortunately, the guy with the gun spotted them at the same moment.

"Drop the gun," Agent Jordan shouted. The other guy turned and, seeing Jordan and two uniforms, started to run into the neighboring yard. The other two officers went after him while Agent Jordan remained focused on the gunman, his own weapon drawn and ready.

Justina watched in horror as the remaining kidnapper turned the gun toward her, pointing it at the opening in the window. "Drop your own gun, or this bitch gets it," he responded. Justina could see his hand was shaking, although his threat sounded real.

Before Agent Jordan could respond, the two uniformed officers returned with the other kidnapper, being walked roughly between them, shouting obscenities and fighting the handcuffs. Justina could see that the man with the gun wavered, distracted. Without thinking, she pushed her car door open as hard as she could, knocking the man forward onto his knees.

Agent Jordan lunged forward as the man fell, but the kidnapper was trying to grab his gun, which had fallen under the car door. Justina stretched her leg out, kicking the gun forward. The kidnapper then tried to grab her leg, but Agent Jordan was on him, pulling him up and away from her. Another agent jumped in, cuffing the man.

While the kidnappers were being subdued and given their rights, Justina ran to the van, yanking the rear door open. Jose was lying on a pile of blankets, with his hands tied. "Tina!" he squealed when he saw her, and she climbed up in the van to pull him out. Agent Jordan came up behind her and helped, untying the knot binding Jose's skinny wrists. As soon as he was freed, Jose threw his arms around Justina's neck, hanging off her. She felt tears flowing down her face and onto Jose as they clung to each other.

48

JUSTINA

Justina couldn't stop the tears flowing down her face as they left the crime scene, with Agent Jordan insisting on taking them home. She was still shaking in reaction to what had just went down, and her immense relief at getting Jose back. And thank God he hadn't been hurt. Despite everything, the men who grabbed him had treated him decently, although all he'd had to eat and drink was junk food and sodas. Out of everyone he seemed to be the least freaked out about the whole thing. But then again, Justina realized, he had been through so much over the past few months, after losing his mother and moving to another country, that he wasn't easily scared.

The FBI were going to be spending some time talking to Jose but agreed to talk to him once he was home. When they pulled up in the black FBI SUV, the vehicle was swarmed by the media, who were in a feeding frenzy filming Jose's return home. Justina marveled that they had gotten wind of the rescue so quickly.

Officer Wilson was there to greet them, and he looked almost giddy as he and his fellow officers pushed back the press. Victor and Therese were out of the house and scooping up Jose as soon as the boy's feet hit the ground. Jose looked around at the chaos with wide eyes, clinging to Victor's neck and then burying his face in Victor's shoulder.

Once they were all back in the house, there was a flurry of discussion about what to do first. Therese wanted to fix something for Jose to eat. Justina wanted to get him into clean clothes. Victor just seemed unable to let go of the boy. And Jose—his first concern was whether the cat had missed him. After rounds of crying, laughing, and hugging Jose, they finally settled him down with a sandwich and glass of juice, letting him sit on the couch and eat while petting the cat, just this once.

Officer Wilson and the other officers took their leave of the house, although the local police said they would continue the outside patrol until the situation was fully back to normal and the case was closed. Because, as the FBI had reminded them, the kidnappers still had plenty of explaining to do, and there were still open questions about who all was involved.

Agent Jordan spent over an hour talking with Jose to see what could be learned from the child. Apparently, the man who had taken Jose from the beach had given him some story, in Spanish, about Victor asking him to come pick him up because Therese had a very important phone call she was on. And they could stop for ice cream. Jose, despite having been warned about talking to strangers, didn't really find it odd; in Mexico his neighbors all helped with the neighborhood kids. So he went along without a fuss. Seeing Therese on the phone made it convincing to him.

He had been kept at the house in Far Rockaway the whole time. He heard the two men argue about getting paid. He told the agent that the men argued a lot, but they did bring him good food from McDonald's and let him play video games. He said he wasn't scared; nobody hurt him, but they did make a lot of excuses about why he couldn't go home or talk to Victor. He asked the agent if they were "very bad men" and if they were going to jail. Agent Jordan didn't get much in terms of new information from Jose, except to learn that the kidnapping plot hadn't been very well thought through and the two men disagreed over what to do with Jose.

Jose seemed unfazed by the whole thing and was eager to finish talking to the agent so he could revisit his room and his toys. And, of course, spend some time with Hercules. Justina thought with amusement that the child seemed to have missed the cat more than anyone else!

Therese had shared the note she had found in her office with the FBI. When she discovered Justina had left in a rush, she called Victor and he came to get her and the note, so it could be handed over right away. Looking at the note, Justina thought it did explain, to some degree, why the kidnappers had thought putting pressure on the family might be helpful, and Agent Jordan agreed. It was so hard to fathom that all this had gone on at a hospital where she was working. It didn't seem real.

Agent Jordan left after talking to Jose, and Justina knew his colleagues at the FBI were grilling the pair of kidnappers. She was still baffled by what had happened, and even her father seemed stumped about what the men had hoped to achieve, with no ransom demand or any communication other than that note left for Therese. Justina had told Agent Jordan, and her father, about the comments they had made about getting money from Powers, but that didn't really make sense. As the house began to settle down for the evening, Justina was finally able to get Jose to take a bath (she was horrified that he hadn't had a bath the whole time he was gone!), and they all called the various friends, neighbors, and colleagues who had been waiting for news. Justina could hear Marci squeal in her father's ear from across the room when he called to tell her the news.

Justina had nearly forgotten about the morning raid at the pharmacy when she got a call from Tim who, of course, had received all the updates from the FBI and the police. According to Tim, the pharmacist had been very willing to talk, once "incentivized." He explained that Dr. Powers, as an owner of the pharmacy, had signed an agreement with a purchasing organization for various drugs, and that he believed that many of the drugs came into the country illegally or, at best, were manufactured in the US illegally. The purchasing company was basically a front to provide illicit drugs to willing pharmacists and, at the same time, create a lot of money for willing "investors."

"So, Dr. Powers was recruiting patients to prescribe to?" she asked, still confused about the scheme.

"Yes, he had a runner. The same guy who kidnapped Jose, in fact. His name is Edgar Jimenez. He's been in jail, deported, and has committed many various crimes, most of them either drug related or petty. Edgar would go to homeless shelters, soup kitchens, bus stations, wherever he could find people who needed to make a little money. They would go into the clinic and say they had a horrible headache or that their back was hurting. They were usually seen by one of the residents, who were instructed on what to prescribe."

It still didn't make sense to Justina. "So why were we seeing all those patients billed to Dr. Al?" she asked.

"It was a very clever scheme, that's why," Tim responded. "Dr. Powers had them bill most of the visits under Dr. Al-Basri, so that any questions would go to the other doctor, who was well known for his temper. Everyone was afraid to confront him. Dr. Al was busy trying to maximize his billing, so he didn't care, and the residents were the ones seeing patients, anyhow. He made more money from the hospital as a result. And there were a lot more patients than just those at the clinic. There were others involved; it was quite the operation. St. Matthew's was just one location." He took a breath, and Justina jumped in.

"So, it was a regular crime ring?" she asked. Wow. She was still struggling to wrap her brain around the size of the operation she had been part of exposing. Unbelievable.

"Yes, it was quite the operation. The 'patients' would get

paid for the prescriptions, in a nutshell. It was a laundering operation of sorts. The hospital clinic would bill for the patient visit, the pharmacy would typically bill Medicaid for the drugs, and the actual drugs would be sold on the street for a much higher amount of money. There were layers of complexity created here to prevent the usual red flags from showing up. That's the simplified version, anyhow."

"Did Dr. Al know what was going on? Dr. Powers was so slimy, he had to have known!"

"Yes and no. There is such a thing as honor among thieves," Tim said with a chuckle. "We've kind of known they were both dirty in their own ways, and that they both had a stake in the pharmacy. But the pharmacist did give us some of the missing pieces." Tim paused, then continued. "The pharmacy was making good money, so Dr. Al was happy to not know. He was also making great money from the hospital and at his own practice, in addition to other 'investments.' At least that's how it appears so far. We are talking to him next. He's already lawyered up."

"What about Dr. Powers? Did you pick him up yet? I would expect him to try to leave the country or something! I still can't believe this."

"We have him. We took him into custody this morning as well. Of course, he has only the best in lawyers." He laughed. "Although he won't have his favorite lawyer, Peter Hancock. We're still trying to find him; he seems to be, um, 'missing.'"

Justina took a minute, trying to process this latest news. "You know Peter Hancock hired me …," she began.

"Yes. This whole thing has been a series of interesting coincidences. The mistake Hancock made, or at least one of them, was sending an honest attorney to St. Matthew's when the CEO called with a concern. Of course, he really thought his colleagues had covered the trail there by chasing away anyone who might know anything and grabbing the files in the compliance officer's office. He's really a narcissist; I think he got a thrill out of thinking he outsmarted everyone."

"Well, they almost got away with it. I mean, if it weren't for the staff and residents coming forward, all we would have had is a billing audit. There would have been issues, but not like this!"

Tim nodded. "Dr. Powers is very arrogant. I'm sure he told Hancock that it was all handled. He would never dream the residents would come forward. And they really didn't think proof of anything would be found, or, if it was, it would all implicate Dr. Al. Unfortunately for them, the residents were willing to speak out and you were there to listen. This easily could have gone differently."

"Does Frank know what's happened?" Justina realized she hadn't tried to contact Frank in several days, with everything else that was happening.

"Oh yes. He's very pleased we are close to wrapping this up. He's one of the best, you know. He notified a few of us while he was on his way to the airport, leaving town. He couldn't leave in good conscience with the board trying to sweep it under the rug."

"Wow. This is all just so unreal!" Justina didn't know

what to ask next—there were so many questions. One thing was still bothering her, though. "I don't understand Peter Hancock's role in all this. Was it just that he was an owner in that purchasing company that supplied the drugs?"

"Well, yes, that's the main issue, given how we believe they were operating. We believe that purchasing company had two sets of books, one for legitimate transactions which can be reported to the government and other stakeholders, and then their real money-making enterprise, which is putting illegally manufactured opioids into the supply chain. We are still digging into that, but Hancock was definitely pulling strings to get that company contracts with various pharmacies where he knew there were unethical pharmacists. Of course, he's on the boards of several large healthcare organizations, as is his wife. She was complicit in all this, too. They are, or were, quite the power brokers for crooked deals. They were laundering these drugs all over New York."

"Unreal," Justina murmured, still trying to process all of it.

"Yes, it is. Look, I need to go. We are doing some more interviews. But just wanted to let you know. Also, good job on getting Jose back! That took some guts, what you did!"

Justina felt her face flushing at the compliment. "Thanks, but no … I didn't have a choice. They had Jose; I couldn't let them leave. We're just glad it all worked out. But thanks!"

"Okay, well, I'll be talking to you later, after we get more details. Now you can relax a bit!"

After signing off, Justina headed upstairs to Jose's room.

Just to see him there. She wondered if any of them would let the boy out of their sight ever again. When she got to the hallway, she could see her father and Therese standing in Jose's doorway, her father's arm draped around Therese. Surprised, she stopped in her tracks. *When did that happen?* she asked herself.

49

JUSTINA

Justina woke early after a dreamless sleep. It was still dark out, and she couldn't figure out why she wasn't still sleeping, until she heard soft footsteps in the hallway and then on the stairs. It took her a minute, then she realized it was probably Jose, still in his habit of waking up too early.

Her heart filled with gratitude, she slid out of bed, pulled on her fuzzy purple slippers, and followed Jose down the stairs. *Was it only a few weeks ago I was mad at him for getting up early?* she marveled. Now she was just so thrilled to hear him sneaking downstairs before the sun was up.

This time, instead of sending him back to his room she gave him some juice and cereal and listened as he prattled on about Hercules sleeping in his room and how he had to call his friend Toby. While she still felt shell-shocked from everything that had happened, Jose had slipped right back to his normal routine and seemed no worse off.

After he had his fill of breakfast, Jose wanted to go watch some cartoons, so Justina made herself another cup of coffee. She figured she would hear from Agent Jordan or someone else at the FBI, since they had spent the day before with the kidnappers. She decided she'd get a little more caffeine in her body and then go up and shower.

Hearing footsteps, she turned to see Therese. "You're up early," she commented to Justina. "I heard Jose. Looks like he hasn't missed a beat!"

"Yup. He already has his day planned. His energy hasn't been affected!"

As Therese went about getting a cup of coffee, Justina pondered how to broach the subject of her father. She decided just to ask.

"So, Therese, what's up with you and my dad? Is there something I should know?"

Therese smiled and looked a little embarrassed. "Your father is an amazing man … ," she began, and then stopped. "Yes," she said. "There is … something. I don't know what yet. Are you okay with that?"

"Wow, okay … Sure, I'm okay with it. I just don't know how I didn't see it!" She thought of the past few weeks, though, and realized she hadn't been paying attention to much of anything except the daily dramas.

Therese laughed. "You've been a bit busy! And really, I don't know what's going to happen. Your dad and I have become good friends, first of all, and neither of us want to ruin that. So we'll see. No matter what, you have all become like family to me." Justina could see Therese getting emotional, her eyes looking a little glassy.

"Don't worry, Therese. You are part of the family. Things are so much better with you here, and my father isn't spending nearly as much time trying to tell me what to do," she joked.

"Okay, well … that's good to hear," Therese said, looking relieved.

Justina could see it was getting light outside and looked at the clock. "I'm expecting to hear from our FBI friends this morning," she said. "I need to go upstairs and take a shower. Plus, I left my phone up there. I'm going to get myself going." She went over to Therese and impulsively gave her a hug. "Enjoy your coffee," she said, and hurried out of the room, wondering if she had already gotten a text from Agent Jordan. And the thing between her father and Therese … she would think more about that later! But it felt natural to her; Therese really had become part of their family and her father had been alone for a long time.

Her phone was blinking when she got to her room, and it was a text from Agent Jordan, letting her know he'd be at the house by ten. *Okay, that gives me plenty of time,* she thought, kicking off her slippers and heading to the shower.

* * *

"Looks like your media friends have lost interest in you," Agent Jordan remarked as he entered the house. Justina looked past him, through the doorway, and saw only one news station van parked outside. *When did they leave?* she wondered, and she realized that ever since they brought Jose home, she hadn't even bothered looking outside. Everything she needed was right there in the house. Except for Daniel, of course. But that would be soon.

"Thank God," she said. "I hope to never go through anything like that again. What a nightmare." She shut the door and offered the agent something to drink, which he declined.

"I really don't have a ton of time today," he explained. "This case has far-reaching tentacles that frankly we are only beginning to unwind. But you were in the trenches bringing it to light, so I wanted to debrief with you about what we know so far."

"Thank you," Justina said, gesturing toward the dining room. "Let's talk in here. Now that we have our dining room back, and Jose's home, that's probably the quietest location."

"First of all," the agent began, "what you did yesterday was incredibly brave." When Justina opened her mouth to respond, he put his hand up. "Brave but really dangerous. Those two men both have long records as well as drug abuse issues. You could easily have been killed. And Jose, too." He paused, looking at her intently. "You probably saved that little boy. I don't know what they would have done to him or if we could have found them in time if you hadn't intervened. Those guys were not on our radar, they are relatively low-level criminals. Not the sort I would look for in complex schemes like this one."

Justina felt a familiar jolt of anxiety thinking about what the agent was saying, thinking about what could have been. She really hadn't processed it all yet, she realized.

"So, who were those guys? Why did they grab Jose? You know we never got a ransom demand or anything? Just that crazy note Therese got in her work inbox. It doesn't make sense."

"It doesn't make sense to you or me, but to these guys … They have both been hired thugs for a couple of years, doing the dirty work for not only your favorite doctor but also Peter Hancock. Any time the bosses wanted a 'message' sent to someone, or a load of new 'patients' brought to a clinic, it was Edgar and Martin doing the deed. The rich got richer, and those two got their hands dirty. They saw Jose as a lottery ticket."

Justina felt she was starting to understand. "So, they wanted a bigger piece of the action?"

"Exactly. They may be thugs, but they aren't stupid. Every day they saw Hancock and Powers with their beautiful wives, powerful cars, boats, vacations, while they did all the work. They got paid well, but not nearly as well as the two fat cats running the show. They know how much drugs cost; they were very familiar with the drug world as regular consumers on top of everything else. So they decided to snatch a kid who, conveniently, belonged to an antidrug politician and his lawyer-to-be daughter, both of whom were part of the problem Powers and Hancock were dealing with."

"But Jose really had nothing to do with them," Justina

said. It really didn't make sense.

"But he does. They figured, correctly, that the scrutiny and media attention would be so much that the two fat cats would pony up big money fast to make it go away." He smiled. "It was actually pretty smart. They knew those two guys would never expose their ransom demands, because they couldn't. And they knew that the longer we were digging, the more nervous those two would be. Think of it as a classic case of blackmail, rather than a traditional kidnapping."

"So Powers and Peter Hancock were behind all those things that have happened, all the way back to Therese and the rock through the window? And Dr. Al?" Justina started piecing together all the various events, tying it together. It was mind-boggling.

"Yup. At first it was just Powers and Hancock wanting to put a stop to the hospital investigation. But when your friend Frank got the CEO to push the board on the investigation Dr. Al-Basri got involved because he realized Powers was bringing all that scrutiny down on both of them. So he had to join forces with Powers to get the investigation shut down, because he's not exactly squeaky clean either, although he had no idea about the full extent of all this. And Al-Basri was guilty of turning a blind eye because it was benefiting him financially. So that's when those two pushed the board to make the CEO resign. The chief medical officer, by the way, has some questions to answer as well." Agent Jordan paused. "You and Frank really opened a can of worms, you know? And there are three residents who have retained counsel, and one sexual assault case filed against Powers. So far."

"Dr. Powers had me snowed," Justina admitted. "He flirted with me and got me to talk about my family, how the case was going." When she saw the agent's eyebrows rise, she hurriedly added, "I didn't tell him anything. But he's very slick. I really thought Dr. Al was the root problem. He was so defensive and hostile."

Agent Jordan nodded. "Yes, that's part of Powers's brilliance. He knew everyone would be intimidated by Dr. Al, so he took some hits to his billing in order to shift any scrutiny over to the guy nobody would want to mess with. And he knew Al was upcoding and doing some unnecessary tests in order to pad bills, so he would be motivated to keep anyone from looking at his charts. Very slick, a sociopath, I would say."

Justina found herself nodding. "Very slick indeed. But he didn't want to pay the ransom, right? One of the kidnappers was talking about that."

"Yes, Hancock paid up quickly. He's as bad as Powers, but at a whole different level. Powers is very greedy and controlling. Hancock didn't start out a crook. We think it probably began when he got on the board at St. Matthew's and befriended Powers. They belonged to the same clubs; their wives became friends. It's still not clear how all that evolved, but my guess is that Hancock was getting bored just running a firm and getting rich. Guys like him crave excitement. And we need to look at his relationship to Jefferson. The campaign contributions and then withdrawals from your father's campaign make me think there may be something there, as well, although we have no reason to believe that Jefferson has any involvement in this drug scheme. But given all of this, we believe that's why he's on the lam when we were able to nab the others. But he can't go far, we'll get him."

"So how many others were involved? Tim said it was pretty broad, not just that clinic?" So many moving parts, and so many people hurt. "And what about the compliance officer that got killed? Was that them too?"

Agent Jordan shook his head. "They aren't admitting to that, but yes, I'm relatively certain it was them. Someone, probably Powers, panicked that she was going to report her information to the government as a whistleblower. That would be my guess. Those two thugs are trying to get a deal, so I expect we'll continue probing and getting more information as they and their lawyers do their negotiating. If we get them on murder, of course, it's much worse than the rest of what they've done. I've gone over all the reports, and I'm wondering if the compliance officer had taken some files home with her, or they believed that she had. It wouldn't be unusual to take files home, if she was trying to keep them secure or, perhaps, was planning to report what she found to the government or an attorney. Powers would be smart enough to know that. From what I hear her resignation wasn't planned, and according to your notes, there were some missing documents. So I suspect they paid her a visit."

"Wow. I had no idea what I was getting involved with. And I agree—it wasn't a coincidence." Justina shuddered, thinking again how close they all were to possibly meeting the same fate. But at least they were caught and couldn't hurt anyone else, she reminded herself.

"No, I don't believe coincidences exist in the natural world," Agent Jordan agreed. "But rest assured, this whole bunch will be getting three hots and a cot, as they say, for a very long time." He glanced down at his phone. "I really need to go. I have a lunch meeting with the DA and your friend from the DEA. Then some more interviews."

"Okay … thanks for coming by. I'm still in shock over all this, but so grateful it's over."

The agent nodded. "I'm sure you are. For us it's just beginning! But I'll check in now and then to keep you posted. The work you and Frank did was instrumental in blowing this all open, and so was the research your father's friend did. It all helped. And even though what you did yesterday was profoundly idiotic"—he smiled—"you got that boy home safe. And that's what counts."

Agent Jordan stood and led the way out of the dining room, pausing to smile at Jose, who was lying on the floor in the living room, coloring and telling a story to Hercules, who actually seemed happy to have the boy's attention. Or at least wasn't running away.

He held his hand out to Justina. "You did good," he said, and shook her hand. "Good luck with law school. Maybe I'll see you again one of these days."

"Maybe you will," Justina said.

* * *

Three Months Later

The atmosphere in the Gonzalez house was lively as the family enjoyed a small gathering after attending Justina's graduation from law school. It was so hard to believe it was finished! It was a miracle, as far as she was concerned, given everything that had been going on. And she had secured a job offer from the law firm. The only thing missing was Daniel, but he would be home soon. They would have the real party then, to celebrate his graduation as well as hers, but for now a small celebration was certainly in order!

Things were going well for her father, too. According to recent polls, Victor had become the favorite, and even Jefferson's campaign seemed to know it, although they hadn't backed off with the attacks for long. Nobody there had ever admitted to fabricating the allegations against her father, but anyone watching local politics had a strong suspicion about it. Nothing illegal had been found in his relationship to Peter Hancock, either, even though the attorney had been caught trying to cross the Canadian border. His case was still in progress, but nobody expected him to see jail time. Although Dr. Powers had been eager to shift blame onto Hancock, there just wasn't enough of a paper trail to prove his culpability. He had been disbarred by the State of New

York, however, which was a small consolation to Justina.

Officer Wilson and Agent Jordan had both stopped by, just for a minute, to wish her well. She had been a little surprised by that, but apparently Marci had put the word out. Justina was flattered they took time out for her little party. They had been such a big piece of her life there for a short while, even though they were just doing their jobs. Frank had sent her a card, from Miami, where he was assisting the Office of Inspector General's fraud task force in some major takedown. She was just honored that he had kept track of her and taken time to send a card.

Things were almost perfect. She thought about her father and Therese. Those two seemed so happy together. It made her even more eager for Daniel to get home. Maybe he would show up early and surprise her; it wouldn't be the first time he had shown up unexpectedly. She knew it was silly, but she kept hoping. Nothing else was missing on this wonderful day!

She shook off her thoughts, noticing a relative lack of chaos and looked around for Jose. Would she ever stop worrying about him? They had allowed his friend Toby to come over, thinking it would keep Jose out from under foot and would also keep him in the house. She headed into the kitchen and was going to ask her father if he'd seen the child when she realized he and Therese were having an in-depth conversation, standing close with hands intertwined, totally unaware of her. She quickly backed out of the room. *Let them have their time,* she thought. *They've earned it.*

She decided to get maybe just a sliver more of cake before finishing her hunt for Jose. The huge pink-and-green frosted cake was in the center of the dining room table, surrounded by several bowls and trays of snacks. Rounding the corner, Justina caught Jose and Toby, making their third or fourth trip around the table. Of course, that's where they were! "All right, you two," she said in a mock-severe tone. "I hope you're leaving something for the rest of us!"

Toby looked at her with wide blue eyes, not sure if they were in trouble, but Jose giggled. "Yes, we will eat it all!" he said, and jumped aside when Justina played like she was going to swat his behind. The boys ran upstairs with their latest round of treats and Justina got her bit of cake and refilled her glass.

Heading to the living room, she plopped down next to Marci, who had brought her husband Jon and baby, Jon Junior, (already nicknamed J.J.), to the baby's first little party. The baby was so beautiful; a miracle by all accounts, and Marci looked tired but very content. Justina wondered if Marci would ever return to the world of politics full-time. Her father's campaign was doing so well with donations now that Marci had helped him hire a full-time person to help take over her job, so she was just advising now.

Justina sat her drink down and held her arms out. "May I?" she asked, and Marci handed over her little bundle. "He's so tiny!" she marveled. She really hadn't been around too many infants, but this one had to be the most beautiful baby she had ever seen.

Marci beamed. "He's our little miracle," she said, exchanging smiles with her husband. "Just wait, Justina. Once Daniel gets home, you'll be on your way to having your own little bambino!"

Justina laughed. "Not any time soon! I am nowhere near ready for that. Keeping track of Jose has shown me how much work that is, and I have my new job! But yes, someday. But first Daniel needs to get home!"

J.J. started to cry, so Justina handed him back. "See? I'm not good at this!" She picked up her champagne glass and took a drink. "Besides, I'd have to give this up!" she said with a giggle. Today was just too much fun, and a huge relief, now that all the stress and drama seemed to be behind her.

Marci started to respond but was interrupted by a shrill peal of the doorbell.

"Who could that be? Do we have any more FBI agents on our guest list?" Justina asked Marci with a laugh. The other woman had already orchestrated an appearance by Officer Wilson and Agent Jordan, so it was hard to say what else she might have up her sleeve. At Marci's shrug Justina stood. "Only one way to find out, I guess!"

She opened the door and stopped short at the sight of an unfamiliar dark-skinned young man in a red hoodie standing on the front step.

"Can I help you?" she asked. His almond eyes looked very familiar, but she was sure she didn't know him.

"I think so. I am looking for Therese Devereaux. Is this

the right place?" He glanced at his phone, then the numbers on the house, shifting his weight awkwardly.

"Oh, okay, yes. Can I tell her who is asking for her?"

He smiled, and she immediately knew. "Yeah, tell her it's Mateo. I'm sure she will remember me."

THE END

ACKNOWLEDGMENTS

For those who know me, you know that *The Hippocratic Deception* took me a very long time to finish! I actually started it right after completing *Finding Maslow*, which was back in 2015. The story has changed mightily since the first draft, and I've had a lot of support, input, and inspiration along the way.

First of all, I want to acknowledge the early help and inspiration I received. In terms of inspiration, the character of Therese was totally inspired by Rev. Dr. Cecily Broderick y Guerra, who was the Vice President of Pastoral Care at Episcopal Health Services in Far Rockaway, New York, when I spent my year working there. She's an amazing lady and an inspiration in every sense of the word. I also never knew that a Reverend Mother could be so much fun!

Another source of early input was Joseline Peña Melnyk, a member of the Prince George's County House Delegation and the Vice Chair of the Health and Government Operations Committee. I reached out to Joseline after meeting her at a local Town Hall, hoping to get an insider's view of running a political campaign. Joseline not only met with me, she even bought me lunch! That was very early on in the process of writing this book, but I've not forgotten the campaign trail experiences she shared.

My first draft had some early readers: Jamie O'Dell, Karin Ballard, and, of course, my poor mother, Velma Lee, who has read at least three versions of this book and critiqued them all. I appreciate all their time, efforts, and input. My mother and I had some healthy debates on the various versions and changes. I'm hoping she likes how it turned out; we didn't always agree!

Once I had a completed draft, I knew I needed help in refining it. I am indebted to a fantastic editor who helped me at this point (and afterwards as well), Bonnie Hearn Hill. Bonnie gave me much more than I could have hoped for in terms of guidance, suggestions, and editing. I've learned so much from her throughout this process, and I wouldn't have written this particular book without Bonnie's support.

I would also be remiss if I did not give recognition to Marilyn Moss, MD. She read the book from the standpoint not only of a physician but one who did her residency in New York. Thank you for your time, Marilyn, and your input! Also, Virginia Hawkins Bennett did me the honor of reviewing the draft and sharing her thoughts. Thank you so much!

Finally, the people who got it past the finish line: Jerry Todd, who did the fabulous cover, Michael Schuler, who did the final editing, and Kelly Carter, who did all the interior design work. You can't produce a good book without a lot of talented help! I've been lucky to find such skilled people.

In a more general sense, I feel so fortunate to have had all the experiences in my career that led me to this point. It's been an amazing ride so far, and I've met so many fascinating people along the way. I'm grateful for every opportunity I've had and every path I've crossed, good and bad. As a writer, I have enough material for a lifetime, and I plan to continue making use of it!

Of course, none of it would matter if it weren't for the readers, family, and friends, who encourage and motivate me. You all know who you are! I'm blessed to have a strong group of supporters. And, if I forgot to name anyone, please know it wasn't intentional. It's been a long and winding road.

Please feel free to reach out to me via my website, susan-walberg.com, and sign up for my email updates, or find me on my Facebook Author page. And, lastly, if you've made it this far, please remember how important reviews are for authors. If you liked this book, please leave me a review on Amazon and/or Goodreads. It's really important and every review matters. Thanks to everyone!

Want to see how it all began? Check out *Finding Maslow* on Amazon, where Justina's journey began.

ABOUT THE AUTHOR

Susan Lee Walberg is an attorney who has spent over 30 years working in the healthcare field. In addition to her attorney role, Susan has worked as a fraud investigator, a compliance officer, and a healthcare consultant, which is her current occupation. Susan is originally from Seattle, Washington, but also resided in Maryland before moving to Florida. Susan received her Bachelor of Arts in Psychology from the University of Washington, then a Master's in Public Administration and a Juris Doctorate from Seattle University. In addition to her novels, Susan has written multiple nonfiction books relating to healthcare compliance, which can also be found on Amazon.com. When she's not working or writing, she's enjoying life in Florida with her mother and various orchids, cats, and chickens. You can find Susan on her website, susanwalberg.com, or email at swalberg@compliancealacarte.com.

Made in the USA
Columbia, SC
14 December 2022

73808295R00221